HOMEGROWN HOLIDAY

A SNOWDRIFT SUMMIT CHRISTMAS

MEGAN SQUIRES

Copyright © 2023 by Megan Squires

All rights reserved.

No part of this book may be reproduced in any form or by any electronic or mechanical means, including information storage and retrieval systems, without written permission from the author, except for the use of brief quotations in a book review.

CHAPTER 1

❄

"This is our year, Sugar Plum. Our noble fir has less than two inches to grow and at the rate it's been climbing this last month, it'll get to the twenty-foot mark in no time flat."

Rachel Joy wanted to share her dad's enthusiasm, and in any other circumstance she would have been more chipper. But only ten minutes remained until her meeting with the executives at December Décor, and she'd pinned her entire professional future upon this presentation, not to mention given up the better portion of the last year creating the prototypes for her exclusive line of holiday greenery.

Her father's unexpected phone call only highlighted that at Christmastime, nothing existed in the Joy family's world if it wasn't red, green, or holiday themed. Sure, her new products technically fell into that category, but her parents weren't aware of that. Rachel had kept her latest work endeavor a secret, like a perfectly wrapped present tucked into a stocking for safekeeping. It was finally time to tear into that packaging.

She wedged the phone between her shoulder and ear and pretended not to hear the request. "I'm sorry, Dad. Now's not a good time. I'll have to call you back. Heading into a meeting."

"You're next up on rotation to sing. Are you ready to do the honors?"

The excitement in her father's voice was palpable, but it was little motivation to croon holiday tunes to an evergreen over the phone. And it did nothing to eradicate the tremor in Rachel's stomach each time her thoughts traveled to her upcoming presentation.

"I'll call back tonight, Dad. Promise. I've gotta run."

"Just a few lines," Stewart Joy bulldozed right through her insistence. "I'm propping up the phone on those leafy, green branches right now. A-one and a-two and a-three....O' Christmas tree, O' Christmas tree!"

Giving up what little fight she had left, Rachel joined in with all the reluctance of a preteen forced to take pictures with a mall Santa. "How lovely are your branches," she humored in a key she couldn't quite find.

She trailed her father a few notes, plodding through the song while she gathered the last of her papers from the printer and placed them into their respective folders. Then she straightened her posture, smoothed down her slate-gray pencil skirt with her free hand,

and threw her shoulders back in an act of manufactured confidence.

"I really do have to go now, Dad." She backtracked across her office to collect her laptop, sweeping her gaze over her desk one last time. "Give Mom all my love."

"Will do," Stewart said. "And thanks for playing along. You know I'm a firm believer that singing to plants helps them grow. I think it's going to be that extra push that ensures our tree will be the one in the town square this year. If we can beat out the Hart's noble, that is. Believe it or not, theirs is creeping up to that twenty-foot mark too."

Rachel's heart and feet stalled, and the young man pushing the coffee cart around their company's floor locked the wheels on his mobile display only seconds before colliding into her. That act didn't, however, lock the large coffee pot into place, and even the scalding splash of liquid dousing her brand new suit did nothing to keep her blood from running cold. She froze where she stood, covered in hot coffee and flushed with sheer disbelief.

"Did you say the Hart's tree?"

"Yep," Stewart carried right along as though he hadn't flung a sack of coal right into their conversation. "Hard to believe those little saplings you and Holden planted back when you were youngsters will be ready to harvest right around the same time. Though I suppose they always were neck-and-neck over the years, weren't they?"

Oh, more than just the trees had been neck-and-neck. Rachel and Holden had been in direct competition with one another their entire lives. From gingerbread decorating contests to snowman building to sledding races down their backyard mountain, Holden Hart had been Rachel's only nemesis. Even after all of these years and nearly two-hundred miles separating them, the fine hairs on her neck rose like hackles at the mention of his name.

"The Harts are not going to win."

"Hopefully not, but only time will tell," her father offered noncommittally. "Suppose it'll just be a race to see which tree gets to the twenty-foot finish line first."

That wasn't good enough. Rachel took a handful of napkins from the barista and blotted the liquid soiling her outfit, suddenly much less concerned with the presentation before her superiors than she was in righting this age-old rivalry. Apparently, that near-knock from the coffee cart had also knocked the common sense straight out of her.

"Not on my watch," she huffed as she crumpled up a napkin and tossed it into the metal waste bin en route to the conference room, her stride and resolve more determined than ever.

"Hard for it to be on your watch when you're in San Francisco and we're up here in Snowdrift."

"Then I won't be. As soon as I'm finished up here today, I'll pack my bags and head up to the summit."

"You know you are always welcome here, Sugar Plum, but don't you have a job to do?"

"I absolutely do, Dad," Rachel said behind both a growing smile and plan, neither of which she could keep from forming. "I'm finally going to win the Christmas Competition, once and for all."

CHAPTER 2

Holden Hart grabbed onto the handles and jerked the snowmobile hard to the left, fresh bits of snow spraying out from the skis in a fan of white powder. The husband and wife duo trailing behind cut along the same path, and their hoots and hollers that reverberated in the winter air confirmed the money they'd spent at Major Hart Mountain Sports hadn't gone to waste.

Another happy customer in the books. Mission accomplished.

Like he did on every backcountry excursion, Holden took the pair through the zigzag of towering conifers, past rushing streams flowing with recent snowmelt, and out into wide, sweeping spaces where they could open up the throttle and really feel the horsepower. This was always the favorite segment of the tour for the true adrenaline junkies. Anyone could travel sixty-five miles-per-hour along a paved highway, but carving a path without the parameters of painted lines—only Mother Nature to serve as a barrier—was an experience only found on the slopes of the Sierra Nevadas.

Holden felt like a winter cowboy, the snowmobile his trusty steed, faithfully taking him everywhere he needed to go, whether that be an hour and a half adventure with paying customers or a day-long mission with his Search and Rescue volunteer team. On days like today, with the sun shining and the air crisp, he was grateful it was the former.

"How are you guys doing back there?" he yelled over his shoulder, slowing up the mobile and curving around in a smooth about-face. The couple leveled off the gas to ease up in front of him, and even though obscured under the dark visors on their helmets, Holden could see the twin smiles plastered to their faces. "You ready to head on in?"

"I could do this every day," the man confessed, chest heaving.

"Well, you're in luck because we're open every day except Christmas. How long did you say you were in town?"

"Only until tomorrow, but our son would never forgive us if we came out here without him again."

Holden gave a nod of recognition. "He'll forgive you next year when he gets his license and he'll be able to drive one of these all on his own."

"I don't think we'd ever get him off of it!" the woman proclaimed.

Holden understood. That had been the case when he was a teenager. He knew the first time he sat on that snowmobile that it was the only mode of transportation he would ever care to use. It had never occurred to him that just ten years later, he would own and operate a winter excursion company with his best buddy, Lance Major. If realized dreams were made of snowflakes, he'd collected an entire mountainside of them.

He took his time leading the couple back to the rental shop, allowing them the opportunity to absorb the scenery previously blurring past their periphery in a wash of trees, logs, and blankets of white. Navigating the High Sierra was a rush, but it also offered a calm that couldn't be duplicated anywhere else. In fact, Holden was pretty convinced the term 'white noise' originated in these very hills. That wind-blown whir of the resting mountain, doing nothing more than existing, and yet providing a soundtrack of tranquility all the same. With the thready hum of the quieting snowmobile engine to accompany it, it was the most beautiful, peaceful sound.

The laughter back at the snowmobile rental shop as his customers shed their borrowed gear and recalled their favorite aspects of the guided tour was also music to Holden's ears. And to his heart.

"What's the verdict?" Lance cuffed a hand onto Holden's broad shoulder and squeezed. "Should I keep this guy on staff?" he asked the customers pointedly. "Or send him on down the hill?"

Lance had a handful of zingers and this was his favorite go-to. He got more mileage out of the tired joke than they had racked up on their snowmobiles. Each time he recited it, Holden gladly played along.

Major Hart Mountain Sports was a fifty-fifty venture. While Holden was competitive at the core, in business, he knew it was best to play fair. Sometimes, he even wondered if that competitive spirit had died out in recent years, a dwindling fire without the motivation of an opponent to stoke the flames.

In his youth, he'd had his rivals: the snowboarding team from the neighboring high school or the kids he'd played ice hockey with on Lake Pinewood when it had frozen over. But those challengers rotated in and out with the sports calendar, and every year there seemed to be a new contender climbing up the ranks to take him on. A new candidate to beat.

The only person to ever consistently challenge Holden and give him a run for his money in practically all aspects of his life had been Rachel Joy.

The name was a complete misnomer. Holden didn't feel a single ounce of joy when he thought back to the determined, if not entirely pretentious, teen girl. Her off-putting confidence had Holden grinding his teeth, even ten years later when he got lost in the frustrating memories.

"Earth to Holden." Lance flapped an empty glove in front of his face. "Where'd you go, buddy?"

Somewhere he didn't want to. Sinking into a past he'd done everything to forget.

"Sorry. Got lost in la-la land for a minute there."

The customers retreated out the door with an enthusiastic wave of thanks, and Holden unzipped his subzero jacket to fold over the bench near the cash wrap counter. He took a seat next to it. He'd worked up a sweat out on that mountain, but unwarranted thoughts of Rachel Joy now had him heated for an entirely different reason. How many years had it been since he'd let her get under his skin like this? He scratched at his arms, the memories crawling over him like a pile of fire ants.

"You've got another group arriving in about a half hour and you shouldn't be out on that mountain unless your head is screwed on completely straight. You sure you're good, buddy?"

At the present moment, Holden couldn't give Lance the answer he needed to hear.

His business partner leaned his elbows onto the counter between them and lowered his chin to a fist. "Alright, man. Fess up. What's got you all distracted in that head of yours?"

Shoving off one boot, then the other, Holden sat back and wiggled his toes within his wool socks. "You remember Rachel Joy from high school?"

Lance's narrowed gaze indicated he did. "Yeah."

"Do you have any idea what she's up to?"

"Last I heard, she worked for some big holiday décor company out of the city. Why?"

"No reason." Jaw tensing, Holden took a tight breath.

HOMEGROWN HOLIDAY

Of course she would work for a Christmas company. Back in the day, the girl had turned everything into a competition, including the entire holiday season. It made sense that she'd figured out how to monetize that now—how to win over the entire month of December in the form of dollars and cents.

One year, she even had their sophomore class vote on the best holiday light display, with their respective houses as the only entrants. She had wanted to beat Holden in everything, and she'd nearly succeeded. Last he'd checked, the score was tied, twelve to twelve. Why did he even remember that?

"You hear from her or something?" Lance pushed back from the counter and fixed a look on Holden that made him wish he'd never brought it up.

"No. Just curious."

"I've heard she's quite a looker these days."

Even if he'd wanted to exercise some semblance of decorum, Holden couldn't keep from snorting. "Doubtful."

"Oh, I don't know. We aren't still the scrawny kids we were in high school. Ten years can do a lot to a person. Look at you, buddy. You've turned into quite the strapping, handsome man."

Apparently, Lance was full of jokes today.

"What's got you suddenly thinking about her?" Lance pressed. "Is it the tree selection for the town square?"

"Why would it be that?" His family had that in the bag, with their fifteen-year-old noble fir standing several proud inches above the required height for consideration.

"I hear the Joy family has a tree they're planning to enter into the running too."

"You're kidding." The blood drained from Holden's face to the tips of his sock-covered toes.

"I'm not," Lance affirmed. "And I'm also not kidding when I say Rachel's not the same girl she was back in high school. I'm serious. Look her up. You might be surprised."

Holden would do nothing of the sort.

No, all thoughts of Rachel remained in the past, along with any competitive desire to put her in her place. He was above that sort of pettiness, and with both the busiest month of the year at the rental shop and Christmas just around the corner, he didn't have time to waste his thoughts—nor his energy—on a silly childhood rivalry.

Some hatchets were meant to be buried, and the one with Rachel was about to be packed under an entire avalanche of indifference.

CHAPTER 3

※

Sleeping on the old pull-out couch in the den of her childhood home was like trying to find comfort while resting on a heap of Slinkys. The coils pressed into her shoulder blades and pinched her skin each time she rotated to find a new sleep position. By sunrise, Rachel had given up the quest for any sort of slumber, thrown on a pair of jeans, a teal cowl-neck sweater, and lugged on the snow boots her parents had thankfully kept stored in the closet since high school.

When was the last time she'd been back in Snowdrift Summit? Three Christmases ago? Four? It had to be more, as the memories were faint and the details fuzzy, like she viewed them through the obscured cloudiness of a shaken snow globe.

Rachel's life was in San Francisco now. Her parents still lived in Snowdrift, but she didn't call that place home anymore. She never quite understood the term 'coming home' referring to the town a person no longer lived in. If she kept thinking of her birthplace as home, then she'd never make one for herself elsewhere. And wasn't that the goal? To branch off from her parents and plant roots of her own in a soil of her choosing?

Rachel chose the city. Maybe the city chose her, with its promises of success and possibilities for achievement as tall as the high rises that pierced the fog-laden sky. Plus, it wasn't as though her business degree would be of much use in a small town like Snowdrift, with its antiquated Main Street shops and owners who valued tradition over innovation and expansion. Opportunity here was about as limited as vision during whiteout conditions. But in the city, there was a new chance to make a name for oneself at practically every turn.

That reality guided Rachel to the local coffee shop that morning. She needed proper caffeinating in order to sort through her notes from yesterday's meeting, as she worried she might be forced to make a new name for herself at an entirely different company sooner than she liked.

Suffice it to say, the presentation wasn't a success. All the buildup she'd amassed—all the energy and passion for her artificial mistletoe—was as elusive as the Man in Red himself. She couldn't summon any sort of excitement for the product at all.

And she blamed Holden Hart for that.

Thankfully, the board agreed to revisit her Mistlefaux product line after the holidays, encouraging

Rachel to take the time to strengthen her pitch over the course of the next few weeks and try again after the new year. It was a gracious offer. One she didn't deserve, and she wouldn't squander it. She looked at it as her Christmas bonus. If she ever wanted to climb her way out of product development and into management, this second attempt would have to be a success. She couldn't afford to fail twice.

With the sun on her face and sleep in her eyes, she drove to Bitter Cold Coffee Bar, delighted to see an open parking spot right along the curb. She would take all the wins she could get today, and a parking space was an easily achievable one.

She opened the door to the shop. A little silver bell above her announced her entry with its songlike chiming. The entire staff behind the barista bar shouted a chorus of off-pitch greetings as soon as she stepped over the threshold. So much for being inconspicuous. Lifting a hand, Rachel waved in return, then directed her gaze about the room to scope an out-of-sight table to set up camp. In the back of the establishment, there was one remaining space and the outlet on the wall next to it would ensure her laptop stayed charged throughout the hours of work.

Bumping past the other patrons crammed into the coffeehouse, Rachel maneuvered to the vacant bistro table, slipped her computer bag from her shoulder, and claimed her spot with her jacket lowered over the back of the chair. She looked around. This would do. There was another customer set up next to her, with an open laptop and spiral-bound notebook turned to a page full of illegible chicken scratch. The owner of the items was nowhere to be seen; likely ordering another round of caffeine, she supposed.

That was the sort of table-neighbor Rachel wanted. Someone similarly buried in their work with no need for idle chit-chat or interaction.

She pulled her wallet from her bag and moved toward the register. A blackboard menu hung at the back wall, a beautiful chalking of the day's specials and hot and cold drink options. Whoever crafted the display was truly gifted, and Rachel found herself lost in the intricate mountain illustrations and clever coffee names.

Ski Lift Latte. Mountain Home Mocha. Chain Control Cappuccino. The list went on and on with unique descriptions. She chuckled to herself quietly at the ingenuity of it all, something she could use a little of herself. Maybe if she stayed in the café long enough, some of that creativity would transfer through osmosis. One could only dream.

"What'll it be today?" A young man in a striped beanie drummed his palms on the refurbished wood counter and flashed Rachel a welcoming smile. "Pick your poison."

"I need a generous dose of caffeine in the largest size available."

The man nodded his understanding. "Ah, so you're looking for something to kick you into high gear? No worries; we've got you covered." He flipped around and peered up at the menu. "Our Black Diamond Cold Brew is a big hit. But if you're not looking for coffee, we can always add caffeine powder to our Holden Hart Hot Chocolate for that extra oomph you're looking for."

Rachel choked. "Hot Chocolate?" She couldn't force the first part out of her mouth.

"Yeah, it's a town favorite, named after the creator himself. Not your grandmother's hot chocolate—it's got sea salt and chili powder in it. Really good stuff."

"Seems like Not-Your-Grandmother's-Hot-Chocolate would have been a fine enough name," she mumbled louder than she intended.

The kid smiled again. "If you know Holden Hart, you know he deserves to have his name up on that board."

Oh, she knew Holden Hart alright. And she knew exactly what he deserved.

"So, what'll it be?"

"Just a large Whiteout White Mocha. Two extra shots." She unzipped her coin purse with more force than required and the handful of change flung out and scattered to the floor like loose marbles.

Thankfully, the man waiting at the bar for his drink stooped to collect the coins before she had the chance for the proper amount of humiliation to form. He dropped them back into her palm and grinned. "I've got you," he said, mouth curving up on the left to reveal a dimple pressed deeply into his cheek.

"Thank you." Angling back to the cashier, Rachel

brandished her credit card instead, unwilling to let another blunder steer her off-course.

When the machine alerted her to remove her card, the cashier said, "We'll call out your drink order as soon as it's ready. Have an epic day."

Rachel shimmied around her coin-collecting rescuer, forcing a smile of thanks as she wedged past his bulky body made even larger by the puffer jacket zipped clear up to his chin. Goodness, these certainly were tight quarters.

Dropping into her chair, she inhaled, pulling her spine taut and shoulders straight. She fished a hair tie from her purse—thankfully keeping all coins and other items within it this time—and wrapped her shoulder-length blonde strands up from her face and into a loose bun at the crown of her head. The last required piece of attire for a day at the computer were her fingerless gloves, and she slipped those on, popped her knuckles, and flipped open the laptop, ready to dive in.

"Holden Hart!" she heard the barista shout from the opposite end of the coffee shop just as she was about to jam her earbuds into place. "Holden Hart Hot Chocolate ready at the bar!"

She still couldn't fathom why they would name a drink after the guy, let alone the fact that someone would actually order it. A grown man sort-of-someone, apparently, as she noted the person who had graciously collected her coins earlier now collecting his drink from the counter.

She harrumphed under a breath, vowing not to let it bother her.

She could have her name up on that chalkboard if she wanted. *Rachel Joy Java. Rachel's Medium Roast.* It wasn't like he had one-upped her by having his name on a silly menu. She wasn't keeping score anymore, anyway. And even if she were, having her family's noble fir as the official town square Christmas tree would be the big holiday win to end all competitions.

Holden's name hadn't crossed her mind in the last decade, so why had it suddenly hung around the forefront of her thoughts like outdoor Christmas lights left up long into February? It was annoying and overdone and entirely unnecessary. But maybe a little of that had to do with the fact that the small town reminded her of his existence at every turn. From the menu, to the sound of his name booming from the barista's lips, Holden Hart kept springing up in her periphery. She would have to shut that down.

Sliding the volume up on her phone, she let the warbling sounds of Bing Crosby's "Santa Claus is Coming to Town" drown out the cacophony of noise within the shop.

During her struggle for sleep the night before, she had taken advantage of that restless time and put together a playlist of holiday carols to keep on rotation for their noble fir. Later today, when she finished working on her business plan, she would head to the general store to pick up an outdoor Bluetooth speaker. While she appreciated her dad's efforts in singing directly to the tree, it wasn't practical, not when the temperatures dipped into the teens and the sun set before five o'clock. If he truly believed music helped things grow, then Rachel would make sure the best Christmas crooners around serenaded that evergreen twenty-four-seven.

She pulled open her document on the screen, took another motivating breath, and began clicking across the keyboard. The volume on her phone must've been too high, as she didn't hear her order when called, and instead startled when a server popped up behind her, beverage in hand.

"I didn't want it to get cold up on the bar," the teenage girl said with a braces-filled grin.

"Oh, thank you." Rachel tugged the earbuds free and took the cup. "I appreciate it."

The man next to her edged a smile in her direction. The intrusion would have annoyed her, but it was altogether impossible not to be in one another's space.

"Excellent service here," he said when their gazes met. She hadn't noticed it earlier, but he'd shed his enormous parka and now sat at his table dressed in a hunter green, long-sleeved Henley that pulled the flecks of jade from his eyes.

Rachel shook her head. She couldn't let the distraction of a handsome man keep her from the day's goals. She redirected her focus to the screen and sipped on her drink, letting the warm promise of energy lift her spirits.

"I've never quite understood those."

She should have put her earbuds back in. "Excuse me?"

The man nudged his chin toward her hands. "Those gloves without the fingers. What purpose do they serve?"

"They keep my hands warm." Brow furrowed, Rachel angled back to the work in front of her, hoping her action served as a period at the end of the unwanted conversation.

"But do they? Really?" The lift in his voice called her out. "Or do they just keep your palms warm while your fingers stay cold? Like toeless socks or something."

"I've never actually heard of toeless socks."

His head bobbed in a deliberately slow nod. "Right. Because they wouldn't really do anything."

Rachel's molars met and clamped together. "If you don't mind, I've got some work to do."

The man scooted his chair back, stretched out his long, jean-clad legs, and crossed one over the other at the ankles. "What kind of work?"

This guy had more questions than a greedy child had toys on a list for Santa. "Marketing and product development."

"Ah, interesting." He lifted his hot chocolate to his mouth, took a sip and held it there, then let out a satisfied hiss after swallowing. "So you'd be able to market fingerless gloves, since that's your line of work."

"If I wanted to." What was this sudden challenge from a complete stranger in a coffeehouse? "Yes, I could market them."

"Give it to me."

"What?"

"Give me your best pitch." He nodded toward her hands again. "For the gloves." His head cocked to the side and a provoking grin perked up his lips. "I mean, you obviously bought them, so you should be able to tell me why I should too. Sell them to me."

She didn't have time for this, and yet everything within her wanted to justify her purchase to the exasperating stranger at the table beside her.

"Fine," she relented. "When I'm typing for a long time, my circulation isn't that great, so my hands get cold easily. But I find I type faster when my fingertips can feel the keys. These gloves help me with that. They keep my hands from cramping up with cold and keep my fingers moving fast," she supplied in a rush. "There. Happy?"

Over the rim of his cardboard cup, the man grinned the most frustratingly appealing smirk. "Very."

He didn't bother her after that; not with words, anyway. But his presence next to her had Rachel as distracted as a dog in a yard full of squirrels. What was with this guy and his insistence that she prove herself to him? She didn't need to prove herself to anyone. Not right now, at least. After the new year, she'd have to prove Mistlefaux's worth in the global market as a necessary piece of holiday décor, but she had some time before that.

And she *would* prove her place as the unofficial Christmas Competition winner once her family's tree shone brightly—front-and-center—at the celebratory lighting in the town's square.

Some might call her competitive, but Rachel labeled it determination. And that wasn't a bad thing, not in her line of work.

Still, she couldn't place the familiar tug toward the coffee shop stranger, nor could she ignore her odd desire to set him straight. She knew the Christmas season should usher in feelings of love and warmth, but each time she glanced over and met his emerald eyes and caught his tempting grin, she turned ice cold.

It was almost enough to make her wish for a pair of normal gloves. *Almost.*

CHAPTER 4

❄

"A puppy!" A young girl with a smattering of freckles and bouncing pigtails raced over to the dog bed, about to smother Scout in a flurry of affection.

"Wait, Emma. You need to ask permission first. It might be a working dog."

Holden appreciated the mother's instruction and smiled at the thoughtful comment. "Scout *is* a working dog. But she's not working right now and she would absolutely love a good snuggle. Go for it."

At that green light, the girl dove onto the dog, getting lost in a blur of golden fur, tail wagging, and tongue licks.

Scout never failed as the main attraction for young children at the rental shop. Something about a happy dog just drew kids in. And a golden retriever? That was like a puppy jackpot. There was a reason the breed was so well-loved. For most people, it was the playful nature that made the canine a top pick as a family dog.

But Holden appreciated Scout for an entirely different reason. The animal had a work ethic and drive like no other, and after almost one-thousand hours of training, she was finally eligible for validation as an Avalanche Rescue Dog. In one week's time, Scout would be tested out on that mountain, and as his handler, Holden knew his girl would pass with flying colors. She was born to do this, made for the search.

"What sort of job does she do?" A man—the father of the young girl, Holden figured—squatted and ran his palm along the top of Scout's fuzzy head, getting a nudge from a wet, black nose in return. "She doesn't lead the snowmobile expeditions, does she?"

It was meant as a joke, but there was an ounce of truth in it. "She's not the best at driving the machines," Holden teased. "What with the lack of opposable thumbs and all." Holden wiggled the two fingers in question. "But she does know how to ride on the back of one, and I'll be bringing her out on our trek today."

"You will?" The girl's eyes sparked with unbridled excitement. "She won't fall off?"

"Nah. She's got great balance."

"So, she's not a tour guide…" The father narrowed down possible professions.

"She's in training to be an Avalanche Rescue Dog."

Both parents bristled in unison.

"And to put you at ease, it's likely she'll never even need to be used as one," Holden reassured. "Avalanches are incredibly rare on this particular terrain. But if there ever *is* one anywhere on this mountain or the ones surrounding us, having a dog like Scout who knows how to find and dig out survivors is like having another tool in our rescue toolbox. She's a tremendous asset."

"You say 'our'. Does that mean you're part of Search and Rescue too?" The man rose to his feet and brushed the dog hair from his wool sweater.

"A volunteer," Holden said. "Both Lance and I are. We've got the snowmobiles, the mountain knowledge, and a good dog. All of that can be really beneficial in the off chance something goes sideways up here in the High Sierra." Holden clapped his hands together. "But that's not happening today. The only thing we're going to do today is to have an awesome time carving up that fresh powder. Who's in?"

* * *

As promised, the tour was a hit. And as predicted, Scout stole the show. She'd caught snowballs launched into her slobbery mouth, donned a beanie and a scarf for family pictures, and ended the adventure with an epic game of tug-o-war. It was the best day for the best girl.

Lance took out the next group of five that arrived at noon, and Holden manned the shop while a few of their employees tuned up the mobiles in the garage in the back, their music cranking over the speakers in a muffled hum that shook the store's walls. Major Hart Mountain Sports was a well-oiled machine, and Holden was grateful for the faithful employees and consistent customers that kept everything running. There was an energy to the place that kept him feeling young.

Not that he was old by any means. His thirtieth birthday was still a couple of years away, but his employees—most of them fresh out of high school—reminded Holden daily that he wasn't a kid anymore with their music, their energy drinks that left him dizzied from the extreme amounts of sugar and caffeine, and their talk of all things related to good-looking girls and Friday night plans.

Holden had aged out of that long ago. A Friday night now consisted of a single cold beer, a game on the television, and a blonde curled up at his side. A furry, golden blonde.

Sure, at one point in his life, he'd figured he'd be settled with a family by now. That house, wife, and two point five kids sort of thing. But relationships never seemed to last longer than the first few dates before they went downhill faster than a skier in the Super-G competition.

Holden was easily bored with casual dating. Bored with obligatory small-talk and introductions. None of the women he met were good matches for him. It was as though they were all cookie-cutter versions of the same person: a nice woman who liked the snow but didn't like to be out in it, liked snowmobiling but only at ten miles-per-hour, liked Holden but not the amount of hours he spent at the shop.

That last one was the typical deal breaker.

Holidays were often spent decorating or watching a marathon of festive movies. Wrapping gifts or addressing holiday cards. The season was one of making Christmas memories, but Holden just couldn't provide that.

It wasn't as though he didn't like Christmas. He was no Scrooge. But somewhere along the line, Christmas had lost its magic. Might've had a little to do with the way it had morphed into a competition back in his high school years.

Instead of paper rings counting down to the beloved holiday, he had a paper chain of wins against Rachel, each victory written on a strip of construction paper and linked in a trivial tally of successes.

Why had he let her steal so much of his joy back then? And why did that still bother him, even now?

The phone vibrating in his shirt pocket rattled Holden out of his reverie. Scout's ears perked up at the soft sound.

"Hey, Mom," Holden greeted. He lowered onto the swiveling bar stool behind the cash register to take the call. "Still on for dinner tonight?"

"I've got the roast in the crockpot as we speak. And I just heard from Sarah. She and the baby are stuck in traffic on Highway 80, but should be in town in time to join us."

Holden hadn't seen his older sister in months, but it

was the thought of squeezing his sweet little niece, Laney, that had him grinning ear to ear. "Scout and I will be there at six. Can I grab anything at the store on my way? Drinks? Dessert?"

"Probably nothing from the store, but that's actually why I'm calling." Holden could hear his mother moving about her cabin kitchen, the open and shut of cabinet doors following her words. "Dad wanted me to ask you if you've got some PVC pipes hanging around the shop. Something we can use to measure Sir Noble Fir."

"So you've officially named him, huh?"

"That's all your father. He's really getting into it, Holden. Like *really* into it," Jill Hart said. "We ran into the Joys at the hardware store the other day and you should've seen your father and Stewart. The glare they exchanged could've cut glass. I've never seen him like this."

"Really? You've *never* seen him like this?"

"Okay, I've seen him like this a time or two," his mother conceded. "But not in years. What is it with those guys?"

The rivalry wasn't confined to the two patriarchs and Jill knew that, but Holden opted not to remind her.

"They're getting a little senile in their old age," Holden chided.

"Something." Jill huffed her annoyance. "Anyway, your father is convinced our tree is finally tall enough to enter this year."

"That's what I've heard."

"And I don't want him climbing up on that silly

ladder to measure it. The last thing we need this Christmas is a trip to the E.R. I was hoping you might configure something. A pole or piece of wood. Something he can prop up next to the tree to measure its height."

"I'll see what I've got around the shop," Holden said. "I'm sure I can come up with something."

"Thanks, sweetheart." His mother paused, and he knew exactly what was coming next. "Can I make up an extra place setting at the dinner table tonight?"

"Sure, you can. But I've told you before, Scout isn't good with utensils and she's perfectly content eating on the floor."

He could feel the eye roll, even through the phone.

"One of these days, you're going to bring home a nice young woman, Holden. And when you do, we'll be here waiting with open arms."

"Your arms are going to get tired."

Another eye roll. He'd bet money on it.

They finished the call with their *'I love you's'* and goodbyes, and Holden replayed his mother's words while rummaging through their storage area in the back of the building. He knew his mother only wanted his happiness. But he *was* happy, wasn't he?

He had his business, a loyal companion, and the best mountain views the Sierra could offer.

So why did his heart catch at the thought of finding someone to share it all with? And why in Saint Nick's name did the woman from the coffee shop suddenly come to mind?

CHAPTER 5

❄

"Don't you think you should turn that down just a touch?" Paula Joy cast a look over her wire-rimmed reading glasses toward her husband busily fiddling with the volume on his phone.

Even with good insulation and double-paned windows, the jingling of bells and soundtrack of holiday tunes carried into the cabin like it was playing on the bookshelf speaker.

"Oh, don't you worry about that, Paula. Our nearest neighbor is ten acres away. I doubt they can even hear it."

Rachel wasn't so sure. Her dad had loved the Christmas playlist idea and spent all afternoon constructing a little shelter for the outdoor speaker so it wouldn't become damaged by the wintery elements. It would have been comical had her father not been so serious about it all.

"I'm sure they can hear that blaring music all the

way to the North Pole," Paula remarked before lifting her book back up and tugging the heirloom Christmas quilt around her middle.

"Even better," Stewart rallied.

Rachel snickered. Her parents weren't the lovey-dovey sort, but they got on just fine. In fact, she'd never really known them to fight, only bicker in the way older couples often did, the many years together shedding their filters and loosening their manners.

But she knew they loved one another. It was clear even now in the way her mother smirked at her father, half-annoyed by his antics and half-amused all the same. Her eyes twinkled playfully and Rachel read that as affection.

Blinking back to her laptop, Rachel tried to focus on the business plan, but the strain from hours spent staring at the screen had her rubbing her fists into her eye sockets.

"Why don't you take a break, Rach?" Paula shut her book this time and lowered it to her lap. "How about I make a batch of hot chocolate and we pull down the ornaments from the closet and get them organized for the tree?"

Rachel's stomach rolled. "Any chance we could have apple cider instead?"

"Sure." Her mother rose from the loveseat. "I think I can arrange that."

Snapping her laptop closed, Rachel moved the computer to the coffee table and sat forward on the couch. "You got that playlist figured out yet, Dad?"

"I've added enough carols that we can get a solid twenty-four hours of unique songs before ever rotating back through."

"I had no clue there were that many Christmas carols."

"There are nearly ten-thousand," Stewart clarified. "But I only have a small sampling of that on the list. Only the very best for our noble."

From the outside, her father's odd enthusiasm could be evidence to check him into the looney bin, but there was always more than what was seen on the surface. Always more to the story.

Rachel knew why her father tended to that precious evergreen day and night. Why he did everything he could to make sure it thrived and flourished under his deliberate care.

Yes, Rachel had been the one to plant it so many years ago, but her older sister, Bethany, had been right there with her, digging that hole in the ground, side by side. It was Bethany's last summer in Snowdrift before leaving for college, and planting that tree was the last act they'd done as a family. The last thing they were able to do before tragedy cut everything unexpectedly short.

There was a bit of her legacy in the towering evergreen, and Stewart made certain he did everything possible to keep his beloved daughter's memory alive in those branches and in its stately presence.

"I should get down those ornaments your mother mentioned." Pressing up to his feet with a groan that seemed to accompany most movements these days, Stewart looked down at his daughter and toyed with the sleeves of his sweater, cuffing them up to his elbows. "And you should take a break from whatever it is you've been staring at on that computer. You're straining those beautiful blues of yours."

'Whatever it is' was her entire professional future, but she didn't care to delve into it. Not now. "Sure. I can take a break." Rachel agreed with a conceding nod. "And trimming the tree is always a good excuse for one."

She followed her father into the spare bedroom—her temporary sleeping quarters—and took each box he lowered from the uppermost closet shelf and passed her way. In truth, it surprised her that her parents had waited so long to set up and decorate their tree. They were typically the put-it-up-the-day-after-Thanksgiving sort of people. And yet it was already into December and Stewart had only gotten the fir into the tree stand that very morning. Something felt amiss, but Rachel had little more to go on than a hunch.

By the time they'd parceled off and stacked the boxes into groups they could easily cart into the family room, Paula came back with a tray of mugs. Tendrils of steam coiled above them, mixing with the aroma of spicy cider. She passed one to Rachel, along with a cinnamon stick.

"Here you go, darling. Careful. It's hot."

"Thanks, Mom." She took that first sip, savoring the heat that moved through her like a holiday hug. She had missed this—being back in Snowdrift with her parents, in this house that held her childhood memories like a scrapbook made from wood and beams. Everywhere her gaze landed, she saw a scene that carted her back to a time she hadn't fully appreciated when she was in the middle of it.

The consistency of family. The comforting routine of a simple schedule. Knowing there was someone to come home to after a bad day.

Rachel didn't have that now. Sure, she had a handful of friends, none of them close. They were the type that she'd go out with for drinks after work. They'd talk about their days at their respective offices on a surface level, never getting too deep. In fact, she didn't even know the professions of half of them, and couldn't confidently say the last names of the rest.

She'd met them in the elevator, all working on separate floors but within the same sky rise.

It was an accident that they had even invited her to join them in the first place. She had been on a phone call when the small group arranged plans, and her perfectly placed, "What was that?" to the caller on the other line led the organizer to believe Rachel was asking for clarification.

They'd insisted she tag along, and she'd been too embarrassed to explain her blunder.

That wasn't like her. And yet, it was the person she'd become.

One who rode the elevator at work and glommed onto people who showed any amount of interest.

Removed from it all now, the sad loneliness of it swept through her like a frigid mountain wind.

"Are you sure you're okay, Sugar Plum?" Her father lowered his mug to a coaster and removed the lid to the first box.

"I'm great," she lied. "Why?"

"The other day—when I called for you to sing to the tree—you seemed…I don't know. A little off."

She took another sip to prolong the time before his question required an answer.

"Go easy on her, Stewart. She had that big presentation this week, remember?"

Her father lifted the first ornament from the box and paused before sliding the hook in the eyehole, a repentant gaze shrouding his eyes. "I didn't remember that." His shoulders fell. "I'm so sorry, sweetheart. That's why you were in such a rush to get off the phone, wasn't it? How did it go?"

"Not all that great," Rachel admitted through a smile she worked hard to give. "But they've given me until the first of the year to rework things and pitch it again."

"That's a very gracious offer," Paula acknowledged, taking the ornament from her husband's hand and placing it onto a branch.

"It is." Rachel knew it was. "But I'm not even sure I should bother trying a second time."

Both sets of eyes locked in on her.

"What?" She suddenly felt self-conscious, like she'd spilled her drink on her sweater without knowing.

"You've never shied away from a challenge." Stewart

handed off another ornament to his wife. "As I recall, you once lived for them."

That was a long time ago, back when winning or losing had little consequence in the real world. Now, a failed opportunity could cost Rachel her entire livelihood, her San Francisco apartment, her carefully curated lifestyle.

It wasn't about ego anymore; it was about fulfilling dreams. Big ones.

She took another drink of cider before abandoning the mug to the table and joining her parents at the almost-bare tree. Someone had strung twinkle lights around it earlier, and the pinpricks of white amongst deep green reminded Rachel of the tapestry of winter stars that peeked through the forest skyline. So different from the city, where lights sparkled and shined too, but with a manmade luster.

It truly was different up on this mountain. Life was different here. And so was the air, which made Rachel wonder if that elevation was getting to her head. She shook hers.

"I'll get started on this box." She squatted low, lifting the brown lid to the box on her left. The ornaments and decorations that looked up at her from their cardboard confinement nearly had her rolling her eyes. Of course, she would choose this box.

"Are those what I think they are?" Paula sidled up behind her daughter to peer over her shoulder.

Rachel's stomach churned. "They sure are."

Each salt-dough ornament mocked her with childish paltriness.

"I can't believe you made one for each contest in the Christmas Competition you had going with that Hart boy."

That Hart boy. Rachel snickered, wondering how she'd never fully recognized her overwhelming immaturity until now. Until a box of ornaments called her out a decade later.

Paula's hand dipped into the box. "Oh, remember this one? You made this for that snowman building contest back in…what grade was it again?"

"That was freshman year, I believe," Stewart supplied. "Yep. See the date right there?" He lowered his glasses and read the year etched into the back of the handmade ornament.

"And this one." Paula took out another. "The year you and Holden competed for ice hockey champion. That was a fun one."

A fun one, until the moment the puck met Rachel's mouth, nearly knocking loose her two front teeth, not something she wanted to include on her Christmas wish list that year. Still, she grinned, absently running her finger over her bottom lip.

Her parents continued riffling through the box and the memories continued filtering back with each trophy-like ornament.

"Whatever happened to Holden?" Rachel broached, curiosity bubbling up within her as each recollection surfaced.

Paula and Stewart exchanged an indecipherable look that had Rachel's gaze ping-ponging between them.

"He's still around," was all her father supplied.

There was more to it than that, but neither offered anything other than to shut the lid on the box, slide it to the back behind the others, and open the next carton of keepsakes.

Rachel wanted to ask more, but it was as though her curiosity was trapped within that box too. When her parents began pulling out new ornaments to hang on the tree, she joined them, leaving questions about Holden in the past, right where they belonged.

CHAPTER 6

❄

Holden was more stuffed than a Christmas goose crammed with all the holiday fixings. His mom always made sure there was enough food on the table to feed a small army, and while he and his dad could pack it away, the amount of leftovers bordered on embarrassing.

Even Scout couldn't clean it all up.

"Once again, I've over prepared." Jill pressed the lid to the container to seal the contents inside, then passed it to Holden.

He stacked it in the refrigerator like a carefully constructed game of Jenga. One misplaced carton and the entire Tupperware structure would come crashing down.

"Before you leave, let me pack up a bag for you to take to the boys at the shop for lunches this week."

"I'm sure they would appreciate that."

Most of the time, lunch breaks consisted of beef

jerky, an apple or other easy-to-eat fruit, and a soda from the vending machine. It was always a grab-and-go sort of situation, their hectic schedules leaving little time to prepare, much less enjoy, a home cooked meal.

"How are things going at the place?"

"Really good, actually." Holden closed the fridge and turned around to lean against it. "We just approved our new storefront logo, so we'll actually have some signage soon. And we're looking into hiring another guide. It's become almost more than Lance and I can do on our own, which is a good problem to have, I suppose."

His gaze pulled from his mother to the stairwell where his sister appeared, holding a freshly bathed Laney in the most adorable reindeer-printed footie pajamas. "How is Lance doing?"

"Great, as usual," he answered his sister. "That guy's pretty unflappable. He took a tour out the other day, and even with a stalled snowmobile and a motion-sick grandma, he still said it was one of the best expeditions yet. He's the eternal optimist. Nothing gets to him."

"I always enjoyed him," Sarah said before bouncing her baby on her hip and nuzzling noses. "Anyway, someone said she wants one last kiss and a bedtime story from her uncle before going down for the night."

"Really?" Holden blinked, unbelieving. "She said all that?"

"Not in so many words, but I could read it in her eyes."

While he cherished his niece and believed she was

the smartest little thing in the world, Holden knew the vocabulary of a one-year-old was limited to 'goo-goo' and 'ga-ga'. And 'no'. That was a big one. But his sister's exhaustion came through as loud and as clear as any verbalized sentence.

He scooped the child from her arms. "Why don't you pour yourself a glass of wine and take a load off while I get this sweetie down for night-night?"

Sarah's shoulders lifted and fell with a massive exhale. "Really?"

"I've got you," he said, then patted the baby on the back of her fuzzy onesie. "And I've got this little one too. Send reinforcements if I'm not back in twenty."

"Or cookies," Jill interjected, pointing a spatula her son's way. "They'll be fresh out of the oven by then."

"I'll be sure to head down as soon as I smell them."

He turned toward the hall and up the stairs, past his parents' master bedroom and closer to the room that was once his, but had now transformed into a full-on nursery. The medals, trophies, and photographs, all boasting his high school achievements, were replaced with plush mobiles, paintings with nursery rhyme phrases, and muted pastel colors.

He didn't mind it one bit. Things changed; life moved on. And the promise of a bright future in the form of this sweet child deserved to be decorated floor to ceiling.

"What'll it be, Laney girl?" He moved her from one hip to the other and scanned the impressive board book selection on the shelf. His mom sure had things down in the spoiling department. "Are we leaning toward something Christmas themed?"

The baby's chubby hand reached up to his cheek, her palm pressing against his stubbly jaw. She rubbed it back and forth and squealed.

"Uncle Holden needs to shave," he teased. "Or maybe I should grow a beard like Santa Claus? What do you think? Ho, ho, ho." He bounced her with the words.

Another bubbling laugh cooed from Laney's lips, her kicking legs joining her delight.

"Hold still, wiggle worm." He secured his grip around her. "Give me one second to find something." Holden ran his fingers along the spines and landed on a tattered book that looked familiar. He tugged it from the shelf. "Rudolph's Reindeer Games," he read aloud.

Moving to the rocker near the window, Holden lowered and rotated Laney so she sat on his lap, facing the book held up in his hands. "If I remember correctly, this was a really good one."

And it was, if you enjoyed reading about a sad little reindeer who lost nearly every competition against his caribou counterparts. How had Holden never noticed the similarities between this piece of fiction and his real life? It was as though Rachel Joy herself had penned the very words on the pages, the illustrations a stark reminder of all the times he'd focused on winning instead of the delight each holiday activity should bring.

He closed the book before finishing, grateful his niece was too young to call him out on that.

"Let's try another one." He hoisted her from his lap and selected another book from the stack, this one about a winter ballerina and her quest to find the Peppermint Patty Forest.

Thankfully, Holden couldn't find any real-life similarities between these pages, and before he came to the closing sentence, Laney was fast asleep in his arms.

He gazed down at her soft lashes fluttering against rosy red cheeks. Even the patch of drool forming on his shirt from her open mouth couldn't ruin the adorably peaceful moment.

The love he had for this little girl ran so deep, he sometimes wondered what it would feel like to have a child of his own. He couldn't imagine his heart housing any more adoration than it already did. And yet, he knew if he were ever blessed with a family, that love would have the ability to crack his heart open in the best way possible.

Shifting from the rocking chair, he carefully transferred Laney to the crib, dimming the overhead light so a muted wash of gold kept the room illuminated.

He left the door open a crack. On an inhale, he caught the sugary aroma of freshly baked cookies, spurring his feet to move back through the halls. Like he had as a child, Holden bounded down the stairs two at a time, the promise of chocolate chip goodness beckoning him to the kitchen.

"How'd she do?" His mother looked up from the

baking sheet. She pried a still-warm treat from the pan and moved it to a red platter with cookies stacked five high. "Did she go down okay?"

"Out like a light." Holden snagged a cookie and popped a bite into his mouth. "Hey, Mom. Remember that old book about Rudolph? The one with all those rhymes and cartoon graphics?"

"Of course, I do. That was your favorite book. In fact, that copy upstairs isn't even the original. I had to buy another because the pages got so worn from you carrying it everywhere you went when you were a toddler. You sure loved all of those reindeer games."

Holden's mouth slipped into a frown. "Have I always been so competitive?"

Jill looked up. "Competitive? Oh, I don't know. I suppose you always liked to be your best. To give everything one-hundred percent. But the apple doesn't fall far from the tree there." She dipped her head and angled her eyes toward her husband, who had suddenly jumped to his feet, shouting emphatically at the football game on the television like he was a coach from the couch.

"I just wonder if maybe I was a little too intense."

"I think you're passionate, Holden. Nothing wrong with that."

"Well, there is something wrong with it when it gets people hurt," he said pointedly.

Jill put the spatula down. She moved the few feet between them and took her son's shoulders into her grip. "Holden Hart, you are not to blame for the things out of your control."

It was a mantra he might as well have had tattooed across his forehead for all the times his parents had imprinted it into his mind.

"I know," he relented. His mother released her grasp.

She turned back toward the cookies. "Things happen and sometimes there's just nothing we can do about it."

"But sometimes there is something we can do about it."

She picked up her utensil and swatted it toward him. "I will not let you go down the path of regret tonight, Holden."

She was right. It made no sense to linger on what-if's and if-only's. And yet, Holden awoke each morning playing out a reel of scenarios that could have changed things in his past.

"I'm serious." Jill shoved another cookie his way. "Eat this and stuff down those thoughts. They're not yours to have."

The cookie made him feel remotely better, but the time with his family in the house he grew up in was the real healing balm. Always had been. And if he continued to be a luckier man than he deserved, always would be.

CHAPTER 7

It was almost an official workspace, and Rachel was grateful that once again, her table at the back of Bitter Cold Coffee Bar was wide open. She set up her things and claimed her spot, ordering an Alpine Americano off of the seasonal menu at the suggestion of the barista.

It was finally beginning to feel like Christmas. Her parents' fully decorated tree—trimmed with heirloom ornaments and adorned in cranberry garland and sparkling tinsel—certainly helped with that. And the constant loop of carols just outside the Joy cabin window did its best to get Rachel in the Christmassy mood.

Even today, she had coiled a green and red plaid scarf around her neck, decorating herself in festive splendor just like a tree.

The café joined in too. Instrumental organ tunes belonging at a Christmas Eve church service piped through the speakers. It was the beautiful and calming soundtrack Rachel needed to ratchet down her anxiety and focus on the work before her.

She pulled out the sprigs of artificial mistletoe and rested them on top of the bistro table, directly next to her laptop. They taunted her, and she winced at the depressing thought that something she spent so much time on could make her feel so inferior.

Over the years with December Décor, she had designed many products for their catalog, most of which became seasonal best sellers. Her rustic evergreen boughs, adorned with pinecones and berries and fashioned into swags and sprays, were a hit last Christmas. As were her farmhouse-themed wreaths that came in the shapes of horses, goats, and even cows.

But the idea of artificial mistletoe was an entirely new venture for their company. Most of the ones currently on the market really dressed up the sprigs, making them resemble holly more than the sparse plant. Some even turned them into little green clusters in the shape of a kissing ball.

But for December Décor, realism was the key to their success. While her farmhouse wreaths were kitschy, the greenery was nearly indistinguishable from real foliage.

And this was where the mistletoe was a miss. Sure, it looked real, but that didn't do it any favors. At the end of the day, mistletoe was simply a parasite on an otherwise healthy tree.

And this project was becoming a parasite in Rachel's otherwise healthy career.

She groaned.

"Hey there, Mittens."

She choked on her drink, head snapping up to attention. The man from the other day stood towering above her, that smile fixed on his full mouth. He slunk an arm out of his jacket, one, then the other, and draped the puffer over the seat back.

Mittens? Really? She didn't even know the guy, and yet his casual familiarity was a little too comfortable. "I do have a name."

"What's that?"

The espresso machine hissed and gurgled loudly at his back, sputtering as it steamed milk for another drink.

"It's Rachel," she said, hardly able to hear her own voice.

"Mind if I join you?" He seemed to completely ignore her introduction.

He'd already settled into the chair at the table next to her. He wasn't really *joining* her, but in this coffee shop with such forced proximity, it was nearly the same thing.

"Go ahead." Her earbuds were in her purse. She could make a move for them as a sign that she didn't care to converse, but he got his out first and popped them into his ears.

Good. Seemed like he had his own work to do today. Looking down at her gloves, Rachel wondered if there would be any more comments other than the odd nickname or if he would let it be. She chanced a look up, catching his green gaze a second before she meant to pull away.

He smiled.

She would have to research the caffeine content of her drink later, because the jitters skittering through her stomach could only be attributed to the buzz, certainly not his beaming grin that transformed his entire face with friendliness.

She forced her eyes back to the mistletoe.

How could she improve upon it and take it from a spindly looking plant to something a couple might actually want to kiss beneath? Maybe it could be scented, some Christmas pheromone that drew potential soul mates together.

She almost laughed out loud at that. Scratch and sniff mistletoe was not a thing.

Lifting it up, she twisted the stems of the fake plant between her fingers, spinning the leaves around like a little disco ball.

The guy next to her popped one earbud free. "You got a thing for weeds?"

The insulting comment hit her in the gut harder than an unexpected smack from a snowball. "Excuse me?"

"You're playing with that weed."

"I'm not playing with it." She dropped it on the table. "I'm studying it."

"You're a botanist?"

"No." Rachel's brow drew so tightly over her eyes it almost obscured her vision. "I'm not a botanist. I'm in marketing, remember?"

"You're trying to market weeds?"

She snagged the mistletoe from the tabletop and shook it vigorously in front of his face. "This is not a weed!"

Like molasses in winter, he slowly tugged the other earpiece free. "Alright. Alright. It's not a weed. It's a dead plant."

"It's not a dead plant!" Rachel smacked her forehead. "It's mistletoe."

The laugh erupting from the guy made the three patrons waiting at the barista bar spin around to locate the commotion. "*That* is not mistletoe, Mittens."

If she wasn't all worked up over the mistletoe debacle, she would've insisted he stop calling her that. But she only had the energy to set one thing straight at a time. "It *is* mistletoe. Or fake mistletoe, at least." She sat up tall. "Mistle*faux*."

Had he been sipping on his hot chocolate, it would have sprayed from his nose, the laugh that flew from his lips that dramatic. "Mistlefaux?" His fist met his chest as he coughed, and he carried on laughing until it petered out into a soft chuckle. His face went blank. "Oh, you're serious."

"Yes, I'm serious." Rachel had a vise grip on the pitiful plant. "It's a prototype, so it's not the finished product. But it *is* mistletoe." She breathed out. "Or at least it's supposed to be."

"Have you ever seen mistletoe?"

"Of course, I've seen mistletoe." Her head twitched a little at the question.

"Have you ever *used* mistletoe?"

She jutted her chin toward him and levied a glare his way. "Sure, I've used mistletoe."

"Like, for kissing under. That sort of thing."

"Yes!" Her hands flew into the air. "I do know what mistletoe is used for, believe it or not."

"Okay, okay." He lifted two palms in surrender. "Didn't mean to strike a nerve there."

"You didn't strike a nerve." Okay, maybe one or two. Or all of them. "This is a product I am trying to pitch to the executives at my company, and I only have a few weeks to make sure I get things right."

"I'd start by creating a new product."

Her eyes were going to tumble out of her head. "Excuse me?"

"I don't know. I just don't think your current piece is all that convincing."

"And what are you? Some sort of mistletoe expert?"

A shrug rolled over his shoulders. "Kind of. I mean, there sure is a lot of it on my mountain."

"On *your* mountain?"

"Well, maybe not *my* mountain. I don't own it or anything like that. But on the mountain where I work," he said, too smug for his own good. "I operate a winter sports rental company up the hill. There's a lot of dwarf mistletoe in the ponderosa and lodgepole pines at the lower elevations in the Sierra. It's all over the place. Looks nothing like your Mistlefaux, though."

This man obviously had more knowledge about mistletoe than Rachel had amassed in her six months of study. She felt sick to her stomach, like the unfortunate time she ate an entire box of candy canes in one sitting.

"I could show you sometime." The coffee cup raised to his face obscured his expression. Rachel couldn't tell if he was flirting or continuing on with his pattern of condescension. She'd put money on the latter.

"Show me this elusive mistletoe? No thanks," she said firmly. "I'll pass."

"Your loss." He shrugged again.

And it would be—the loss of her job. Her eyes slammed shut for a beat and then she forced them back open. "Fine."

"Fine?"

"Fine," she repeated with an exasperated breath. "I'll go see this magical mistletoe you're talking about."

"It's not magical. Just a disease on a plant."

Rachel huffed. "Well, it must hold some form of magic if it makes people want to kiss beneath it."

"I suppose maybe there's a little magic." His eyes sparked as he caught and locked onto her gaze. He raked his fingers through his disheveled hair and lifted a brow to a point when he added, "But I suppose there's only one way to find out."

CHAPTER 8

❄

This was a bad idea. A Santa's sleigh-sized sort of bad idea.

Why had Holden impulsively invited this stranger up to his place of work? And why—against all forms of logic—was he so unbelievably nervous?

He didn't even know this woman's name. But he had to admit, something about that was a little exciting. It served as a reason to keep the conversation going. To continue learning more about one another. Or maybe the fun was found in keeping things a mystery. Whatever the reason, Holden's interest had been piqued in a way it hadn't in years.

"Am I crazy?"

Scout's ears stood at attention atop her furry head.

"Don't answer that."

The door to the rental shop flung open, and with it came Lance and a whirl of mountain air. Holden zipped his jacket. No matter how high they cranked the heater, it wouldn't take the edge off the chill on the summit. Staying warm on a mountain peak in early December was, more often than not, a losing battle.

Despite the cold, Holden's face flushed, the disparity between his internal temperature and his nerves at polar opposite ends.

"That last group sure was a hoot." Lance limped toward the register and nodded at his buddy. "Who would've thought a bunch of women in their sixties would give me a run for my money on those hills?"

Holden couldn't help but detect the residual pain in the wince that chased Lance's laughter. His business partner rubbed his kneecap absentmindedly, mouth bending into a grimace.

"You know? I find I'm rarely surprised out there anymore," Holden said. "The mountain seems to bring out the daredevil in everyone, regardless of age."

"Isn't that the truth?" Lance yanked his beanie from his head, wild strands of cropped blonde hair springing into place. "We rode hard out there today, and of course my knee is acting up because of it. I'm going to go in the back room and ice it for a bit. If you need me, that's where you'll find me."

Holden hated seeing Lance in pain, and it truly bothered him that even after all the years since his skiing accident, his discomfort only seemed to worsen.

"Can I do anything for you?" It was an offer he'd been reciting longer than he could remember, but Holden already knew the answer.

"I'm fine, buddy. Promise. Just need to ice it."

Holden dipped his head in understanding. "Mind if Scout tags along? I've got someone coming in soon, and I don't plan to take her with us."

Pulling on the knees of his pants, Lance crouched down to the dog's level with a grunt. "This sweet little lady is *always* welcome company."

The wave that tumbled through Holden's stomach at the thought of his own approaching company had him feeling a sudden and foreign giddiness. What was that about?

"I'll be in the back if you need me," Lance said again before slipping down the hallway toward the break room, Scout following jollily on his heels.

It wasn't a minute more and Holden heard snow tires crunching over the slushy parking lot. He lifted his gaze to glimpse the beautiful blonde steering her Jeep into a spot just on the other side of the big glass window. She flipped down her visor, ran a tube of gloss over her mouth, and pressed her lips together in an act that had Holden's shoulders tingling. Even the hairs on his neck stood on end. He shuddered.

"Pull yourself together," he admonished under a breath as he rounded the checkout counter to stand in front of it. He lifted a heel to prop himself against the wooden structure, trying to look casual but feeling ridiculous. His arms wove across his chest and he cocked his head coolly, another silly effort at conveying calm when everything within him jumped with nerves.

"Hey," he said before she'd even fully entered the

building. He needed to temper his enthusiasm. "Hey," he tried again once she was within earshot.

"Hi." Her smile was hesitant, but lovely all the same. She came closer and stopped in front of Holden, slipping her hands into the pockets of a periwinkle jacket that matched the sky blue tone of her eyes.

"Have any trouble finding the place?"

"No." She shook her head. The tuft of yarn at the top of her beanie bobbled like a spinning top. "Your directions were great. And I actually think I've been up here before."

"Oh, yeah?" Holden leaned an elbow onto the counter, then yanked it back when he realized how forced he looked. "You've been to our shop?" He figured he would have recognized her.

"No, not the shop. But before it was here, I think." Her shoulders flinched in a shrug. "It looks familiar."

He echoed her smile and stood there a wordless minute. "Okay." He clapped his hands. "Just a little paperwork before we get on our snowmobiles—"

"Our what?" Her eyes sprang open wide.

"Snowmobiles. The trees with the mistletoe grow further down the mountain. We'll take the snowmobiles to them."

She tugged her bottom lip between her teeth and Holden read it as an act of frustration, but it had his heart doing cartwheels all the same.

"You didn't say anything about snowmobiling." Her voice trembled.

"I didn't?" He knew he hadn't. If he had, she wouldn't have agreed to the invitation.

"No, you didn't." She whipped her head back and forth, making that ball on her beanie go crazy. "I thought you would have a collection of mistletoe up here to show me or something like that. I didn't realize we'd be hunting for it."

"Well, lucky for us, mistletoe is an easy shot, what with it not moving and all." The joke fell flat in the increasingly awkward space between them. "I'm sorry. I should've been more clear."

She slipped a hand from her pocket and fluttered his comment away. "It's fine. Where's the paperwork?"

He led her to the register to retrieve the folder of blank waiver forms. Conversation was stilted between them, and his next question wasn't going to do anything to remedy that. If he was going to ask for her name again, he'd have to do it now. He thought he'd heard her introduce herself at the coffee shop, but the noise and commotion had completely drowned her out. Plus, she'd seemed so annoyed with him then. He had a feeling asking her to repeat herself would only add to that irritation.

But he had to try one more time. "So, this is going to sound sort of strange since I'm sure you already told me, but—"

"Buddy?" Lance's voice crackled over the speaker. "Would you mind coming back here for a second?"

Holden flicked an index finger toward the ceiling. "Sounds like I'm being paged. I need to check on my business partner really quick, but while I'm gone, if you could fill out the information on this form"—he slid the sheet over the counter—"that would be great."

He passed her a pen, and the way their fingers brushed when she took it from his grip had him dizzied. He spun around, needing to catch himself on a rack of men's snowboarding pants so he wouldn't topple completely over.

Momentarily steadied, Holden inhaled for five solid seconds before rushing to the back room, but even that wasn't long enough to get any oxygen into his clouded brain. What was happening to him?

"Sorry," Lance apologized as soon as the door cracked open. He had his heel elevated on a metal folding chair and a pant leg rolled up clear to his thigh, a bag of melting ice draped over his knee. "I left my phone out there, otherwise I would've texted. Just wanted to remind you we've got that guy coming in after closing for an interview. I forgot to mark it down on the schedule. Wanted to make sure you knew."

"Got it." Holden shot two thumbs in the air. "Anything else?"

Lance shimmied in his seat, trying to peer out the door. "You got someone out there?"

"Just a woman I met at the Coffee Bar. We're heading down the slopes to stock up on mistletoe."

Lance's eyebrow made an impressive arch that almost touched his hairline. "You're going on a date?"

"It's not a date. Just helping her with a little research for her work assignment."

"Her work assignment involves kissing under mistletoe?"

Holden's chin jerked back. "What? No. We're not kissing. Just gathering mistletoe."

"To do what with?"

"To study."

Lance snorted. "Buddy, I know it's been a long time since you've taken a dip in the dating pool, but this really isn't how you do it."

"I'm not dating. Seriously. I'm just taking her to collect some mistletoe. Completely innocent."

"If you say so." The ice pack slipped from Lance's knee and Scout shoved up from her curled position on the floor to collect the baggie with her mouth. She trotted up to Lance and passed it off. "Good girl." He patted her appreciatively and gave his friend a devious look. "And you be a good boy."

"Are we done here?"

Lance just smirked and Holden hightailed it out of there before the guy could get in another aggravating word.

His new friend from the coffee shop had her back to him, her eyes tracking over the apparel portion of their store. When she made a full rotation, she faced Holden. "You're back," she said with a warm smile, no longer wearing the frustrated expression from earlier.

So much for asking her name. He wasn't going to chance landing back in awkward territory, not when she looked almost excited to see him again. He'd have to find out some other way.

"Sorry. That took longer than expected."

Her hands ran up and down her biceps. "It's not a problem."

"Are you cold?" He noticed a small shiver jostle her slender shoulders.

"No. I'm not cold," she said, dropping her arms to her sides. "If I can be honest, I'm a little nervous."

"Me too!" Holden blurted before any sort of filter could dam up the words. "I don't know why being around you makes me feel that way."

She didn't blink. "I meant I was nervous about riding a snowmobile."

"Ah." He scratched the back of his neck. "Right." All saliva evaporated from his mouth and he forced a parched swallow. A cough cleared his throat. "If it would make you more comfortable, we can ride tandem."

"Like…together?"

"Yeah," he said. "That's what tandem means."

She gave a wary pause. "I don't know."

"I ride with clients all the time. We've got snowmobiles that can easily accommodate two adults. And that way, you don't need to be so nervous about the ride. I've got you."

This new proposition did nothing to combat the nerves that had been assaulting Holden's senses from the moment she stepped into the store, but they might assuage hers.

"Only if that's not weird," she replied.

"It's not weird. Promise." He moved toward the wall

and took a helmet from the women's rack. "Not any weirder than marketing plastic weeds." He pressed the helmet toward her stomach and she took it, her mouth tightening in an annoyance that also hinted at amusement.

"Touché."

Holden's shoulders jounced. "I'm sorry. I had to. That was low-hanging fruit."

"Okay, Buddy," she said as she pulled the beanie from her head and replaced it with the helmet. She balled up the knit cap and tucked it into her pocket. "Let's go see if we can snag ourselves some low-hanging mistletoe too."

CHAPTER 9

❄

When the snowmobile engine cut off, Rachel prayed she wouldn't be found out. The steady purr had masked her erratic heart rate well during their journey down the mountainside. But now, with nothing but the soft, open stillness of winter surrounding them, she feared complete exposure.

In his element, Buddy was even more good-looking. Sure, she had recognized his undeniable appeal back at the Bitter Cold Coffee Bar the first time she'd encountered him. But riding a snowmobile, her cheek pressed to his solid back as he maneuvered the small vehicle and whittled a path along the mountain, she saw him in an entirely new light.

A light that nearly blinded her with attraction.

Hiking a leg over the seat, Buddy lifted off the mobile first, then extended a hand to help Rachel onto the snowpack.

He didn't really look like a Buddy, but that was the name she'd heard clearly over the intercom when his coworker had called him into the back room. In truth, it was a relief that she no longer needed to ask for his name outright. It wasn't a date, but there was a familiarity between them that hinted at more than just two strangers conducting a simple research project. The timeline for introductions had come and gone, so the clue into his identity had been a welcome gift.

And Buddy seemed perfectly content calling her Mittens. The playful nickname even started to grow on her.

"There it is." He lifted his chin toward a sparse pine tree a few yards ahead. "See that cluster on those bottom branches?"

Shading her brow, Rachel directed her gaze along the same path until the tree in question intersected her line of sight. "I'm not sure what I'm looking for."

"Because you're looking for something that resembles your little art project."

Her chin drew back sharply. "My little art project?"

"I'm sorry." Buddy backpedaled. "That was rude. I didn't mean it like that. I just meant, don't look for that exact type of mistletoe. Look for something different."

"I honestly never realized there *were* different types of mistletoe."

"Of course there are. There's mistletoe for first kisses. Mistletoe for forbidden kisses. Even mistletoe for stolen kisses."

She pinned him with a skeptical look.

"Okay, fine." He ran a hand over his helmet-matted hair, offering a sheepish grin that pressed both dimples into place. "I just made all of that up. But it sounded good, didn't it?"

She couldn't lie. The thought of a stolen kiss on the slopes had her heart racing faster than their snowmobile, and that machine had reached speeds she'd never even achieved on the freeway.

It sounded *very* good.

"Any chance you played that game called chicken when you were a kid?" he asked out of nowhere. He slipped his thick gloves from his hands, shook the bits of snow free, and tucked them into an inner pocket within his jacket. "The one in the pool?"

"Have I played chicken? What kind of question is that?"

"A relevant one." Rachel failed to see the connection. "I need you to get on my shoulders."

Her jaw unhinged. "What? Why?"

Striding toward the pine with long, determined steps, Buddy kept talking. "How else are we going to get that mistletoe down? I don't have Go-Go-Gadget arms, Mittens."

It was a fair question, but she didn't like the answer. "You didn't bring anything to cut it down with?"

"Sure, I did." Unsheathing a small knife from his back pocket, Buddy smiled. "I brought this. And I brought you."

She groaned. That didn't feel like a viable solution. "What other options do we have?"

"I can get on your shoulders, but I'm six-three and two-hundred pounds, so unless you're a champion in weightlifting, it might be a struggle."

The only thing Rachel was currently a champion in was turning as red as a holly berry. Her cheeks flamed with a blush that had her loosening her scarf.

"Fine. I'll get on your shoulders."

"I promise I won't drop you," he assured, crouching down. "That only happened once. And don't worry, her nose healed just fine."

Rachel's snow boots rooted in place.

"I'm kidding." He waved her closer and snickered a low laugh. "Come on. Hop on up."

She sucked in a confident breath, but the cold air only tightened her lungs and burned her chest. What did she have to lose? Reaching deep for motivation, she hiked one leg over Buddy's broad shoulder, then the other. She wasn't sure why she was altogether unprepared for his hands to reach up to clasp onto hers while he gently pressed up to full height, but even with her gloves as a barrier, Rachel's palms sweat.

"How you doing up there?" His head tilted back just enough to catch her gaze but not set her off-balance.

She gulped. "Air's a little thinner."

He chuckled, then shuffled across the snow toward the pine tree, each shaky step forward making Rachel wobble from her perch atop his shoulders. She clamped her hands harder around him.

"I will not let you fall."

"I know." She nodded, but abruptly stopped when the slight movement made her sway.

She'd never been much of a tree hugger, but once that evergreen was within arm's reach, Rachel released his grasp and shot her hands up over her head to cling to the closest branches. The action anchored her slightly, but her stomach still felt as though she was on a sailboat, tossed around in tumultuous waters.

When Buddy also transferred his grip to her ankles, Rachel gasped.

"See that right there?" he indicated with a tip of his chin.

"Right where?" She scanned the tree.

"Right in front of you. The part that looks a little different from the rest of that branch."

It all looked the same to her. In fact, everything on this mountain looked the same, a winter wonderland full of snow-dusted conifers and fresh-powder peaks. Rachel wasn't even sure how Buddy had known which route to take down the hill. It was all a sea of indistinguishable white.

At one point in time, she'd known her way around Snowdrift. Knew the scenery hidden under the blanket of snow that cloaked the landscape for months at a time. But years away removed that familiarity, and it was as though the veil of snow tucked the memories beneath it too.

"Do you see what I'm talking about?"

Rachel drew herself out of the nostalgia and set her

focus on the task at hand. The sooner she could identify the mistletoe, the sooner she could get her feet back onto solid ground and off of the sturdy shoulders of the man that had her heart ticking much too quickly for her liking.

"All I see are some clusters of greenish-orange needles, but nothing that resembles mistletoe."

"That's it."

She blinked. "*This* is what you brought me all the way down this mountain to see?" She reached for the ugly barbs and touched them with the tip of her glove.

"Cut some off and I'll make sure it's what we're looking for, but that should be it." Holding onto just one ankle with a firm grip, Buddy passed off the knife with his other hand. "I told you it looked different from what you're used to."

Yeah, no kidding. It looked like a clump of grass clippings. Swallowing down her disappointment, Rachel angled the knife's serrated edge along the woody stem and began to saw back and forth. Even though only her arms moved, her entire body shifted with the effort, and Buddy slid his large hands further up toward her knees to lock her in place.

"You good?"

"I'm good," she replied. "Almost got it."

With another strong swipe of the knife, the mistletoe broke free and Rachel suddenly snapped back, the tension holding her in place releasing like a broken rubber band. Her upper body swung backward. Buddy staggered sideways to counteract her falter.

For seconds that felt like minutes, they swayed across the icy ground as one ridiculous, top-heavy unit. It was as if she were suddenly on stilts, with no control over the legs and feet that ensured she wouldn't end up face first on the ground. Her body, her brain—it all came untethered.

"Hang on!" Buddy shouted. He moved his hands up to her waist and when he dropped to the ground and lifted her off, Rachel's head whooshed like she'd crested and then dipped the highest arc of a rollercoaster. "I've got you."

Her boots met the snow first, then her knees, then her palms.

"Whoa there!" Buddy stooped and took her elbow to urge her cautiously to her feet. "You okay?"

"Fine." She flattened a palm and brushed the snow from her clothes, shoulders squared. "Totally fine." Then, hoisting the piece of mistletoe between them, right above eye level, she seethed when she asked, "*This* is better than the prototype I've been working on?"

Buddy took a step back, dusting off tiny flakes of snow from his own jacket. "It's different."

Indignant, Rachel stomped closer, coming face to face. "Different? Um, yeah. It's different alright." Her words released on a hot breath. She shook the mistletoe with vigor directly above their heads. "No one in their right mind would want to kiss under this!"

His slow gaze traveled from Rachel's wild eyes, dipping and lingering the briefest moment on her mouth before drifting back up. "You sure about that?"

he said in a tone that had her knees threatening to unhinge and drop her back into the snow.

She yanked the plant down. "We should get back."

"You're right." He looked almost disappointed. "I've got an interview in about an hour and I should probably prepare for it."

"You're looking for a new job? But I thought you owned the rental store." She crammed the mistletoe into her pocket and took the helmet when Buddy passed it her way.

"I'm not the interviewee, I'm the interviewer. We're looking to add to our staff."

"Oh." Rachel found her place behind Buddy on the snowmobile and threaded her arms around his waist, wishing for a quick ride back up the mountain so she could finally be done with all of this physical contact. It had her dizzier than a pirouetting Sugar Plum Fairy. "I may need to pick your brain about that."

"About the interviewing process?" He turned the key over on the electric start snowmobile.

"I'm pretty sure I'll be looking for a new place of employment after the new year, and I haven't interviewed with anyone since I was right out of college. I'm out of practice." She paused, thinking better of it. "On second thought, I don't know how much confidence I should place in your 'expertise'." She let go of his waist and hooked her fingers to make air quotes around the words. "After all, you brought me all the way down here only to harvest completely useless mistletoe."

His neck craned back and he smirked. "We haven't tested it out to see if it's useless yet, though, have we?"

Before Rachel could register his words, he released the choke on the snowmobile and whisked up the mountain at breakneck speed, her protest suddenly gone with the alpine wind.

CHAPTER 10

❄

"Come on, girl!"

Snow kicked out from Scout's legs like the fine grains of sand tossed from a child building a beach castle.

"Almost there."

Holden's eyes bounced between his dog and the stopwatch on his phone. If Scout could locate the piece of buried wool within the next thirty seconds, she'd beat her fastest time yet.

"So close."

Dipping into her carved-out snow cave, Scout disappeared. Holden held his breath. Waiting was the hardest part of it all. He wanted to rush over to make certain she was okay. To confirm that the very trench she'd created didn't trap her within it too. But Scout was working, and she was good at her job.

Better than Holden.

The tip of a furiously wagging tail backed out first,

followed by Scout's body, which wiggled side-to-side in celebration. She trotted over and dropped the fabric onto Holden's lap, ready for a game of tug-of-war as her reward for another job well done.

"Good girl!" Holden praised, cupping her fuzzy cheeks in his hands. He pressed a kiss to her head and ruffled up her fur. "Very good girl, Scout. You did it again!"

A flat tongue on his cheek had his eyes watering with pride.

He prayed she would never have to, but Holden was confident Scout could prove her worth as a top Avalanche Rescue Dog if the need ever arose. She'd "rescued" countless pieces of fabric during their simulations, learning to ignore the human scent on the surface of the snow and sniffing around for it buried beneath instead.

Holden had gotten Scout as an energetic puppy and knew right away she'd never be happy with the lazy lifestyle of a shop dog. She needed more. She was driven, competitive. Sure, she appreciated rest and a good nap by the fire, but it was the challenge and ensuing reward which really motivated her.

It wasn't lost on Holden that Scout was his canine counterpart. Maybe that was why they got along so well. They understood one another in an unspoken way that he often couldn't replicate with people.

As odd as it was to admit, something about the woman from the coffee shop reminded him a little of

Scout. That competitive, yet endearing, nature. Warm, but determined all the same.

Holden reached behind his back for the hidden chew toy. Scout's golden eyes danced with delight the moment it appeared. She chomped down on the rubber, her backside swishing to and fro. A throaty growl gurgled from her mouth as she bared her teeth and tossed her head.

"So ferocious." Holden couldn't keep from chuckling. Scout was all bark and no bite, and Holden had a feeling the coffee shop girl was the same. She had been yesterday, at least.

He'd had fun with her, showing her around the mountain from the back of the snowmobile. Maybe he'd even had a little too much fun, really poking the bear about the mistletoe. She'd been right. It was ugly. Much uglier than he'd remembered. But he still didn't regret taking her down to see it. The only thing he *did* regret was that they didn't get another adventure on the calendar before she left.

By the time they'd made it back to Major Hart Mountain Sports, the guy coming in for the interview had already arrived. Lance had been waiting on Holden to get things started, so they'd said their goodbyes in a rush. Holden couldn't ignore the pit forming in his stomach as he watched her Jeep drive off the property. She knew where to find him, but he had no clue where to find her, other than the Coffee Bar. He couldn't stake out the place; that wasn't his style.

No, if they were to cross paths again, it would have

to be serendipity that brought them together. Chance. Fate. Whatever you called it. Holden had tried chasing a girl before, and that had resulted in more than just a broken heart.

He wouldn't do it again.

"Should we go inside and get cleaned up before we head to Mom and Dad's?" Scout didn't answer, but she loosened her grip on the dog toy and held it obediently in her mouth when Holden let go on his end.

His house wasn't as large as his parents, but it was home all the same. It was a steep A-frame cabin with the kitchen and living room downstairs, along with a full bath and large closet for his linens, jackets, and snow gear. Upstairs, he'd converted the loft into a bedroom. It didn't have doors or a closet, so he couldn't label it as one if he ever sold the place, but it functioned the way he wanted it to and fit his queen-sized bed just fine.

Who needed doors, anyway? That would only block his unobstructed view of the sunrises over the Sierra, the majestic wash of morning light filtering in through a stretch of floor-to-ceiling windows. It was like a new painting each day, layers of pinks and oranges and purples that deserved to be framed.

"Wipe your paws," Holden reminded Scout after they'd ascended the small front porch deck. She shuffled her four little feet along the bristled mat before bounding into the cabin once Holden unlatched the door.

He dropped her toys into the wicker basket near the

fireplace, then filled up a dog bowl with fresh water from the kitchen sink. She lapped it all up as soon as he lowered the dish to the ground.

Holden could use a drink himself. Tugging on the refrigerator handle, he studied the contents within it, coming up empty.

Maybe he should go to Bitter Cold and get himself a to-go hot chocolate on his way to his parents' house. Or maybe not to-go, depending on if a certain someone was there.

He shook his head.

What was he thinking? This desire to make something happen with a practical stranger was crazy.

Scout nudged her empty food dish across the wooden floor until it met Holden's foot.

"You've already had breakfast."

Puppy dog eyes challenged him to say no. He couldn't do it.

"Fine, fine. Just a snack."

Scout didn't get kibble or dried food. No, Holden made her full-on meals. He'd read once that fresh food was significantly more nutritious for dogs than the store-bought, bagged stuff, so he'd tried his hand at preparing a few at-home meals. At first, it was just boiled chicken and steamed rice. But then he added to the list of ingredients. Sweet potatoes. Broccoli. Even eggs. Of course, Scout devoured it all, tail wagging appreciatively in non-stop motion. It was her way of saying thank you, and for some silly reason, it made Holden feel good.

It felt good to cook for someone other than himself.

He reached into the cupboard to collect the container of peanut butter dog biscuits he'd baked earlier in the week. He broke off a large piece from one, almost tempted to take a bite for himself. "Only this for now. I don't want you to spoil your appetite before dinner."

Scout gently took the treat and nibbled it down. Her tongue came out to lick any stray crumbs from her lips. When she lifted a paw for a shake, Holden caved.

"Okay. I suppose that was only half, so here's the other portion. But this really *is* all you're getting."

She wolfed down this piece faster than the first, eyes pleading for more. Looking up at Holden, she spun around in a full circle. Then rolled onto her back. It was the playing dead part that had him doubling over in laughter.

"I don't know where you get it from." Relenting, he tossed her another half of a cookie. "But that's it. For real. I'm serious."

He sealed the container and stowed it in the cabinet behind a shut door before he had the chance to give in to her adorable antics once again.

Satisfied, Scout curled up on her dog bed by the radiator while Holden took a quick shower. He wasn't even in there long enough for the water to heat up fully, so when he emerged, he tugged on the warmest sweater he owned, followed up with dark denim jeans and his argyle print wool socks. It was scarf weather up on the summit, so he looped the one his sister had crocheted him last Christmas around his neck and collected his jacket from the hall closet.

Blinking up at him, Scout cocked her head.

"I know, I know. I'm all dressed up, and you'd like to be too," he answered the question she clearly couldn't speak. "Come on over."

Bounding across the room like a jackrabbit, Scout skidded to a stop right before taking Holden out at the knees. He reached into the closet and withdrew Scout's Christmas sweater, the one detailed with alternating dog bone and candy cane shapes. If a dog could smile, Scout's was an ear-to-ear grin.

"Gimme your paw," he instructed. He fit the neck opening over her head and pulled one leg through. "And now the other."

She obeyed, then sat back proudly on her haunches.

"Now we both look our holiday best."

Following her owner out the door and into the detached garage, Scout leapt into the passenger's side of the vehicle. Holden came around the back to load the PVC pipe measuring stick he'd constructed into the truck bed. It easily broke down into three, eight-foot sections, and he'd notched both inches and feet into the plastic tubing to make the measurement as accurate as possible.

Holden was admittedly curious about the tree. When he'd planted it as a kid, he'd had the hope it would one-day serve as the town's prestigious Christmas tree during the annual lighting. It was an honor to have a tree selected, their small town's version of a Rockefeller Center evergreen.

In the beginning, he did everything he could to encourage its growth. Bought special fertilizer. Constructed a tarp to keep the snow off its branches in the winter and the sun from burning its needles in the summer. But over the years, that wish and effort dwindled until the dream was entirely extinguished.

In truth, he assumed the noble fir wouldn't get to the twenty-foot mark required for consideration. It wasn't until this last year, when it had a surprise growth spurt, that he let his heart latch onto that last little portion of remaining hope.

But his parents were all in. Especially his dad, who stood in the driveway, ready to greet Holden the moment his truck angled onto their hillside property. It didn't matter that it was twenty-eight degrees outside with steady flurries of snow and predictions of whiteout conditions, Zeke Hart was like an expectant child awaiting Santa Claus himself.

"Did you bring it with you?" Zeke met Holden at the truck and waited for Scout to jump down from the cab before shutting the door behind them.

"In the truck bed." Holden didn't want his father rushing around in these elements. With slick ice coating the ground, he risked a fall or worse. "Wait here and I'll grab it for you."

"I'm telling you, Hold, this is our year."

"So you've said," Holden replied. "But I've heard it could be the Joy's year too."

"Don't you use that kind of language around here, son," Zeke teased with a solid thwack between Holden's shoulder blades. "Keep it up and I'll have you heading inside to wash your mouth out with soap."

Stepping up onto the wheel well, Holden reached over and pulled the pipes from the bed, then passed them off to his father. "And what happens if we don't win?"

Zeke looked offended. "This win is fifteen years in the making, Hold. Our tree deserves center stage. It deserves to be ornamented with the finest decorations, strung with the most brilliant twinkling lights."

He hadn't seen his father like this in years. "And doesn't the Joy's tree deserve the same?"

"Ah, they can have it next year." He flapped a dismissive hand and tucked the long pipes up under his arm.

Holden didn't understand what was so special about this year in particular, but he let it rest.

"Mom's got some mulled cider on the stove if you want a mug before we do the honors," Zeke offered.

"That sounds great, actually," Holden said. "Let's go inside to grab that first."

"You go on ahead. I'm just going to fiddle with this before we make it official."

Holden lowered a brow. "Dad, promise me you'll wait to take the measurements until I'm out here with you."

"Scout's honor." The dog perked up at the mention of her name. "I'll wait."

Holden trusted his father's words about as much as he trusted a young child left unattended with a roomful of Christmas-morning presents. But that cider called to him, and when Holden swung the entry door open and caught a whiff of the spiced scent, his watering mouth steered him straight into the kitchen. Apple cider, cloves, and nutmeg simmered over low heat on the stove, a holiday aroma that harkened to past Christmases that took place within this very home. It was strange how a smell could be its own transportation device, depositing you squarely into the middle of a memory.

The last time their family had shared a kettle of the savory drink, his sister had a little something of her own to share: the news of her pregnancy and upcoming birth of the family's first grandchild. Or niece, in Holden's case. He couldn't think of a time when an announcement had filled him with such overwhelming joy. Maybe when Sarah and Darren had gotten engaged. That was a close second.

The beloved memories made Holden wish he had his own good news to spread. When he'd gotten Scout, he'd made a big show of it with a large, pink bow around her neck rather than a collar. And while the pup was as loveable as could be, the announcement of a dog paled in comparison to Sarah's declarations of love expanding their family through marriage and birth.

Holden wanted that. And yet, he feared he'd never get there. Never get to a place in his life where he could open himself up enough to let someone else in. And he'd witnessed the hurt that occurred when Darren unexpectedly left shortly after Laney was born. Holden saw his sister's heartbreak firsthand. Sarah had said she didn't regret any of it. Darren had given her a beautiful daughter and a brief love story she would cherish, even if he'd closed the book on his part in it. She knew she deserved better—that her daughter deserved better—and it was best that Darren's true colors showed earlier rather than later.

Her resilience was inspiring, but it still made Holden wary when it came to love.

"Please tell me your father isn't out there by himself measuring that silly tree." Jill removed her son's jacket from his shoulders when he entered the kitchen.

"He promised he'd wait."

"Well, we all know how that goes." She folded the coat over the back of a barstool at the kitchen island and tipped her head toward a collection of holiday mugs on the counter. "Go ahead. Help yourself. I made a huge batch, more than we can possibly drink." She paused. "Is there anyone you'd like to invite over to share it with?"

"Nope," was all Holden said, and he lifted a full mug to his mouth to put a period at the end of that conversation.

Jill dipped down to the retriever's level to cradle the animal's face within her hands. "Oh, Scout, sweetheart. You look just precious. I love that sweater on you. Red is your color, girl."

Jill Hart had so much love to give, it poured out

from every part of her. From her constant need to make sure the people she cared for were well fed, to the way she doted over her grandbaby and even grand-furbaby. She always said the apple didn't fall far from the Hart tree when referring to Holden's competitive nature, but the way his own heart swelled with love for family had Holden thinking maybe he'd inherited just a portion of that caretaking nature too.

At least, he hoped he had.

A sharp howl from outside suddenly cut short the peaceful moment in the kitchen.

Jill and Holden locked eyes. And then it was a race toward the back deck. Holden reached the sliding glass door first. He threw it open.

"Zeke!" Jill shouted, coming up behind him.

"Dad!" Holden echoed.

"Woo hoo!" His father danced with the teetering pole in his grip, looking like a holiday elf doing a jig in the snow. "Town square tree lighting, here we come! Sir Noble Fir is an official twenty-feet, three-inches tall! Beat that, Joys!"

His overjoyed voice carried through the mountain air, ringing with glee.

Scout barked.

"I know, girl," Jill said. She patted the dog's head and rolled her eyes. "I know."

CHAPTER 11

❄

Rachel stood from the dining table and moved to the other side, hoping if she came at it from a different angle, things might look better.

Nope.

Uninspired, she returned the piece of artificial mistletoe to her tote and pressed her hand to her forehead with a belabored sigh.

"How's it going this morning, sweetheart?" Paula appeared in the doorway. Her fingers fiddled to insert a pair of holiday earrings, the large clay wreath ones Rachel often stole for her dollhouse when she was a child. It was a wonder her mother still had the matching set. Paula clamped the backs on and grinned. "Any progress?"

"Sadly, not a lot."

"You know what you need?" Paula squinted her eyes like she was in on some secret. "You need to give that brain of yours a break from all of this work stuff. It's all you've been doing since you got here. How about you come with me? I'm heading into town for a holiday knitting class. Sue from church was supposed to join me, but she's come down with an awful head cold. Care to take her spot? I wouldn't want it to go to waste."

Rachel wasn't sure if an afternoon spent in a knitting circle was the prescription for her mistletoe melancholy, but she didn't have any other invitations.

"You know what? I think I will join you. Thanks, Mom." As a child, she'd always loved the In Stitches Yarn Shoppe, the kaleidoscope of colorful, soft skeins arranged on shelves like a rainbow made of yarn. "Let me grab my jacket and I'll meet you out in the car."

"Take your time," Paula said. "I'll go warm it up."

Rachel moved quickly through the house, retrieving her coat from the hall tree where she'd left it the day before to dry out. Her hands found the pockets as she slipped it on, and the brittle crunch of mistletoe against her fingertips made her smile.

She didn't know what Buddy had been thinking. That piece of sad mistletoe was even worse than the one she'd created. She snickered under a breath, the memory of yesterday heating her cheeks and squeezing her heart in a way that had it faltering out of rhythm.

Removing the dried plant, she placed it onto the small table by the door where her father kept his wallet and keys, then joined her mother in the car, leaving her frustrations with work behind. Maybe a day spent fashioning something entirely new was just the ticket to get those creative juices flowing.

The Joy property was a quick drive to Main Street, made occasionally longer when stuck behind a snowplow, like they found themselves today.

"That was a big storm last night." Paula snapped on her blinker to turn left, skirting the plow and picking up speed on an open stretch of white road. "Your poor father was outside at the crack of dawn, shaking the snow from the branches of that tree with a broom. I keep telling him nobles are built for these conditions, but he won't listen."

"He's really got it in his head that it's going to win this year, doesn't he?"

"He's got it in his head and in his heart." Letting her gaze leave the windshield for a brief moment, Paula's eyes met her daughter's across the cab. "This Christmas would've been Grandma Birdie's ninetieth birthday. I think he's looking at this win as a gift for her. A tribute of sorts."

How had Rachel not remembered? Had she been so wrapped up in her own world that she'd completely forgotten the one she came from?

Grandma Birdie's birthday was always a cause for celebration, and even after she'd stopped having them here on this earth, the family still acknowledged the day with fanfare and festivity. It was a tradition that spanned the many years since her passing, and Rachel suddenly understood her father's determined passion.

"Ninety years old." Rachel inhaled slowly. "I wonder what she would be like."

A single chuckle parted her mother's lips. "Oh, I

imagine she'd be even more opinionated than she already was, and her collection of fancy gloves and scarves even larger."

It was true; the woman had more opinions than a candy cane had stripes, but Rachel loved her all the more for it. It was at Grandma Birdie's consistent nudging that Rachel even applied for college in the city. Her encouragement was the push she needed to step out of her comfort zone and spread the wings that would ultimately carry her away from Snowdrift Summit.

"At one point in time, these hills were the land of opportunity for our family. But it wasn't our ancestors' intention that we settle here and never leave," Grandma Birdie had confessed to Rachel one night over a pile of college applications and scholarship submissions. *"Every generation needs to forge their own path, Sugar Plum. And that brain of yours is big enough to take you anywhere you want to go. Let the only limit to your dreams be the wide open sky."*

"You okay, sweetie?" The car rocked back at the four-way stop. Paula paused, glancing over at her daughter once more.

"What do you think would've happened if I stayed in Snowdrift?"

Even though it was their turn to go, Paula's foot hesitated in finding the gas pedal, her words taking time too. "Oh, I don't know." She shrugged her shoulders to her ears, catching her dangling earrings. "You would've gotten bored here, constantly competing with that Holden kid. You needed a bigger challenge."

"What even started that?"

"Started what?" Paula maneuvered the SUV onto Main Street and, after a quick search around the block, angled into an open spot along the curb. She shut off the engine.

"That whole thing between me and Holden?"

"You honestly don't remember?"

Rachel's front teeth pressed into her lip. She shook her head.

Her mother's mouth sputtered with a breathy laugh. "It all started when he asked you to the Winter Ball in eighth grade."

"He didn't ask me. I went with Cody Walters."

"But he *did* ask you. It was this whole elaborate ask too." Paula slid her purse onto her shoulder, her hand pausing on the inside door handle, about to exit. "Don't you remember the whole cookie decorating thing? All those cut-out letters you had to unscramble and arrange into the words, 'Will you go to Winter Ball with me?' It took you almost an hour to figure it out.'"

"Yes, but it was Cody who put all of that together." Rachel got out of the car first.

"No." Her mother shook her head. She left the vehicle to join her daughter on the sidewalk. "Cody just happened to come over for tutoring the same night you had the cookies on the counter. He thought you were asking him." She laughed a little. "And apparently, you thought he was asking you."

"Because he *was* asking me. We went to the dance together."

"You went to the dance together, but he wasn't the one who originally asked you."

Rachel's brow tightened. "How do you even know all of this?"

"Because Jill Hart sometimes comes here too, and things have a way of getting around the knitting circle."

Before Rachel could snap her unhinged jaw back into place, Paula grasped the handle to In Stitches and waltzed into the shop, a chorus of cheery greetings from the women inside drowning out the question on the tip of Rachel's tongue.

"Paula!" A woman bearing an uncanny resemblance to Mrs. Claus bounded toward them, her white bun on her head like a perfectly rounded snowball. "You made it." After squeezing Paula in a hearty hug, she swooped around to bring Rachel into her arms too. "And you brought a friend."

"I actually brought my daughter."

The woman thrust Rachel out at arm's length. "Well, frost me with icing and call me Cookie! This isn't sweet little Rachel Joy, is it?"

"The very one," Rachel said, recovering from the lung-crushing hug. She'd met Ruth, the owner, long ago, but the years between introductions had changed them both.

"Goodness! Look at you!" Ruth's twinkling eyes suddenly shrouded behind her tortoiseshell frames. "Where did all that mousey-brown hair of yours go?"

She pinched the tips of Rachel's curled strands between her fingers.

"Same place her freckles and baby fat went. She's all grown up," Paula answered for her daughter.

"In fairness, I paid the hairdresser a pretty penny to make it this way."

"Platinum blonde suits you, darling. You're every bit the Sugar Plum princess your sweet granny always called you. Just gorgeous."

Talking while walking, the woman guided Rachel and Paula toward two empty folding chairs at the edge of the circle. A bundle of deep evergreen yarn reserved the vacant places on each seat, along with several pre-cut strands of cranberry red. Many women were already happily crocheting, their hooks moving in and out of the threads in their hands while their mouths yapped and gossip traveled.

"Saved these spots just for you, dearies."

"Thank you," Paula acknowledged, finding her seat.

"We're making some mistletoe bunches today!" Ruth clapped her hands together in front of her chest. She reached for a sample and passed it off. "Aren't these just precious?"

Rachel couldn't escape. Mistletoe madness accosted her at every turn.

"Honest," Paula said in a hush as soon as Ruth left the two to their crafting. "I promise I didn't know."

"It's okay, Mom. Mistletoe is an integral part of the holiday season. I get that."

But so were candy canes, snowflakes, ornaments—

all of which would have made for equally festive crocheting projects.

"This will be fun." Picking up the hook and yarn, Rachel gifted her mother an assuring smile, even if the words were false.

"Are these seats taken?" Another mother-daughter duo came over, their faces familiar but names misplaced somewhere in Rachel's lost memories of hometown acquaintances.

"They're all yours," Paula answered without looking up from her project. When she finally lifted her attention, she froze. "Oh, Jill. I didn't realize it was you."

"Hi, Paula."

The greeting was obligatory, and Rachel noticed an apologetic half-smile form on the mouth of the daughter, as though she could also sense the tension that settled between the women like a sudden squall.

"I can sit somewhere else if it's more comfortable for—"

"Nonsense." Paula tapped the metal chair with her hook. "Please, sit. Join us."

What had happened between these families? And why did Rachel have the sudden, sinking feeling that she was entirely to blame?

"I'm not sure if you remember my daughter, Rachel." Paula pressed her hand to Rachel's knee. "She's in town for the tree lighting."

It wasn't entirely a lie. Rachel had returned home to help ensure their win, but coming face to face with the competition suddenly had her stomach tumbling like a washer filled with sodden clothes.

"And it's going to be an utterly stunning tree this year. I have that on good authority," Jill answered, likely referring to her own homegrown fir, but having the politeness necessary to keep from saying it outright. Something Rachel's father didn't possess. She waited to see if her own mother could show a similar amount of restraint.

"Yes, it is," was all Paula replied, but the smug look she brandished when Rachel caught her eye conveyed all she needed to know.

The Christmas Competition was back in full swing, whether Rachel wished to be a part of it or not.

* * *

Rachel needed a drink of the caffeinated variety, pronto. She had declined a ride back to the house with her mom, opting instead to make the short walk to Bitter Cold Coffee Bar up the street. She required the fresh air to clear her head and ease the tightness from her chest. Who would've thought a day of knitting would have the ability to tangle her own stomach into knots too?

At the end of it all, Paula and Jill had been civil, even bordering on cordial. But there was a band of tension between them that stretched tighter as the hours went on. By the time the women had completed their mistletoe activity, Rachel worried her mother's forced graciousness would snap her fake smile right in half.

Shaking off the frustration, Rachel rolled the yarn project in her hand. It had turned out even cuter than she imagined it would. She could envision it in a shop on the corner, one that specialized in handmade items and one-of-a-kind designs. But that wasn't Rachel's industry. Easily duplicated, bulk manufactured items were December Décor's claim to fame. Sometimes, she wondered if those parameters actually stifled her creativity, knowing she had to fashion something they could mass market.

It wasn't as though she'd be satisfied making and selling homemade items in a quaint mountain town, but the story behind a product like this sure held more meaning than the ones she'd created over the years.

She tucked the sprig of yarn into her purse, all the while taking in Main Street at its holiday finest. Large red bows adorned every lamppost, a repeating of scarlet red that made the entire town feel wrapped up like a present. And the window displays—those were her favorite. Every storefront boasted winter scenery, from fluffy fake snow to twinkling lights to displays filled with little villages and moving trains. Even her parents' small grocery store, Main Street Market, got in on the holiday action with stacks of green pasta boxes constructed in the shape of a Christmas tree and links of cased salamis adorning the window like strands of garland.

The outdoor music piped through the square was a

welcome treat too. Not unlike the carols on constant replay back at the Joy house, these melodic holiday tunes aided in a little growth of their own. By the time Rachel reached the Coffee Bar, her Christmas spirit had expanded by several sizes and her step felt instantly lighter, like a weight lifted from her once-weary shoulders.

She'd had a bad attitude about everything, but that was about to change. Work could wait, competitions could continue without her involvement, and a cup of hot coffee would help put everything in perspective.

The handsome face beaming up from his table near the back of the café helped a little with that too.

"I was wondering if I'd find you here," he said, rising halfway to stand. "Would you care to join me?"

Until that point, they'd only shared workspaces side by side, but Rachel gladly took the chair opposite him. "I would love that." She placed her purse between them. "That, and a massive cup of coffee."

"Rough day?"

"Weird day."

"Weirder than ours yesterday?"

She laughed. "Yesterday wasn't weird. It was different."

"Like the mistletoe."

"Speaking of." She slipped her hands into her bag and unveiled her crocheted project. "I came across another variety."

His head tilted slightly and a lock of hair swept over amused eyes. "And what's that type used for?"

"I don't know yet," she said before stowing it back in her purse, a grin challenging her lips. "Haven't tested it out."

His lips parted. He blinked a few times. "Can I get you something to drink? My treat."

"I would love one of those holiday specials. That peppermint one, if they have it."

"Coming right up."

She didn't mean to pry, but his open laptop beckoned her gaze. The results from an internet search filled the screen with images of large noble firs resembling the very one growing in her parents' backyard.

Sooner than she had expected, he came back to the table. "Should be up in just a couple of minutes."

"Thank you. I appreciate it," she said. "You doing a little Christmas tree research?"

He looked at his computer, then at Rachel. "No, why do you ask?"

"Your computer screen. I wasn't meaning to snoop. I just happened to look over and saw all the trees."

"Oh." He clamped the laptop shut. "Nah, that's for something else. But would you believe it's almost the second week of December and I don't even have a tree up yet?"

"I don't have one either. I mean, I do at the place I'm staying here. But not at home."

He leaned back. "And where's home for you?"

"San Francisco." Rachel folded her hands in front of her on the table. "I live on the twenty-fifth floor of my building, so it's not even that feasible to get a

Christmas tree all the way up. I usually settle for one of those small tabletop ones instead."

"You should never settle when it comes to a Christmas tree."

"Says the guy who doesn't even have one."

"You got me there." The barista called out the drink, but before he stood to collect it for her, he asked, "Hey, would you maybe want to join me in remedying that?"

"Go Christmas tree shopping with you?" she clarified.

"Actually, on second thought, maybe not," he retracted the invitation. "If your Christmas tree selecting is anything like your past mistletoe choices, I could be in trouble."

"Hey Buddy, I'll have you know, I *do* know a little something about Christmas trees. Let's just say that expertise has been passed down in my own family tree."

"Oh, really?" One brow pitched up. "I could say the same. So I guess this means that together, we have the potential to select the best Christmas tree this town has ever seen."

Rachel grinned. She didn't doubt that one single bit.

CHAPTER 12

❄

He was going to have to ask her name again. It wasn't a date per se, but she would be coming over to his house. Sitting next to him in his truck. Hopefully helping him decorate his newly purchased Christmas tree if the evening went well.

Holden could only get away with calling her Mittens for so long. In reality, she hadn't even been wearing mittens the last time he saw her. The nickname only bought him so much time.

"I'm sorry, I didn't quite catch your name," he rehearsed in front of his bathroom mirror. Fog steamed up the glass, so he took a hand towel to swipe it clean. He'd showered—even shaved—and thrown on a splash of cologne, all the things he would do if this were an actual date.

But it wasn't one. You couldn't date someone if you didn't even know their name.

"What am I going to do, Scout?" Cozied up on the

bathmat near the shower, Scout's jowls flapped with a breath. "I know. I know. I'm totally ridiculous."

He could go the formal route and call her miss or ma'am, but Holden had learned from both his mother and sister that regardless of age, few women enjoyed being called the latter. That wouldn't work.

It was much too soon for a term of endearment like sweetheart or honey. Plus, neither of those were really his style.

He would have to find out her name some other way. Maybe he could steal a look at her driver's license. If they went to Snowbound Brew on Main Street, Hank, the bartender there, would card them. If Holden was quick enough, he could try to sneak a peek before she tucked her I.D. back into her purse. He would have to be fast, but it could be done.

But Holden wasn't a big drinker, and from what he knew of her, coffee was her preferred beverage. Maybe he could ask the baristas at Bitter Cold to start calling out drink orders by the customer's name rather than the drink's. Right, he could totally ask an entire coffee establishment to alter the way they did business just to help him out a little in the dating department. That was completely acceptable.

Holden groaned.

"Could you ask her for me?" He looked down at Scout.

The dog side-eyed him, picked up her stuffed chew toy, and trotted out of the bathroom.

"Alright, I can take the hint."

He feared his date might do the same as his dog, and the thought of her hightailing away from Holden had his pulse skittering along his neck. They had only interacted a handful of times, and yet there was an instant connection that had Holden feeling like they'd known one another their whole lives. And that was crazy; he would have remembered her.

Women like Mittens didn't come around Snowdrift Summit often.

Man, he really needed to stop calling her that.

By the time he peered out the window to see her Jeep climbing up the slushy driveway and settling into park, Holden had talked himself in circles. He was just going to be honest and ask for her name. In reality, it wasn't as though she knew his either. She'd called him buddy a few times, and the sweet term of endearment had him feeling as warm and fuzzy as…well, a pair of Christmas mittens. But he figured it was her way around admitting she hadn't the foggiest clue his given name either. They were both in the same awkward predicament.

Meeting her at the front door, Holden pulled it open before she even knocked.

"You made it." He paused. "Come here, *you*."

She stepped over the threshold, and Holden interpreted the move as going in for a hug. His two arms wrapped around her tightly and the scent of warm vanilla met his nose when he pressed his face near her wavy blonde tresses. Goodness, she smelled like a Christmas kitchen, sugary and sweet.

"Hey, *you*," she echoed his generic greeting.

Withdrawing from his embrace, she grinned. Her lips were painted a darker pink than normal. Holden noted the sweep of shimmery powder over her eyes and a rim of black coating thick lashes, like she'd prepared for their evening with more makeup than usual.

So this *was* a date then, wasn't it?

"You ready to go?" he asked, shouldering into his jacket. "I figured we would take my truck so I can just toss the tree into the back."

"That sounds like a good plan to me."

"Scout!" Holden whistled. "You ready, girl?"

At the call, Scout bounded down the stairs from the loft, loping toward them with the accompanying jingle of her collar.

"You have a dog?"

Holden scratched along his jaw. "I do. Scout meet—"

He'd hoped for a little help with the introduction, but Scout smothered her with a shower of kisses that jammed up any ability for Holden's date to offer her name in reply.

"She's adorable!" The two were a tangle of happy giggles and tail wags.

"That, she is. And she knows it."

The woman rose to her feet and picked the stray dog hairs from her coat.

"You want a lint roller?" Holden suggested. "I can grab you one."

She waved him off. "I figure I'm going to get pine needles all over me too. A little dog fur never hurt anyone. What a sweet girl."

"She is. And a smart one. She's in training to be validated as an Avalanche Rescue Dog next week. We both are in training, I suppose. I'll be getting certified as a search-dog handler if all goes well."

"Really? That's incredible. I didn't even know that was a thing."

"Yep. There are a half-dozen certified search dogs in the area. They're deployed in the case of an avalanche or missing skier. Things like that."

Holden moved toward the door leading to the detached garage.

"How does that work?"

"Locating missing persons?"

"Yeah." She followed and joined Holden and Scout in the truck's cab. "With the help of a dog and all."

"Scout's trained to locate the scent of someone under the surface of the snow. Dogs like her can cover multiple acres in the time it takes us to search just a small space. It's a game for her: she finds the person—or in the case of training, a piece of scented cloth—and then gets a reward."

"And what's her reward of choice?"

"A vigorous game of tug-of-war, of course."

"So another competition," she smiled, clicking her lap belt across her middle. "Sounds like she's incredibly driven."

"She is. We both are. I've been with the volunteer

Search and Rescue team for about five years now. I'm just adding on the dog handler part."

Holden pressed the button on the garage opener and waited for the door to slide up before reversing his truck. He maneuvered around Rachel's Jeep parked along a berm of packed snow walling in the driveway and set out for the tree farm.

"So I've got two almost-certified Search and Rescue volunteers with me on a hunt for a tree? I'd say we should have no problem finding one."

Holden laughed. He sure liked the woman sitting beside him, liked how she made him feel seen in a way he hadn't in years.

"Caribou Conifers has quite a selection this year. It may be more difficult than you think."

"I'm confident we will locate the perfect one."

She folded her hands and when Scout nudged close, sliding her head onto her lap, she released her clasp to pet the insistent animal.

"You can tell her no if she's bothering you," he offered. "She's not super great with boundaries."

"Are you kidding me?" She ran her nails through the retriever's thick coat of fur. "I'm loving every minute of this."

"You're an animal person?"

"I am, but I can't have any in my apartment per the lease's strict rules."

"So you can't have a tree and you can't have a pet." Flakes of snow began to flutter down like iridescent pieces of confetti. Holden flipped the windshield wipers on low to swish the flurries from his line of sight. "What's keeping you there?"

"Well, I *can* have a tree. It's just that it's not all that convenient." Her shoulders lifted an inch in a shrug. "But your question is a valid one. One I've been thinking about a lot lately."

"Is it your job, then?" He looked over his shoulder as he switched lanes. "That's keeping you there? You must really love it."

"If loving something is the same as dreading it, then I'm head over heels."

Holden noted the biting sarcasm that infiltrated her words like a splash of strong brandy in eggnog. "So if you don't love it, then why do you continue doing it?"

"There's this thing called an income. It's really helpful for things like paying rent. Keeping food on the table. All that good stuff."

"I understand what you're saying." He laughed softly. "I'm just wondering why you're in a job if you don't love it one-hundred percent. Life is too short to be spent doing something that doesn't bring you joy."

"But it does bring me joy," she insisted, her hand stilling over Scout's back a moment. "At least the thought of a management position does."

"You think once you climb your way up the corporate ladder, you'll achieve happiness? From what little I know of you, I'm not convinced that you'll be satisfied with that."

"No?" Her gaze confronted him. "Why's that?"

"I think you're motivated by the challenge. The race

to the top. But what happens once you finally get there?"

"Then I'll look for something different, I guess."

"Yikes."

Her jaw set. "What?"

"I'm just hoping you don't adhere to that same line of thinking regarding your relationships. Being all about the chase and everything."

"I don't really do relationships."

Holden's heart nosedived clear down to the truck's floorboards. "How come?"

"I don't have the time."

"Everyone has time for love."

"Maybe not everyone has the capacity for it."

That statement shut the lid on the conversation, but it didn't keep the questions from forming in Holden's mind. There was certainly more mystery to this woman than just her name, and suddenly Holden worried none of it was his to discover.

CHAPTER 13

❄

"That's the one."

Rachel knew the moment she laid eyes on the tree that it was the winner. Sloping green branches led from a perfectly pointed tip down to a full, leafy skirt. There was enough density to handle a heavy ornament without being crowded, and yet it wouldn't be considered at all sparse. It was pine tree perfection.

And the smell. Spruce and cedarwood met her nose when she took a deep inhale. It had all the natural characteristics of Buddy's cologne, that woodsy, somewhat spicy scent that had Rachel feeling Christmas vibes to the tenth degree.

"I agree with you. This definitely is the one." Buddy tipped his chin toward the grand evergreen. "What do you think, Scout?"

The dog let out a single bark.

"Looks like we have a winner." He folded the perforated line on the tree's tag and tore off the bottom section. "I'm going to take this up to the barn to pay for it. Would you mind staying here with Scout to stand guard? Believe it or not, I actually had a tree stolen one year when I mistakenly let it out of my sight."

"A Christmas tree caper?"

An appreciative laugh pulled Buddy's lips into a dimpled grin. "You could say that."

"Don't worry. Scout and I will make sure no one absconds with this beauty."

His eyes locked with Rachel's for a few breaths, then he cut his gaze up the hill. "Great. I'll be back in a jiffy."

Rachel sighed as she watched him jog through the rows of greenery.

She'd said too much in the car without really saying anything at all. It was strange how that could happen. Their conversation had slipped into territory she wished to avoid, and yet she'd found herself teetering dangerously close to confession's edge.

Love wasn't in the cards for her, and she knew it.

Goodness, her entire history had proven that. Even the recent tale her mother had shared about Holden Hart asking her to the dance all the way back in the eighth grade. Rachel's competitive nature sure had a way of clouding everything even remotely romantic in her life, shutting the opportunity for it completely out.

What would have happened if she'd gone to the dance with Holden instead of Cody? Would she still have spent the better portion of her teenage years seeing him as an academic, athletic, and all-around threat?

Rachel had silenced all of that back when she'd knocked him out of the running for valedictorian and earned the only scholarship offered from the small town's Chamber of Commerce.

She still remembered the essay prompt: *What does success mean to you?*

Back then, it meant getting into a top school with competitive internships that funneled into prestigious professions. It was a route Rachel had gladly taken.

And yet, she found herself at a dead end.

Her fingers absentmindedly stroked the tree's branches. A few needles fell into her palm.

"Rachel?" The shrill voice at her back pulled her spine ramrod straight. "Rachel Katherine Joy, is that you?"

She'd had trouble placing the faces and names of her hometown neighbors, but that nasally voice brought with it a flood of adolescent memories. "Monica Hastings. How on earth are you?"

The old high school acquaintance stood there, holding the midline on the trunk of a freshly cut tree. Her overly lipsticked mouth gaped like a fish, eyes bugging like one too. "How on earth am I? I think I should be the one doing the asking. What on earth are *you* doing here? Never in my wildest dreams did I think you'd set foot back in this town. You were in such a huge hurry to get out of here!"

"I'm just back for the holidays. My parents needed a

little help with some tasks around the house for Christmas. I'm not staying long."

"And by tasks, you mean that Christmas tree competition?"

How had she known? And why did Rachel's stomach wrench at being found out so easily?

"Not sure I can really help them in that department," Rachel attempted to justify. "Pretty sure Mother Nature has it all taken care of."

"Well, we know that's not entirely true." Judgment flashed through Monica's eyes. "I can hear that constant rotation of Christmas songs all the way up at my chalet on the ridge."

Embarrassment flushed Rachel's cheeks a warm pink. Her shoulders gave a little hop. "Whatever helps, right?"

"You're not the only crazy Christmas people around here." Monica leaned in and cut her volume in half, speaking behind her hand when she whispered, "I hear the Harts are just as fanatic. Would you believe they make a compost tea for their tree? It supposedly has nutrients and microbes and a bunch of other stuff I can't pronounce. I don't even make tea for myself; I can't imagine brewing up an entire batch for a backyard tree!"

Monica looked down, suddenly noticing Scout's presence at her feet. "How adorable. Is this your dog?"

"It's a friend's."

"What a sweet little face." The woman's adenoidal tone warped into baby talk. Scout's ears flattened against her head. When she reached down for a scratch, Scout bared her teeth behind pulled lips. "Oh! Goodness."

"She's a little protective."

"I can see that." Pressing her hands to her abdomen, Monica shuddered. "Well, it's been good seeing you, Rachel. Best of luck with the tree competition."

"We don't need luck!" Rachel found herself shouting when Monica moved to go. The woman didn't turn back around.

"That's all taken care of." Holden's voice breached Rachel's attempt to call out for Monica a second time, and it was a thankful interruption. "Everything okay here?" An evaluating gaze swept the area.

"Just saw someone I knew from years ago." Rachel regained her lost composure. "Did you say we're all set?"

"Yep. I told them we didn't need to bother with bundling or anything since I'm just going to toss it into the truck bed. Let's get this thing home and decorated. What do you say?"

* * *

THEY HAD UNLOADED and settled the tree into its stand, right in the center of a wall of expansive windows. It was as though the previously empty space begged for a Christmas tree to be placed in the middle. Even the slope of the A-frame cabin mimicked the triangle taper of the evergreen.

Locating a tree skirt in the hall closet, along with a box labeled **Holiday Decorations** written in fat, black marker, they'd adorned the tree with glass baubles and beaded, wooden coils of cranberry-hued garland. And, as luck would have it, the strands of lights were all in working condition, nothing short of a Christmas miracle.

"I'm going to make a hot chocolate for myself. Can I get you anything?"

"What's with you and hot chocolate?" Rachel moved to the couch and tucked her legs beneath her on the leather cushion, settling in.

She'd seen him order the specific drink multiple times at Bitter Cold and knew it had to be a favorite.

"What's not to like? It's a mug full of liquid chocolate, topped with gooey blobs of marshmallow sugar."

"When you put it that way." She released a laugh. "Sure, I'll take one. Thank you."

"Of course."

She watched him gather the ingredients, moving about his kitchen as he hummed softly under his breath. They'd stripped out of their large jackets, which left him in a cream colored, cable-knit sweater paired with dark jeans. Goodness, he sure was handsome, that rugged mountain man physique exemplified in his strong stature. Rachel felt heat sweep through her before he even came over to pass off her mug of hot chocolate.

"You'll want to let it cool down before you take a

sip," he instructed, finding his place next to her on the couch. "No burnt taste buds on my watch."

She blew across the dark surface, pushing tendrils of steam across the mug, then took a sip. Hazarding a guess, she asked, "There's a little something else in here, isn't there?"

"A dash of chili powder and a pinch of sea salt."

"Like the one they serve at Bitter Cold."

"The very one."

His look lingered over her face. It might have been from the drink in her hands, but a flush of warmth traveled up her neck.

"I had a lot of fun with you today," he said.

"The fun's not over, Buddy." She gulped down another sip of the sweet drink. "That tree is only half-decorated. It's not going to finish itself."

"You don't have anywhere else you need to be?"

And where would that be? Back to her parents' place, stewing over her mistletoe project? Or worse yet, losing herself and her mind in the Christmas tree competition?

"There's nowhere I'd rather be than right here."

The words were true and tumbled out more freely than she would have liked.

"You've mentioned a few times that you're staying with your parents," he said. "Any chance I know them?"

Rachel stilled. "Oh, I doubt it. They like to keep to themselves. Don't get out much."

If keeping to oneself was the same as owning the only

market on the summit, the sort that allowed customers to keep a running tab and offered friends and family discounts to practically all of their shoppers. Main Street Market was a well-known staple in the mountain town community, a Mom and Pop store in the truest of senses.

Rachel didn't want Buddy putting those pieces together. It had been embarrassing enough when Monica called her out, drawing attention to her parents' odd obsession over their tree. She didn't want Buddy sharing those same judgmental thoughts too.

Reading her boundary, he left it at that.

"Any progress with the mistletoe?" He placed his mug on the armrest next to him.

"I've decided to take a break from it for the time being. I've got a while before I need to hunker down and figure all of that out. For now, I just want to enjoy my time in Snowdrift."

"And are you? Enjoying your time?"

"I am."

He might've edged closer, or it could've been Rachel's thumping heart that propelled her toward him. They were suddenly shoulder to shoulder on the sofa. But when Buddy's arm draped across her back, his hand curling around her to draw her near, her breath hitched.

"Is this okay?"

She nodded. She moved her mug to the coffee table, then angled her body back into his on the couch. He had the perfect arm for sliding under and curling up beneath, that protective, secure strength that blanketed her with calm.

"I feel like I have to ask…" His words and volume trailed.

This was it. This was where he discovered her identity and her cover was blown. He'd asked her name before, but had never called her by it. Had he even heard her? Was this going to be the point where he learned of her ties to the Joy family noble-fir-nonsense and he politely asked her to leave? Sure, it sounded farfetched and vastly out of character from the man she'd gotten to know over the last few days, but stranger things had happened.

Should she just make up an entirely different name? Some undercover alias?

Her brain scrolled through a list of viable options, only interrupted when he finally asked, "You're not already in a relationship, are you?"

She exhaled so loudly, Scout startled from her place on the floor next to them.

"Relationship? Goodness, no."

"Because you don't do relationships," he inferred.

"Because I've found I don't have much time for them."

His mouth remained a thin line. "Or interest?"

Until meeting Buddy, she would have said no. But each encounter had her thinking differently about her priorities. Had her pondering the true definition of success and if she'd had it wrong all along.

"I have the interest." Snuggling deeper into his side, Rachel's mouth twitched into a grin.

"Good to know," was all he said in response, and Rachel suddenly wanted to know more about the man next to her. Wanted to know everything she could.

Starting with his full name.

"This is going to sound really strange, but—"

The sharp trill of his phone ringing with an incoming call lopped off the end of her sentence.

"You can get that," she encouraged with a nod to the cell phone discarded on the table.

He grunted a sigh and glanced at the phone screen. "It's my mom. I probably should. It'll only be a minute."

"Take all the time you need."

He offered his apology with a brief squeeze of her arm and soft smile before bending forward to lift the phone and accept the call. "Hey, Mom. Can I call you right—?"

Color instantly drained from his face, his features going slack.

"Slow down, slow down." Buddy stood from the couch and within the span of five long strides, had his jacket on, keys in his palm, and his grip on the door handle. "I will be right there. Tell everyone to stay calm."

Rachel jogged up to him. Even Scout scurried over.

"My dad fell while shoveling out the driveway. Thinks he might've broken his foot. At the very least, sprained his ankle. They're at Urgent Care now." A touch of ruddiness came back to his ashen pallor as he rallied his breathing into a consistent rhythm. "I should probably go be with them."

"Yes. Of course," Rachel agreed. "Go."

"I'm so sorry." His pained gaze lingered on hers. "I hate to rush out like this."

"Family always comes first."

He nodded his head slightly, then drew her into a swift hug. "Thank you for understanding."

"Absolutely."

Rachel understood family emergencies more than he would ever know. That decade's old feeling of utter desperation washed over her, memories of her sister's accident crashing into the forefront of her mind. Her stomach roiled, and she tamped her emotion down with a forced smile. "Let me grab my keys and I'll follow you out."

He gave her another helpless look. "Can we get a rain check on our evening?"

"I'm holding you to it," she said, also holding onto a hope she hadn't let herself feel in more years than she could count.

CHAPTER 14

❄

"*If* he rings that bell one more time..."

Jill Hart typically had the patience of a saint, but even saints had their limits, Holden figured.

"Yes, dear?" His mother came up behind the couch and looked over the edge at her invalid husband—all sprawled out and bandaged up—with sympathetic, kind eyes. "What can I get you now?"

"This jingle was actually meant for Holden," Zeke clarified. "Maybe I should have an entire set of bells, each with a distinct sound. One for you. One for Holden. One for Sarah."

"Let's not get carried away." Jill walked back to the kitchen, passing her son on her way. She tagged him on the shoulder. "He's all yours."

As requested, Holden moved across the room toward his father, taking up position on the arm of the couch. "What can I do for you, Dad?"

Holden had stayed the night after the emergency

visit. His dad had been right; his foot was, in fact, broken. In two places, to be precise. Luckily, Zeke had retired as a fire captain years earlier, so the unexpected injury didn't throw a monkey wrench into his work plans. But it did seem to hinder his tree tending, and Holden had a hunch that was the cause for the most recent bell ringing.

"It's Sir Noble Fir." His father heaved an overelaborate breath.

"I figured as much."

"There is no way your mother is going to let me out there to take care of him. Not like this."

"And she shouldn't." Holden drew out his words and the point. "You need to keep off of that foot and let it heal. Plus, didn't you say the tree already exceeds the height requirement?"

"It does," his father affirmed. "But it's not our tree I need your help with."

"I'm not following, Dad."

Zeke Hart's train of thought had more twists and turns than a snowboarder on a halfpipe.

"I need you for a covert operation."

"Why does this sound illegal?"

"It's not illegal, son. Just maybe slightly unethical."

Holden lifted his hands. "I'm out."

"Oh, come on, Hold. You're my only heir to carry out my last dying wish."

"Hey now," Sarah piped up from the floor, where she and Laney stacked ABC blocks into a wooden tower. "What about me?"

"You're not dying, Dad," Holden redirected. "You're in a cast. One that you will get off in six to eight weeks if you just allow yourself the time to heal."

"I might not be dying, but my dream of winning this tree competition will, unless you can help me get some intel."

Holden didn't like the sound of this, but he had to give his old man credit. He had a knack for playing up the theatrics.

"What do you need me to do?"

"Do you have night vision goggles?"

"What?" Holden jerked his head at the odd request.

"Okay, those might not be entirely necessary. But what about all-white clothing? Something to camouflage you in the snow."

"I have a jacket and we sell white snow pants at the shop. I could probably get a pair there, if I really need them."

"You do, son. You do." His dad's calloused hand came over the top of Holden's, emphasizing his point. "You'll need that measuring stick you made too."

"Dad, what are you going to have me do? What are we talking about here?"

Zeke's chest expanded. "Son, I need you to sneak over to the Joy's property to measure their tree."

"What?" Holden yanked his hand out from his father's grasp. "You've got to be kidding!"

"It's my final wish."

"Again, Dad, you're not dying," Holden reiterated. "This is crazy."

"It's crazy for an old, feeble man to think his one and only son could help him achieve his holiday dream?"

"Are you all hearing this?" Holden turned to his mother, then his sister.

"Unfortunately, yes," Jill said. "Loud and clear."

"How many painkillers are you hopped up on, Dad?" Holden inquired in all seriousness.

"Not nearly enough," Zeke deadpanned. "I need you to do this for me, Hold. I have to know if we stand a chance this year."

"And why can't you just wait until the tree lighting officials make that call like everyone else?"

"I've never been all that good at being patient."

"I'm sorry." Jill cupped her ear, leaning in dramatically. "Did you just admit that you're not a good patient?"

"No time for jokes, Jill." Zeke cut his wife a solemn look, then swung his gaze back to Holden. "Whatever you got for me for Christmas, son, please feel free to take back. All I want is to know if our noble is in the running. That'll be the best gift anyone could ever give."

It was a simple enough request, even if the absurdity of it all had Holden pinching back laughter. "Fine. I can go over tonight."

"Thank you!" Zeke swiveled up from his lying position on the couch, knocking his heavy boot against the side table in his haste. "Oomph."

"Be careful, Dad." Guiding his father back to rest on

the couch, Holden asked, "What'll you do if their tree is taller?"

"Let's not even plant that idea in his crazy brain," his mother advised. "And Holden, please don't get caught."

"Do you honestly think anyone else is taking this whole tree competition even remotely as serious as you all are?"

Three blinking stares pinned him with disbelief. Even Laney leveled him with an incredulous look.

"Okay, okay. I will get this tree measured for you, but then you're on your own. If Sir Noble Fir is going to be center stage on Main Street this year, it'll be without my involvement."

But it was entirely too late for that. Holden was already in as deep as the summit snowpack.

*** * * ***

"WHEN DID you take Rachel Joy out on an excursion?"

Holden glanced up from his container of reheated leftovers, his mother's lasagna tasting every bit as good the second day. Lance stood in the doorway to the back room with a single sheet of paper in his hands and a befuddled look on his face.

"Not sure I know what you're talking about there, partner," Holden said.

Lance flapped the paper against his palm. "We've got a waiver here with the name *Rachel Joy* written at the top. Found it when I was cleaning up the front desk. By the way, our organization around here leaves much to be desired."

Eyes narrowed, Holden dropped his fork onto the plate and pushed up from his chair. He took the sheet Lance passed to him and scanned the form, his mind drawing a blank.

"I never took…"

Like he'd sucked on a sour candy, Holden's mouth suddenly tingled with acid. He nearly choked.

"That woman you had your little mistletoe hunt with!" Understanding dawned, and Lance gave Holden's unsaid revelation words. "That was Rachel, wasn't it? That's why you were asking all about her the other day."

"No," Holden blurted. "No." It wasn't that way. "It couldn't have been Rachel."

"What do you mean it 'couldn't have been'?" His friend's steel-gray gaze trapped Holden's, challenging him. "It was Rachel or it wasn't."

"There's no way that woman was Rachel Joy."

"Are you trying to tell me you didn't know the name of the woman you took out on the snowmobile? And that you're just now discovering her identity?"

If the Easter Bunny, Tooth Fairy, and Santa Claus all walked into their rental shop, Holden couldn't have been more surprised than he was in that very moment. Even toss in a leprechaun; it wouldn't have added to his shock. Disbelief sucker-punched him in the gut.

"This can't be." His fingers speared through his hair. He paced the small break room, head shaking.

"Oh my word. You're dating Rachel Joy, aren't you?" Lance's mouth lifted into a haughty grin.

"I am *not* dating Rachel Joy."

"But you kissed her under the mistletoe."

Holden's chin drew back. "What? No! I didn't kiss her!"

"You're telling me you went on a mistletoe expedition with a beautiful woman and you didn't even kiss her? Wasted opportunity, buddy. Big time."

Holden had a harder time wrapping his head around this situation than he'd had wrapping the lights on his ten-foot Christmas tree, and that had been a huge struggle.

"This can't be happening."

"What? That you're falling for your worst enemy?"

"I'm not falling for my worst enemy! It might not even be the same woman."

Lance struck Holden with a dubious look. "Blonde hair? Blue eyes? Beautiful smile and cute, little ski slope nose?"

"There are a lot of women who fit that description," Holden asserted unconvincingly. "And how do you know so much about her appearance?"

"I told you, I looked her up a while back. I was shocked to see how different she looks from back in high school. Hard to believe it's even the same person. I went down quite a rabbit hole just to make sure it was actually the Rachel we knew way back when. Probably something *you* should've done before you started dating her."

"I'm not dating her!" All the years of rivalry and spite swirled around Holden in a blizzard of emotion. "We're not dating."

"Well, that's probably a good thing, since your parents are sworn enemies. Montague and Capulet style. Rumor has it this Christmas tree competition has knocked all of them completely off their rockers."

"Let's not get carried away." But it was too late for that. This unwelcome discovery even had Holden's thoughts scooping him up and depositing him straight into crazy territory. What was he going to do?

"You know? I find it really hard to believe Rachel Joy would willingly date you. I'm pretty sure you were her least favorite person back in high school."

"Like I said before,"—Holden emphasized—"we're not dating. And she might not be entirely clear on my identity either."

Lance let out a hoot that had Scout's ears cocking at the uproarious sound. "This is wild, buddy!"

"That's it!"

"What's it?" His friend's face went neutral.

"That's why she keeps calling me Buddy! She probably heard you call me that the other day when we were in the store together." It all started to make sense, like the missing pieces fitting into a very convoluted puzzle.

"She thinks your name is Buddy?" Lance let out another hearty guffaw. "What are you? An elf?"

"This is a mess," Holden groaned.

"Little bit."

"What am I going to do?"

"For starters, you could clear up the whole name thing. You really want her thinking you build toys at the North Pole for the Man in Red?"

Holden grimaced. "I'm serious, Lance. This is not good. I'm supposed to go over there tonight."

"Another date?"

"No." Swallowing around the tight lump wedged in his throat, Holden said, "To measure their Christmas tree."

"Really? I'm surprised her family would want someone with your last name anywhere near their precious evergreen." Eyes rounded, Lance added, "But that's right. She doesn't know you're a Hart."

"And she doesn't know I'm coming over."

Lance's raised brows indicated his unspoken need for clarification.

"I'm doing a favor for my dad," Holden expounded.

"You mean you're sneaking onto private property to measure a tree that doesn't belong to you for a competition that's gotten way out of hand?"

"Something like that."

Holden rubbed his shoulder, massaging the tension that pulled all of his muscles. He felt like he could snap.

"What time?" Lance asked quickly.

"Huh?"

"What time do I need to be ready?"

"You're coming with me?"

"Course I am, buddy. Snowdrift Summit hasn't seen

this much drama since the year I busted my knee during that terrible ski race you organized."

Holden didn't need the reminder; it was something he thought about every day. "I don't think this is a good idea."

"None of it is a good idea, but that doesn't mean I don't want a front-row seat for it all when things go down."

Holden had had his share of bad ideas in his life, but this one might just take the cake.

"If you're serious, I actually could use the help," he relented. "I can't get caught, Lance."

"Because then Rachel Joy will finally find out that you've never let things go."

That was a part of it, but not the whole story.

"I've got your back, buddy," Lance assured, capping off his statement with a solid slug on his best friend's arm. "Always. That's something you can count on."

Some days Holden wasn't sure why Lance still had his back, but it was an undeserved blessing he'd forever be grateful for. And one he hoped to repay someday.

CHAPTER 15

❄

It wasn't even noon and Rachel had reorganized the Christmas candy display twice. The morning at the market had been a quiet one. Overnight snowfall and resulting sunny skies had a tendency to slow things down on Main Street. The promise of a ride down a mountain of fresh powder lured most residents to the ski resorts, pausing things like errands and grocery runs until a later time.

"Thanks for covering Marcel's shift, Sugar Plum. Something's going around. That's the third illness we've had this week." Stewart Joy walked down the bread aisle carting a box of fresh loaves from the local bakery. He moved the container to his hip. "When was the last time you clocked in here?"

"High school. So at least ten years."

"Really?" He rubbed his forehead. "No kidding? Has it been that long?"

In some ways, it felt like an eternity, and in others,

just yesterday. Back then, after Rachel finished up her school day, she would head into town for the last shift of the day at the Main Street Market. And as soon as they would shut the doors to the public and close for the evening, she would sneak a gingersnap cookie from the display case, knowing they would be in the 'day-old' bin the following morning. It was the perfect treat to cap off a day of work at her parents' store.

"It's nice to see you wearing that apron. Suits you."

She knew he intended it as a compliment, but nothing about the red apron—stitched with white, embroidered lettering—felt like it suited her. No, *suits* suited Rachel. She could only imagine what her superiors at December Décor would think if they could see her now, donning the uniform of a small town grocer.

"I have to head over to Snowdrift Deli to pick up an order of meat for the cold case." Her father lifted the loop of his apron over his head and folded it before placing it onto the counter. "Would you mind holding down the fort while I'm gone?"

"I think I can handle that," Rachel offered with a smile.

"Thanks, Sugar Plum. And if Joe Daulton comes in, that turkey rub he's been looking for is under the counter. Tell him it's on the house."

"Got it."

Rachel watched her father skip out the entrance, his step jovial and light. Through the windows, she glimpsed him greet passersby on the sidewalk, a tip of his hat and a warm smile for each person he encountered.

Did Rachel smile at the people she passed in the halls at work? Did she greet those she sat next to on the bus or exchange pleasantries with the neighbors who lived in her building?

She'd set out for the city for a chance to become part of a bigger world, and yet, her world still felt so small. Sometimes, it was as if she was the only one in it.

Refilling the container of straws near the fountain soda machine, Rachel sighed. It would be nice to have that—to be friendly with those around you, sharing in life and laughter. But Rachel hadn't even been that way when she'd lived in Snowdrift. As a teen, she had kept to herself unless it involved academics and achievement. She made little time for relationships, a pattern that seemed to plague her even now. Her stomach soured as she thought of the girl she once was, fearing she hadn't come very far in the last ten years.

Moments later, the little bell above the door chimed, and a man she recognized as Joe stepped into the store. He shuffled his snow-dusted boots on the mat bearing their logo and moved further inside. Swiveling his head, his gaze searched the grocery, landing on Rachel at the checkout stand.

"Well, if it isn't Snowdrift Summit's big city success! Rachel Joy, is that you all grown up?"

"Hi, Mr. Daulton," Rachel acknowledged with a grin. "How have you been, sir?"

"The good Lord's given me another day, so I can't

complain." His merry face lit up as he came closer. "You know, your daddy brags about you every time I stop in here. Says how well you're doing in San Fran with that fancy job of yours. Never seen a papa as proud as that one, I tell you."

Had her father really said all of that? The thought made something sharp catch in Rachel's chest.

"He also said he's holding some of that turkey seasoning for me." He drummed his hands on the counter. "I've been meaning to stop in, but haven't had the time until now."

"Yes." Lowering to look at the shelving beneath the register, Rachel scanned for the item. "He said he set it aside for you. Let me see if I can find it."

"That stuff sold out fast before Thanksgiving, but he mentioned another shipment came in. Think I'm probably the only person in Snowdrift planning to cook a turkey for Christmas, but it's what Trinity requested, so it's what she gets."

"How is Trinity?" Rachel asked over the counter, still bent down. "I haven't seen her since graduation."

"She's wonderful. Gave me two precious grandbabies and the best son-in-law a father could hope for. She's got a beautiful little life up here—a modest one, but that suits her just fine."

Trinity had been a classmate of Rachel's, and Rachel remembered her sweet nature and kind heart fondly.

"Always thought the two of you would've made good friends. Trinity's a real gem."

The man was probably right, had friendship been something Rachel invested in back then.

"Here it is!" Locating the bottle of seasoning, she popped back to her feet.

Joe moved for his wallet.

"Dad says it's on the house."

"Does he really? Well, that's mighty nice of him. Tell him I'll smoke a turkey just for him as a thank you."

Rachel chuckled. "I'm pretty sure an entire turkey is worth more than a bottle of seasoning."

"Not all exchanges of kindness are measured the same. Your father's been good to this town. The least he deserves is a turkey."

It was an odd way to phrase it, and the tear it brought to Rachel's eye was even more peculiar. She pushed her palm to her cheek with a sniff.

"How long are you in town for?" Joe asked, his heel turned to go.

"Through the holidays."

"I'm going to tell Trinity to look you up. Maybe the two of you could go to coffee or something. I know she could use some time out of the house, what with those little rascals running her ragged. I'm sure she'd love to see you and catch up."

Rachel surprised even herself when she said, "I'd really like that."

He pinched the brim of his hat and beamed. "Happy holidays to you, Rachel."

"And to you, Joe."

Even moments after the door closed behind him,

Rachel's thoughts lagged back, replaying their conversation.

How many friendships had she missed out on? How many people had she overlooked? She was still sorting through thoughts of her past when a rush of frosty air tunneled through the entrance, bringing with it two large men. The windy blast rattled the Christmas card display on the counter by the register, and several cards and envelopes caught air, sailing across the store like paper airplanes.

Rachel skirted the stall to tidy up the sudden mess. She was crouched low, gathering the cards, when a pair of huge boots planted directly in front of her. Her eyes trailed up the legs and body, her gaze finally landing on the face of yet another person from her past.

Rachel lifted to her feet. She attempted to collect her composure but found it as scattered as those silly greeting cards.

"If it isn't Rachel Joy."

She swallowed thickly. "Lance Major. How are you? It's been a while."

Turning to set the stack of cards on the counter, she fiddled with her apron strap. She could have sworn she saw two men enter the market only moments ago, but now, the other was nowhere to be found. She was honestly beginning to think this mountain air was making her loopy.

"I've been great. And it looks like you have been too," he said with all the confidence she'd remembered from his teenage years. Unlike his best friend, Holden

Hart, who was rail thin with glasses and a crooked smile, Lance had been one of those guys that matured early in high school, his final size and height achieved when he was merely a freshman.

"I've been...good," she supplied with what she prayed was a convincing grin.

"You look it. Man, if I didn't know any better, I would hardly even recognize you. But it is you," he said, his volume unexpectedly increasing as he angled his head, almost calling out over his shoulder. "Yep, definitely Rachel Joy. Standing right in front of me. Rachel. *Joy.*"

"That's me." She flashed her hands in the air, jazz-hand style, and then quickly tugged them down. "Can I help you find something?"

"I'm just here grabbing a few snack items to restock the break room at work."

"And where's that?" She swiped the card stack from the counter and collated them again, her idle hands making her anxious. "Where's work?"

"Major Hart Mountain Rentals. You heard of it?"

Her eyes fell open wide. "Yes, actually. Believe it or not, I was just up there the other day. I went out on a snowmobile ride with one of your coworkers."

"Oh, really? And who would that be?" Lance did that strange, near-shouting thing again.

"Buddy."

His mouth cracked into a smile so large, she could no longer see his gray eyes pinched above his cheeks. Lance bent at the waist with a single, punctuated laugh and then straightened. He dragged a hand through his hair. "Buddy? You don't say? Buddy is the best."

"Seems like a pretty good guy."

"Oh, most definitely. That Buddy…he's a real keeper."

Rachel wasn't sure where this odd conversation might take her.

"Buddy, Buddy, Buddy," Lance said on repeat, a laugh tacked to the end like an echo. "Some people say he's got one of those familiar faces."

"Yeah?" Her hands clamped around the cards. They were going to be mangled if she didn't just set them down.

"Yes, they do." Lance thumbed the divot in his chin. "What do you think? Does he remind you of anyone?"

Rachel scanned her brain, but it was currently on pause. She couldn't compute anything. "Not that I can think of."

"Doesn't remind you of *anyone* you know?"

At that moment, a thunderous clatter resounded from two aisles over, like an avalanche of canned food and boxed cereal. Dozens of aluminum cans rolled across the linoleum floor, several coming to a stop at Rachel's feet. She stooped to collect a jar of pasta sauce.

"What on earth?" she mumbled.

"I'll take care of that." Lance grabbed her by the shoulders, locking her in place. Another patron—an elderly woman—came through the front door and Lance flicked his gaze behind him quickly. "You just take care of her and I'll get things put back."

"What do you think even caused that?" Rachel made a motion to step forward again, but Lance blocked her like a linebacker.

"Probably just another earthquake."

"An earthquake?"

"Oh, yeah." He jogged backward. "We get them all the time up here. You don't remember?"

There was a lot Rachel didn't remember about Snowdrift Summit, and earthquakes definitely fell into that category.

Being up on that mountain made her loopy, alright. And judging by Lance's unusual behavior, she wasn't the only one affected.

CHAPTER 16

❄

"I still can't believe you."

Holden cut the engine a quarter mile from the Joy property. They would hike the rest of the way in. With the help of a full moon reflecting on alabaster snow, he didn't think they would have any trouble locating the mammoth tree. Or hopefully not-so-mammoth tree, if his father's wish came true.

"You can't believe *me?*" Lance gripped the edges of his beanie and yanked it over his ears. He released his seatbelt. "You're the one who nearly blew our cover with all of that commotion. What a racket. You knocked over half an aisle's worth of food. You were supposed to be hiding."

"I had to stop you! It was the only thing I could think to do. You were being ridiculous with all of that *Rachel Joy* shouting."

"I just wanted to make sure it was her. Someone had

to do their due diligence because you didn't think to before you started falling in love with her."

"I'm not in love with her!" Even within the confines of the closed vehicle, Holden was positive his shout was loud enough to rustle a bear out of hibernation. "I don't see why we had to go there, anyway."

"We needed snacks for our mission." Lance pulled a packet of M&M's from his pocket and lifted it to funnel the colorful candies into his mouth. He chomped down. "And I figured there was a chance she might be there. She used to work for her parents back in high school, you know. Thought maybe she'd clock in a few hours while back home. Plus," Lance continued, "I wanted to get a look at her for myself. I've only seen pictures online. But man, she really has changed, hasn't she?"

More than just Rachel's looks had changed. Her entire demeanor had transformed. Sure, she was still determined as ever, but when that drive wasn't directed at Holden, it wasn't off-putting in the least. It was actually attractive.

"I think we've all changed," Holden said.

Lance got out of the truck. His boots met the snow with a slushy, wet crunch. "So what's the plan here, buddy?" He snorted. "Buddy. Ha! I think you need a new nickname."

"I think I need more than that, starting with a reality check. Should we really do this?"

Lance leaned across the hood of the truck separating them. "If you're asking if I think this is a good idea, no, I don't. But if you're asking if I think we should abort the mission, that is one big, fat, absolutely not. You made your old man a promise and we're going to see it through."

Holden rounded the vehicle to grab the pieces of the makeshift measuring stick. "We probably need a code word or phrase. Something to use if things go south."

"I've got one. How about 'Buddy the Elf'?"

"Will you please let that drop?"

"Okay." Lance hunched his giant shoulders and huffed. "Cornucopia."

"That's a mouthful."

"Fine. You come up with something."

Holden blurted the first word to come to mind. "Mistletoe."

Lance's eyes tumbled one full roll. "Oh, sure. So original. Fine. Mistletoe it is." Taking two gloves from his pocket, he fit them on and zipped his jacket up to his chin. "So, what's our game plan?"

Holden had already given this some thought. "We're going to come at it from the east, make a big arc, fanning out toward the back of their property, and scope out the situation from that angle. If I remember correctly, they planted the fir closer up by the house. And from what I can already hear, they've got outdoor music playing, so that should help with our cover."

Even though they were still several blocks out, the faint hum of Christmas tunes filtered through the winter night like a trail of stardust behind a comet.

"We'll assemble the pole when we get closer," Holden continued, taking the lead as he started up the street. "I put a piece of tape around the twenty-foot, three-inch mark, which is the height of my parents' tree. Anything under that, and we win. Anything over, and my dad might have a conniption."

They trekked along the plowed edge of the road single file, cloaked in solid white attire and armed with a plan that felt as solid as Jell-O.

"So, you think you'll ask her out again?" Lance piped up after a long quiet stretched between them.

"Ask Rachel out? That'd be a no."

"But I thought the two of you were having so much fun together."

"We were, but that was when I didn't know who she was."

"It's when you didn't know her name," Lance clarified. "There's more to a person than their name."

"Rachel and I have a complicated history. And by complicated, I mean we pretty much loathed one another throughout our teenage years."

A few more seconds of silence passed, then Lance asked, "Would you be opposed to me asking her out?"

The heel of Holden's snow boot slipped out from under him and he had to use the pipes in his grasp like walking sticks to steady his stance and keep from landing squarely on his backside. "You want to ask Rachel out? Like, on a date?"

"I mean, only if it's okay with you. But judging by your overly dramatic reaction, I'm taking that as a no."

Holden didn't have any sort of claim on her. They weren't dating or in a relationship, and yet the thought of Rachel going out with someone else had his throat closing and heart stuttering. He almost felt sick.

"You can ask her out, Lance. Of course. That's fine."

"No way. I'm reading between your lines loud and clear, buddy. She's all yours."

But she wasn't. Not even remotely.

They climbed the rest of the way up the hill, "Santa Claus is Coming to Town" and "Jingle Bells" spurring their movements along with the Christmassy beat. When the log cabin came into view behind a crest of evergreens, Holden signaled for Lance to follow him. They took cover behind an old shed.

"This is the place," Holden whispered.

"Wow. That's one good looking tree," Lance said, his hushed words floating on a frosty breath that hung in the air between them. "I can totally see that on Main Street. Look at how dense those branches are. And what a solid trunk!"

Holden cut his friend an 'are-you-kidding-me?' glare.

"Sorry." Lance coughed. "I mean, it's nowhere near as nice as yours."

"The tree isn't mine. It's my family's."

"Same difference, but whatever." Lance swiped his hands together. "What's the next step?"

With his knees pressed in the snow, Holden inclined forward and squinted. "We're going to army crawl over to the tree. Stay on the back side of it so if anyone is home, they won't spot us out the window. I'll assemble the measuring stick when we get to the tree and we'll get a quick read on the height. Then we'll make our way back here and regroup."

"Aye-aye, captain." Lance snickered with a flick of his fingers to his forehead in salute. "Hey, how about Captain? Now that's a good name."

"So is Holden."

"Aw, but that's no fun." Jamming his hand into his pocket, Lance pulled out a fistful of red licorice. He snapped off a bite between his front teeth. "Want one?"

"I'm good."

Truth was, Holden wasn't sure he could keep anything in his stomach. It churned with regret over the sneaky act he hadn't even committed yet. Some might call that a conscience, and if Holden had half a brain, he would listen to it. But they were in too deep already. He just needed to get it over with.

"On my count." He lowered himself to the ground, belly pressed to the snow, and tucked the long pipes under his arm. "Three, two, one."

It was an anticlimactic countdown. They didn't set off racing, rather, they wriggled at a snail's pace over the fresh snow. Their flattened bodies left a trail of ugly snow angels, all linked in a line that led from the shed toward the lofty noble fir.

Lance took the lead without the cumbersome poles to hinder him. Holden spat the slush that kicked up from his friend's boots and landed in his mouth. He should've worn goggles. Or a ski mask. He didn't anticipate the many inches of recent snowfall to cause such a flurry around him.

It couldn't have been more than a couple minutes, but by the time the two men reached the tree, exhaustion racked Holden's entire body. He was used to physical exertion in the snow, but usually the rush of adrenaline accompanied it. Apparently, dread had a different effect. It was as though even his own muscles fought him, protesting their involvement.

"That was a workout." Lance sat up and rolled back onto his haunches. "I need another snack." He pulled a bag of trail mix from his jacket slash snack storage and ripped into the packaging. "Want some?"

Holden took him up on it. "Sure. I'll have a handful."

The two sat beneath the canopy of branches, chomping on their mix of raisins and nuts like a pair of wild squirrels.

"We shouldn't be doing this." Holden fit the poles together. "Right? I mean, sneaking around their property? It's wrong."

"Santa does it." Lance lifted a shoulder. "And he even goes into people's houses. We're not doing that. In a way, that makes us better than Santa Claus, and everyone *loves* Santa Claus."

The logic was convoluted, but gave Holden the flimsy encouragement he needed.

The last notes of "Rocking Around the Christmas Tree" blended into the beginning sounds of "Silent Night" around them. It had always been one of Holden's favorite songs, the words sung in his mother's beautiful voice at Christmas Eve church services year after year.

But right now, nothing was calm, and Holden didn't feel all that bright.

This was royally stupid.

"Let's get this over and done with." He erected the pole and hoisted himself up. Like a reed swaying in the wind, it teetered until he plunged it into the snow, meeting solid ground several feet below. He craned his neck skyward. "Can you read it? What does it say?"

Lance narrowed his eyes. "I can't really get a good read from here. We're too close."

He was right. It was like looking up at a high-rise building from ground level and trying to calculate the number of floors to the top. The higher it got, the fuzzier the details. How on earth had his father been able to measure their own tree with such accuracy?

"I need a better vantage point," Lance said.

Holden tracked Lance's eyes toward the cabin. At the back of the house, there was a large deck. Holden didn't like where this was going.

"Not an option," he answered before Lance had the opportunity to ask.

"Come on. I can sneak over there real quick and get a good read. It's the perfect vantage point to view it from."

"Or you could head back to the shed and take a look from there."

Lance tossed his head in a 'no'. "It's too dark. I need

the porch lights from the cabin to see the markings on the pole. I'll be fast."

This was a bad idea, another tally on the regrettably long list of them. Holden shouldn't have agreed to help his father. They shouldn't have stopped by the market earlier in the day. Those were bad decisions. But creeping onto the Joy's deck in the still of night to measure their tree? That was downright idiotic.

"Come on, buddy. We're already in this far. Might as well see it through."

"You can't let them catch you, Lance."

"I'll be faster than a speeding bullet, Superman style. Promise. They won't see me."

Maybe the Joys weren't even home. Sure, their porch lights were on, but it was night and most people left their outdoor lights illuminated all hours to keep critters away. The house itself was dark inside, not even a table lamp left on. If they were home, they were likely sleeping. With the continuous soundtrack of music to muffle their noises, Lance and Holden just might pull this off.

"You have to be quick," he instructed. "And quiet."

"Quick and quiet. Got it."

Holden gave one clipped nod, signaling go-time.

Bent at the waist, Lance maneuvered through the snow. His boots sank into the layers, coming clear up to his shins. He looked like a fisherman wading upstream. He wasn't remotely fast, but he hadn't made it to the deck yet, and from the cabin, he still couldn't be seen.

Holden trapped in a stinging breath.

Lance's tread met the first step. He gripped onto the railing to find purchase and keep from slipping on the icy boards. He looked like one of those cartoon capers sneaking about, their movements slow but dramatic all the same.

Almost there.

Holden waited for a light to flicker on. If they were found out, that's how it would happen. Rachel would sense the commotion and venture outside to locate the source. She'd flip the switch and shine a light on their foolishness.

Holden had watched enough movies to know the script. He wished he could write himself out of the scene entirely, but he had a job to do. Securing his grip on the pole, he held it upright.

Lance continued to slink his way across the deck until he stood squarely in front of the tree, but at a distance of a dozen or so yards. His forehead buckled as he strained to read the measurement.

"Hurry," Holden hissed.

"I can't see. Move the stick to the front."

Grimacing, Holden clomped his way around and jammed the pole back into the snow. "Now?"

"Twenty feet…." Lance's gaze tightened again. The guy needed a trip to the optometrist. "Three inches."

"You've got to be kidding me," Holden groaned.

"Yep. Twenty feet, three inches."

"You're sure?"

"Yes," Lance sneered. "I'm sure."

Holden tugged the pole out of its rut and untwisted the pieces. "Okay. Hurry back. And be quiet."

How was it possible that the two trees were identical heights? It was as if they were back to square one, neither family having an edge over the other. His dad was going to lose his mind.

A blip in the track had "God Rest Ye Merry Gentlemen" suddenly morphing into "The Twelve Days of Christmas." It also had Holden's heart faltering out of rhythm. When the new song stuttered and repeated day eight three times in a row, Holden took that as a sign to hightail it out of there. The wheels were falling off.

"No army crawling," he said when Lance came up to his side. "We make a run for it."

The music shut off completely.

The light Holden had anticipated from earlier flashed on, flooding the mountainside.

"Run!" Holden whisper-yelled.

The two raced toward the rickety shed. Lance got there first. Holden threw the poles behind the structure.

"Hello?" The sound of Rachel's voice had Holden's stomach doing somersaults. "Is someone there?"

CHAPTER 17

❄

*S*he saw them. Two men, just like back at the market. She was certain of it.

But when Rachel ran into the house to tug on her snow boots and jacket, the shadows that crouched behind her dad's old work shed were gone, the only things left behind three long pieces of plastic pipe.

"Could this day get any weirder?" She blew into her cupped hands. Her fingers were freezing. It was the coldest day of December yet. No one would dare to be out in these elements unless they had good reason to be.

Her eyes must have been playing tricks on her. It was the only plausible explanation. But the fresh tracks in the snow made her feel a little less crazy. Someone or something had been out there.

But she hadn't heard anyone. The only reason she even ventured outside was to investigate the malfunctioning speaker. Apparently, keeping the power on for a full week wasn't an ideal use for an electronic item. Her father wouldn't be thrilled, but they'd have to come up with another Christmas carol plan.

Heading back inside, Rachel cast one last extensive gaze over the yard, coming up short with explanations.

The full moon hung in a blanket of navy above, accented with shimmering stars that glittered like rhinestones. It sure was beautiful country up here. The atmosphere was unpolluted, the air clean. Christmas in the city was an extravagant event filled with decorated stores and fancy shop windows, but the summit provided a different backdrop. One where even Mother Nature got in on the celebration.

She took one last look at their tree. It was perfect, even more majestic than the one she'd picked out with Buddy. Oh, how she wished her sister and sweet grandma could see it. Angling her gaze heavenward, she hugged her arms close. Maybe they could. That hope filled her with a warmth like no other, and when she finally trekked back into the cabin, even the fire in the hearth couldn't compete.

Rachel heard the footfalls first and then saw her mother's figure coming down the stairs. Paula buckled her robe around her middle with the fabric belt and grinned. "You couldn't sleep either? Something wake you?"

"You know? It was actually the lack of noise that did. Dad's speaker is on the fritz and the music cut off."

She moved with her mother to the kitchen, knowing the routine. Back when she was a child, a sleepless night called for a cup of lemon tea and a splash of honey. Paula got the kettle ready while Rachel snagged the bear-shaped squeeze jar from the cupboard. She pulled out a barstool and took a seat.

"I was getting so used to that loop of music as constant background noise that I didn't even notice it had still been going until it stopped."

"Funny how we don't truly miss something until it's gone." Paula angled her head. "Do you ever miss it here? Because it sure is nice to have you home, sweetheart."

It had been nice—and confusing and even a little weird. "Yeah, I have missed it."

"Do you ever think of coming back?"

"To Snowdrift?" Rachel perked up in her seat.

"Yes. I mean, for longer than just the holidays. Your father was going on and on all night about how much he loved having you back in the store, working side by side again."

"Mom..."

"I know." Paula shed the smallest smile. "It's not like you'd be content here, living a simple life. I've always known that."

"It's not that," Rachel said. "It's just that I'm finally so close to living the life I've worked so hard for."

"And is it the life you want?"

That question was more loaded than Santa's bag of presents. "I think so." Her shoulders scrunched to her ears. "I don't know."

"I know Bethany always dreamed of the city, ever

since she was a young girl. I just never fully realized it was your dream too. Growing up, you girls shared a lot, from bedrooms to clothes. But you both had your own gifts. And you're allowed to have your own dreams."

The teapot on the stove trilled a whistle. Paula snagged it from the burner before the screeching increased to full volume. She poured a generous mug for Rachel, sliding it over the granite island between them.

"I have my own dreams." Rachel squeezed a dollop of golden honey into the hot water. "And my gift is that I get the chance to achieve them, even though Bethany no longer can."

Her mother's hand smothered Rachel's and pressed down. "I know losing her changed you, sweetheart. It changed all of us. I just want to make sure you're not losing yourself too. You have every right to fulfill your own destiny, one that you dream up all on your own. You need to know that."

"I do know that."

They shared a cup of tea, but no more words after that. Paula headed to bed and Rachel retreated to the spare room, her mother's confession working its way right past her brain and straight into her heart.

Losing her older sister had steered everything in Rachel's world off course, like a snow globe turned upside down and never righted. She had been a mess of wayward emotion that year. Throwing herself into her studies helped, and latching onto the path Bethany had once hoped to take marked out a journey Rachel could easily follow. A blueprint she could read.

As kids, they had always talked about sharing an apartment in the city. How they'd each have designer purses and dogs, with more money than they would ever know what to do with. It was a game of pretend, until the point Rachel made it reality.

But without Bethany to share it with, it all felt utterly pointless.

Rachel fell asleep that night wondering what her life might look like had she forged her own way instead. Carved her destiny and set out on her own journey.

With these thoughts, she slowly slipped into a dream, and the place her heart took her sure looked a lot like Snowdrift.

* * *

"What project are you working on with those PVC pipes, Dad?"

Stewart's fork, loaded with scrambled eggs, stalled several inches from his mouth. "What are you talking about, Sugar Plum?"

"Those pipes behind the old shed. With the markings on them like a tape measure."

Her father's utensil met his breakfast plate with a clatter and the nails-on-a-chalkboard screech of his chair legs had Rachel's shoulders jumping to her ears. Stumbling out of his slippers and into galoshes,

Stewart barely had one arm in his jacket and he was out the back door, not even bothering to close it behind him.

Paula and Rachel locked eyes, brows raised.

"Should we go?" Rachel started to say and then they were both outside, similarly clad in a mix of outdoor gear and flannel pajamas.

The women scurried to catch up.

"Someone's been snooping around here. I can feel it," Stewart grumbled, head swinging. He sniffed the air like a bloodhound on a scent.

"And see it." Paula pointed to the tracks leftover from the night before. A dusting of snow had filled them slightly, but they were still easily visible. "Looks like it was two snoops."

Stewart had the pipes in his grasp. Nose tipped, he eyed the marks over the top rim of his glasses. "Someone's been trying to get a measurement on our tree!"

"How do you know that?" Paula asked.

"Because this here is a manmade measuring stick. The only reason anyone would need something this tall would be to measure something tall...like our noble fir."

"Who would want to do that?"

That above-rim gaze moved from the tool to his wife. "Do I really need to answer that?"

"The Harts wouldn't stoop that low."

"Oh, really?" Stewart nudged his glasses back up his nose with his knuckle. "You don't think so? They're still boiling over the fact that Holden's essay was disqualified for that college scholarship. They think Rachel stole their son's only chance at a fancy education. Well, you know what? They're not going to steal our tree's rightful spot as the town Christmas tree, that's for sure."

"Wait." Rachel lifted her hand like a crossing guard. "What are you talking about, 'I stole Holden's scholarship'?" She made quotes around the question with her fingers.

"They think Holden was unfairly disqualified, which made you the uncontested winner. Zeke brought it up at a Super Bowl party a few years back after he'd had his share of punch, which was no doubt spiked."

"Why would they do that?"

"People do it all the time," Stewart said matter-of-factly. "You can hardly taste it."

"Not spike the punchbowl, Dad. Why would they accuse me of taking his scholarship?"

"Because there could only be one winner and you were it. The Harts are sore losers, Sugar Plum. Always have been. But they better ice up because they're about to get even more sore when we finally beat them once and for all."

Paula shuddered and crossed the opening of her jacket over her stomach. "Don't you think we could fix all of this if we just sat down with one another and talked things through?"

"You can't fix crazy, Paula," Stewart said in a maniacal tone that had Rachel questioning who the real crazy one was. Then, as though snapping to attention, he threw the pipes aside and darted back to the house double time, heaving with breaths that forced a cough from his lungs.

"Stewart, slow down!" Paula yelled. "You're going to hurt yourself."

"I don't know why I didn't think of it!" Her father was in mad-scientist mode.

"Didn't think of what?"

Ambling back into the house, Paula and Rachel discovered Stewart at the kitchen table with his cell phone in his trembling grasp.

"The cameras." He swiped over several applications and pulled up the one in question. "Remember? We installed them to catch the raccoon that kept getting into the trash bins. If I rewind far enough, we should be able to get a view of the perpetrators."

Even though it felt crazy, Rachel couldn't tamp down the anticipation that had sweat beading on her forehead. She peered over her father's shoulder, breath caught.

"There they are! There's one on the deck right here!"

"Lance?" The outline was fuzzy, but Rachel could clearly make out the shock of white hair peeking out from a beanie. Of course, it had helped that she'd seen him just the day before, his appearance fresh in her mind. "Why would Lance care how tall our tree is?"

"It's not Lance who cares," Stewart zoomed in on a

shadowy figure at the edge of the frame. He tapped the screen. "It's him."

"Buddy?" Rachel's mouth went dry, his name grating on her tongue.

"I don't know who Buddy is," her father continued, "but this right here explains everything." He paused the video and pulled up the image even bigger. "Looks like all the Harts are in on it this time. Even that sneaky, no good son of theirs."

CHAPTER 18

❄

Sarah stretched back from the table and bounced her baby on her lap, eliciting a fitful of giggles from the child. Laney had made an absolute mess of her breakfast, but it really couldn't be avoided when all food was considered finger food.

"I'm going to grab a few napkins from the counter and clean up this disaster so the poor busboy doesn't have to. It looks like a breakfast tornado."

Holden's sister scooted out her chair, but he stood first.

"Let me. You have your hands full."

"Isn't that the truth?" Pressing a kiss to her daughter's mop of corkscrew blonde curls, Sarah beamed with motherly pride.

Before Sarah and her ex-husband had transferred from Snowdrift to Sacramento for Darrel's work as a legal assistant, Holden had made a point of weekly brother-sister breakfasts. It was a designated time on the calendar to touch base, even if it had become more of a "Can you believe Mom and Dad?" gab session in recent years. Though the meetings were fewer, Holden was still thankful for his sister and their shared history. No one knew you like family.

He moved through the Cornerstone Café and snagged a stack of folded napkins from the dispenser on the bar, right next to a Santa that bellowed *"Ho, ho, ho"* each time a patron moved past and triggered its motion sensor.

"How was everything today?" Holly Calloway, the restaurant's manager, pressed over the counter and seized Holden's attention with her cheery greeting.

"Pancake perfection, Miss Holly. Like always."

"Did the little gal enjoy the snowman shaped ones? I made those special, just for her."

"She certainly did. And I might've even commandeered one for myself. I couldn't resist."

Laughing heartily, Holly flung a checkered print dishtowel over her shoulder. "All you need to do is ask, Holden. I'll let you order off the kid's menu anytime you like. You already know that."

Miss Holly had been in charge of the establishment since Holden was Laney's age, and the memories he had of sitting around the table in her café ushered in a nostalgia he couldn't ignore.

That's what he loved about Snowdrift Summit. Sure, it was a small town, but that phrase felt so limiting. Nothing was small about the relationships formed here. About the memories created with people who shared not only the same zip code, but a rich history of celebration and tradition. On the outside, Snowdrift offered mountain views with sweeping, natural landscapes of pristine white. But it was the people who called the place home who provided the real beauty, their generosity and love every bit as spectacular as the scenery surrounding them.

And it was why Christmas was such a big deal around the place. And why having a tree chosen to represent the town truly meant something.

For over one-hundred and fifty years, the Christmas Committee scouted and selected the finest local tree, fit to be adorned with brilliant lights and antique ornaments. They would place the lucky evergreen directly at the end of Main Street, so everyone who passed through could effortlessly glimpse its grand splendor on full display.

Legend was that the first Snowdrift Christmas tree even had a little to do with the town's founding. For years, Snowdrift served as a trading post for settlers brave enough to venture through the High Sierra on their route toward the Sacramento Valley. Crossing these mountains in the dead of winter was a risky, dangerous endeavor. But promises of gold lured many over those hills and toward a future filled with land and riches. For most, Snowdrift was a pass-through on the route to the fulfillment of bigger dreams.

Only a handful of pioneers called the place home back in those days. There were a few shops on what was now Main Street, and only a scattering of cabins lining the ridge surrounding town.

But that first year, the townspeople thought weary travelers deserved a tree of their own. Covered wagons barely had room to house the basics, and a Christmas tree wasn't an essential item. But one glimpse at that lovely tree had voyagers setting up camp. And the hospitality of the townspeople and spirit of the season caused many to change course with their plans and plant down permanent roots in Snowdrift instead.

Over the years, Holden sometimes wondered if the tale boasted more bits of folklore than the original telling, but it didn't matter. There was something special about a town like Snowdrift Summit and he was grateful every day that he was fortunate enough to call the place home.

"Thank you," Sarah said when he finally came back to the table with the requested napkins. "Any chance you want to trade jobs and hold her for a bit instead? She's about to wiggle right out of my lap."

"Clean the table or snuggle my adorable niece? Is that even a question?" He scooped the baby into his arms. "How about I take her outside for a change of scenery?"

"That would be great." Sarah swiped the crumbs into a pile. "I actually need to put in an order for a couple of Holly's holiday pies, so if you don't mind taking Laney on a little stroll, I'll meet up with you when I'm all finished here." She pulled the strap of the diaper bag from her seat back and passed it her brother's way. "And take this. Always good to be prepared."

Holden moved the large bag onto his shoulder, swiveled Laney to his hip, and gave Sarah a quick hug before heading out the door.

Fresh mountain air skated over his skin in an invigorating welcome.

"What do you say we go for a little walk, Laney girl?" He lifted the hood of her puffy jacket over her head to keep the wind out of her ears. "Main Street is all decked out, so there's lots to see."

He took her to the bookstore first. They stopped in front of the window display and admired the tower of hardcover books, all stacked and positioned to form a literary tree. Even the door to the shop had a wreath fashioned from old, worn books with a large, festive bow made from pages tied right at the top.

There was Christmas creativity on every corner. Laney especially liked the General Store's display, with its moving train that whistled and chugged. She pressed her chubby hands to the glass, leaning in to get a closer look.

"Want to go inside?" Holden suggested. His mother had asked that he pick up an icepack for his father, so Holden figured he could kill two birds with one stone: keep Laney entertained while also checking the errand off of his to-do list.

A bell chimed his entrance and Laney looked up to locate the ringing sound.

"Ding, ding, ding," Holden mimicked, which got the

squeal he'd hoped to draw out from the child. "Ding, ding, ding."

He continued ringing away, his volume getting louder and intonation sillier with each repetition. He even added a little dancing shuffle to the melody, and the two boogied their way through the aisles.

Laney mimicked her uncle's antics, really feeling it.

Holden was all in. He trotted backward as he shimmied to their made-up song, losing himself in the sheer goofiness of it all.

He'd lost himself so much, in fact, that he didn't notice the customer behind him in the same aisle. Not until he smacked straight into them, nearly knocking them over.

He spun around.

Icy blue eyes as wide as glass ornaments pinned him with a look of disbelief.

"Oh!" Holden stopped dancing, but Laney kept on reciting *ding, ding, ding* like a needle caught on repeat in the groove of a record. "Hey."

"Hey there, *Buddy*," Rachel said. She had a Bluetooth speaker in her hands and a heated look on her face that could melt a snowman.

"This isn't what it looks like." He shifted Laney to his other hip.

"What do you think it looks like?" Her head angled so far, her ear almost touched her shoulder.

"It looks like I have a baby."

Her eyes tugged from his down toward Laney, and Holden suddenly realized it wasn't the child's presence that had Rachel so upset. It had to be something else entirely.

"You do have a baby."

"I mean, yes, I have a baby in my arms, but she's not mine."

"And what's her name?" she asked, then lifted a hand and her mouth flipped into a sarcastic frown. "Oh wait, never mind. I'm not sure I would believe you, even if you told it to me."

The back of Holden's neck prickled with heat. "What's going on?"

"Why don't you tell me, *Holden*?" She spun away from him.

He gulped. "I'm sorry. Rachel, listen—"

She whipped around. "What? You mean to tell me you've known *my* name this entire time, but I had to find out from my parents who you were?"

His head shook side to side so quickly, his vision lagged a second behind. "No. I didn't know it was you. Not until Lance figured it out."

"Ah, your partner in crime."

Laney wriggled, bending to reach a nearby display of stuffed animals. Holden stepped out of arm's reach. "What are you talking about?"

"I saw you both last night, sabotaging our speaker and measuring our tree."

"What? We didn't sabotage your speaker."

"But you *did* measure our tree?"

Chest ballooning with a breath he needed for

courage, Holden admitted, "We did. And that was really dumb and I'm really sorry."

"You mean you're sorry you got caught?"

"But we didn't get caught. I thought we made it out of there without being seen."

"There's this fascinating little technology called home security," she said bitterly. "My dad saw you on the cameras."

One-part embarrassment, two-parts regret pulsed through Holden's veins. "I'm really sorry you had to find out who I was that way."

"I mean, it's fitting, isn't it? That I would discover your identity like that? With you attempting to take this competition from us?"

"I'm not trying to take this competition from you. I was doing a favor for my dad. Remember that broken foot? He asked that I do it for him."

"So you're telling me your entire family is in on this?"

All words disappeared right out of Holden's brain. He went mute.

"Of course they are!" She flung around again.

Holden jogged around her and Laney must've thought it was some game because she let out a loud belly laugh. "Listen, Rachel. I really am sorry."

"I can't believe I thought your name was Buddy." She shook her head and looked at the ceiling.

"I'm a little too big to be an elf," he joked, but it fell flat. Too soon, apparently.

"Ding, ding, ding," Laney suddenly interjected when another patron entered the store.

Holden lowered his volume. "Rachel, I really don't know how else to put it. I snuck onto your property and I measured your parents' tree. That was dumb. I'm sorry."

"And you led me to believe you were someone else this whole time."

"I don't remember you being very forthcoming about your identity either, Mittens."

Her eyes practically shot icicles at him.

Noted. He needed to retire that nickname altogether.

"All I'm saying is, I think we were both having a little fun with the mystery of it all."

"And that mystery is completely gone. I know exactly who you are, Holden Hart."

"And who's that?" he challenged. "Because I don't know about you, but I think I'm different from the kid I was in high school."

She gave him a clipped once-over. "You might look different, but the fact that you trespassed onto our property and lied about your true identity shows that deep down, you're still exactly the same kid who will do anything to win."

"I think you're wrong."

"Well, that's a shocker. We never have agreed on much."

Holden breathed in sharply. "I get that you're mad. And I get it if you never want to speak to me again. But can't we at least be civil? I mean, our parents aren't really acting that way. Don't you think we should be the voices of reason in this whole ridiculous thing?"

"I don't want to be the voice of anything with you, Holden," she said, chin high. "We're done here."

With determination in her step and her head held high, she stormed out of the store and out of Holden's life. For a second time.

CHAPTER 19

❄

She needed to calm down. Rachel hated what the unexpected encounter with Holden had done to her previously untroubled mood. What she hated even more was how—despite all logic—she still continued to find herself attracted to the man. It wasn't just physical. The way he'd danced around the store with that baby in his arms, as though they were the only two in the entire place, had Rachel's insides melting like chocolate candy.

She could not reconcile what she knew to be true with what her heart felt. They were at the greatest of odds.

The brisk walk to Bitter Cold didn't provide the clarity she'd hoped to achieve. In the city, when her mind got hung up on a work problem, a few laps around the block were usually all it took to unravel the situation and see things clearly. Not so this morning. And when she entered the coffee shop and saw Trinity

Tillman already at the bar waiting for her drink, she had an idea.

"Trinity," Rachel greeted. It had been years since she'd seen the woman, but a hug felt appropriate. Trinity's chestnut brown eyes were warm, the embodiment of the friendly and open spirit Rachel remembered so fondly.

"Hi, Rachel." She took her drink from the counter and fit a plastic lid onto the cup, then slid it into a sleeve. "I'm so glad you could meet with me. It's been so long. It's wonderful to see you."

"Same to you," Rachel reciprocated. "Do you have a table?"

"Not yet." Trinity's gaze moved about the room. "It's really busy here today. We might need to wait a little bit for one."

"It is, which is why I was thinking maybe we could go for a walk." Rachel shrugged, wondering if the request was an odd one since it was barely above freezing outdoors. "Unless it's too cold."

"I've been cooped up in my house with two toddlers all weekend. I will take all the winter sunshine I can get."

Rachel placed her order at the register and within minutes, the drink appeared at the barista bar.

Trinity filled her in on her life as they headed onto Main Street. The woman had the type of easy going nature that made picking up right where they left off an effortless thing to do.

"What brings you into town?" Trinity asked before

pressing her lips to her cup to take a drink. She skirted a man with a small, curly dog tugging at the full length of his leash. The dog yapped as they strolled by. "It's been a few years since you've been back, no?"

"I came home to help my parents with the holidays," Rachel said without divulging too much. "And to research a project for work."

"What sort of project?"

With her free hand, Rachel fiddled with the frilled edge of her wool scarf.

"I design artificial greenery for the company I work for. This one is for a new line of fake mistletoe."

"Oh, that sounds so fun," Trinity said, and if her enthusiasm was false, Rachel couldn't detect it. "What an amazing profession. You've always been so good at everything you set your mind to, Rachel. Your company is lucky to have someone as driven as you," Trinity said, then added, "I know if you stuck around Snowdrift, I would've utilized that big, creative brain of yours when we opened our shop."

Rachel hadn't even asked Trinity what she did for a living, and embarrassment about her lack of politeness pummeled through her. "You have a store?"

"I do. Floral shop just around the corner. I run it, along with my mother. It's a slower time of year for us bouquet-wise, so we've been focusing our efforts on creating arrangements more in line with the holidays. I know you said you make artificial greenery, but I figure it translates the same."

"I would love to see your shop sometime."

An appreciative smile formed on Trinity's mouth. "We're closed today since it's Sunday, but we'll be open tomorrow. You should come by. I usually have the little ones with me, but they keep busy playing with the flowers and filler." She laughed. "What about you? Any kids?"

"No husband, no kids," Rachel said behind her cup. She pulled in a sip and held it there. "Just me and the big ol' city."

"Sounds amazing." Trinity's voice harbored a twinge of jealousy. "Living the dream."

Someone's, sure, but Rachel was beginning to doubt it was her dream anymore.

They looped their way down Main Street on one side and up it on the other, stopping into the bookshop and the gift store for Trinity to do a little Christmas shopping without her children in tow. To Rachel's surprise, nearly every shopkeeper recalled her specifically by name and acknowledged her with wide, welcoming smiles that had her feeling seen in a way she never had in San Francisco.

The unanticipated reunions had her emotions rising to the surface. She recalled each friendly face too, until they bumped into a woman Rachel couldn't pinpoint right off the bat. She scrolled through her recent memories.

The younger of the two women from the knitting shop. That was it.

"Trinity," the woman addressed. "It's good to see you."

Lowering her coffee cup to her side and with her other hand busy holding her shopping bags, Trinity pressed an armless hug to the woman. Their cheeks met in greeting. "Sarah, it's so nice to see you back in town. How are you? And where's that sweet little cherub of yours?"

"With Holden," Sarah replied, and suddenly, it all snapped into place.

Trinity turned to Rachel. "Sarah, you remember Rachel Joy." She waved her cup up and down Rachel as an introduction.

"That, I do. Hi," Sarah said. She stretched her hand out for a shake. "I'm sorry, I didn't recognize you at first from the crocheting class the other day. It's good to see you." She paused for a breath, then smiled. "I should probably track down my brother. He's a wonderful uncle, but it's been a while since he's been on baby duty."

"I just saw him at the General Store. He seemed to have things under control."

"Well." Sarah's shoulders bounced in ambivalence. "That's the thing about Holden. He's really good at appearing like everything's fine when things are falling apart just below the surface. It was nice to see you both. Merry Christmas."

"Merry Christmas," Rachel and Trinity echoed. Even when Sarah was several yards from them, Rachel found her gaze lingering on her, as though the meaning of her words would become clearer the more she focused on them.

"You and Holden never quite made nice, did you?" Trinity shifted the shopping handles within her grip.

"No, we never did," Rachel confessed, wondering how things had gotten so convoluted over the years and if they would remain that way forever. But she already knew the answer.

Her rivalry with Holden Hart would endure until one of them caved first. And if history could tell her anything, she wouldn't be the one to do it.

CHAPTER 20

❄

"Any questions?"

A redheaded boy's hand shot into the air.

"Yes, young man," Holden said, nodding to the student in the front row of desks.

"Does she get paid? Since you said she's a working dog?"

"These Search and Rescue dogs aren't motivated by money like people are. For Scout, once she locates her item, an immediate reward is a game of tug-of-war."

"I love tug-of-war," another boy piped up from the back of the classroom.

Every winter, Holden would visit Miss Morgenstern's first grade class to give a quick lesson on snow safety basics. It started years back when he became a Search and Rescue volunteer, but the students' interest definitely piqued when Holden began bringing Scout along with him. That golden gal always stole the show.

A quieter young girl obscured behind another

student slid her hand into the air. Holden called upon her next. "What can I answer for you?"

"Are we allowed to pet her?" She quickly tugged her hand down.

"Absolutely! Part of Scout's training is socialization, which means she needs to learn to be on her best behavior in all sorts of situations."

"And a classroom full of energetic kids is a good place for that," Miss Morgenstern said. A murmur of excitement quickly grew into shouts of glee and the teacher clapped her hands three times to rally her tiny troops. "Class, if you'd like to pet Scout, please line up two by two with your lunch line buddy. We'll file through quietly and on our very best behavior. No rough-housing and no shoving to get to the front. We all wait our turn. Yes, students?"

"Yes Miss Morgenstern," all twenty-four voices replied in sing-song accord.

Holden stepped to the side to stand by his old teacher. "Thanks for letting me bring her in."

"Are you kidding me? This day is always a favorite for the students—right up there with corndog day in the cafeteria."

"Corndogs are worth the excitement. I get it."

He slipped his hands into his pockets and leaned against the whiteboard while keeping a watchful eye on Scout. She held her proud head high as each child came through and stroked her fur. Some wrapped her neck in a hug. Holden even saw one sweet girl plant a kiss on the tip of her wet nose.

"You know," Miss Morgenstern began, "I'm not at all surprised by this, Holden." She gestured toward the golden retriever and then brought her gaze back to her former student. "I'm not one bit surprised you became a Search and Rescue volunteer and that you're now training your dog to be one too. Even as a young boy, you had a heart for helping others."

Holden shrugged within his jacket. "Really?" That wasn't how he remembered it. He remembered getting in more trouble than the rest of his first grade class combined.

"Oh, definitely. I remember you once brought in that poor kitten you found out on the playground during recess. It was stuck up in a tree. Do you remember that?"

A laugh rose with the memory. "How could I forget Miss Kitty?"

"You scaled that fifteen-foot tree to get her down. I remember not knowing whether to give you detention or a gold star."

"I think a phone call home was the final decision."

"And I remember that call. Your father was so proud of you. Said you were in line to be the next great Hart firefighter."

"That had been his hope," Holden admitted. He knew his father was proud of the life Holden had made for himself, even if he disguised that praise under sarcastic jabs, often comparing Holden's job to a child that essentially got to play in the snow all day.

For Holden, it was the best of both worlds. He got

his adrenaline fix out there on his snowmobile, but he also got to give back by volunteering his time to help others when needed.

And having a good dog by his side throughout it all was just the icing on the cake.

"I know you originally wanted to go to school to study medicine." Miss Morgenstern continued their sidebar conversation. "What ever happened with that?"

"It wasn't in the cards." Or in the bank account. "Plus, I don't know that I'd ever be happy in a doctor's office. I think I've discovered that the best prescription for most any ailment is a large dose of fresh mountain air."

"For what it's worth, I think you could have taken your pick when it came to your profession. With that smart brain and relentless drive of yours, the sky was the limit." Her hand came down over his shoulder. "I love to see my students doing so well for themselves. It's been wonderful following your journey all these years, Holden."

"Having teachers like you who believed in me and saw my energy as more than just something to wrangle made all the difference."

The redheaded boy from earlier spoke up. "Can we go back through and pet her again?" His mouth stretched into a pleading grin that had his little neck straining. "Please?"

Miss Morgenstern returned to her place at the front of the classroom. "I think we need to let Mr. Hart and

Scout be on their way. Class, can we give them one more thank-you for coming in today?"

"Thank you, Mr. Hart and Scout," the class tried to echo, but the words jumbled into a conglomeration of out of sync voices.

"Anytime," Holden replied. "And hopefully next time you see Scout, she will be a fully validated Avalanche Rescue Dog."

"Paws crossed," Miss Morgenstern said with a smile.

* * *

Lance withdrew a hanger from the box and slipped the jacket onto it. They'd received a new shipment of winter gear, just in time for the 'Storm of the Century' that the locals—along with every meteorologist within a hundred-mile radius—predicted would come rolling through any minute.

Things like bottled water, toilet paper, and spare generators flew off the shelves first, but Holden knew last-minute shoppers would pack their store, hoping to purchase a few necessary items before the storm hit. When you had to dig your way out of your own home, it was best done in the warmest, cold-weather clothing possible.

They'd already had a few phone calls that afternoon checking on their wool sock and long underwear inventory. When they'd opened up Major Hart Mountain Sports years ago, Holden figured they would stick to the adventure side of things: snowboards and skis, helmets and goggles. All the gear for a run down the hill.

It had been at Lance's urging that they integrated more everyday items. They even stocked blankets, and currently, they were down to just two remaining. Vacationers and travelers visiting the mountain for a short period of time rarely brought the extra items needed to weather an epic storm. It was a smart business decision to have these products in the shop.

They unboxed the first delivery and moved on to the next. They'd already had two snowmobile tour cancellations that day, and Holden figured more would follow suit.

It hadn't stormed yet, but the threat of it loomed over the summit in a heavy cloak of gray.

"What did you think of the guy from the other day?" Lance asked as they continued to price new inventory and get it onto shelves. "The one we interviewed."

Holden had liked Brady. He shared a similar love for high-elevation sports and his resume corroborated his wealth of experience on the slopes. And he seemed easygoing, a necessary trait in their line of work. He was personable, professional, and down-to-earth—the perfect fit.

"I say we make him an offer. We've only got a few months left in the snow season and I think we could use him on staff." Holden folded a stack of beanies and moved them to a lower shelf along the wall. "And he's an avid mountain biker, which will bode well for our summer crowd."

Neither Holden nor Lance were all that into mountain biking: Lance with his bum knee and Holden with the memory of the time he went over the handlebars and landed in a nest of angry hornets. That memory stung in more ways than one. But when all the snow melted and winter passed, their hill transformed into an entirely different sort of playground. Where snowmobiles once carved across packed slopes of snow, bike tires formed new grooves in the dirt.

Holden usually led hiking expeditions on foot, and even the nearby horse stables utilized the terrain for mounted, guided tours. It would be good to have another adventurer on staff, one with a set of skills they currently lacked.

"I'll call him this evening." Lance used his pocketknife to cut through the packing tape on another large box. "Speaking of, you planning on making any phone calls? Maybe to a certain someone named Rachel?"

"That was the lamest transition ever." Holden groaned at his friend.

"I know. Not my smoothest."

"The answer is no. I haven't called her. But I did run into her at the General Store and let's just say, the cat is completely out of the bag and there's no way I can wrangle it back in without getting my eyes clawed out."

"You're going to have to translate that for me."

"She knows who I am. And she knows we were at her parents' place measuring the tree."

Lance looked up. "How is that possible? We got out of there without anyone seeing us. I'm sure of it."

"Her parents have a security camera and captured us on it."

"And she figured out you aren't actually Buddy?"

"You guessed it."

Lance broke down an empty box and moved it to the pile of folded cardboard boxes headed for the recycling dumpster. "There's got to be a little relief in that, right? That you both finally know the other's true identity?"

"Maybe a little." Holden sighed. "I mean, she just seems so different. It's hard to believe she's the same girl I disliked so much back in the day."

"They say there's a thin line between love and hate."

Holden bristled. "Who says that?"

"People." Lance squared his shoulders confidently. "Scientists."

"Scientists say love and hate are the same thing?" Holden sincerely doubted that.

"Not that they are the same thing, but that the brain registers the emotions the same. Something like that. I don't know. I didn't come up with it."

"But it sort of sounds like you did."

"All I'm saying is that maybe this animosity you've built up toward Rachel over the years was really something else in disguise," Lance conceded with his hands up.

"You think I've been in love with Rachel since high school? I'm pretty sure I would have known if that were the case. Plus, don't you think I would have recognized her if I supposedly had all these feelings for her?"

"Blinded by love—that's another term for it."

"Sounds like you're just reciting a lot of mumbo jumbo you've heard on a Dr. Phil show."

"It was a Dear Abby article, but whatever."

"I'm not—and never have been—in love with Rachel Joy. All I've ever wanted was to put her in her place."

"And that place is right in your arms," Lance crooned.

Holden balled up a scarf and chucked it at him. "I'm putting an end to all of this."

"All of what?"

"This family feud. It's one thing for Rachel and I to have our differences, but both of our families are in on it now. And I think the only way to finally resolve things is for there to be a clear winner. That'll happen when my family's noble fir is selected for the town tree."

"You think that'll really put an end to it?"

"It'll have to," Holden offered. He ripped into the packaging on another box. "Rachel will go back to the city again and it'll be over for good."

"I remember the first time she left Snowdrift. It was like someone told you there was no Santa Claus. I've never seen you so aimless. A ship without a rudder. A horse without a carrot to lead it."

"You're on a roll with the analogies today, bro."

"I've been doing a little light reading lately. I think it's opened up my mind and expanded my vocabulary. Thank you for noticing."

Holden snorted under a breath. "You're really sure their tree was the same height as ours?"

"Yeah, unfortunately. And I don't know how you can get yours to grow any taller in…how long do you have until the selection?"

"A few days."

Lance thumbed his chin. "Maybe we could do a tree dance? Like a rain dance, but for plants. Or cast some sort of miracle-growth spell."

"I'm honestly willing to do anything at this point," Holden said. "Losing is not an option."

When it came to Rachel, it never had been and never would be.

CHAPTER 21

Trinity's floral shop was enchanting. Long-stemmed red roses in cut crystal vases filled the big bay windows, combining the colors of the season with a touch of romance in the most beautiful way. Rachel inhaled deeply the moment she set foot in the shop. It had everything her San Francisco office lacked. That sharp aroma of freshly cut greenery. The soft, calming fragrance of dried lavender. The vibrant scent of roses that transported you straight to an English garden.

The area was painted a bright white, with distressed tables and shelving that allowed the colorful floral arrangements to remain the focal point, no matter where your gaze landed within the room.

"Rachel!" Trinity settled a pair of shears onto the counter and brushed her hands against her apron. She scurried across the store and took Rachel in her arms.

"I'm so glad you were able to stop in. I was hoping you would."

"This place is so lovely, Trinity." The compliment barely scratched the surface. "What a gorgeous storefront and even more gorgeous interior."

"That means so much, especially coming from you." Trinity released her. "Our flowers are perishable, so they aren't perfect like the ones you create. But I do love arranging them, and our customers always seem to be happy with the finished product."

"I can easily see why." Rachel took in another long breath. "It smells amazing in here."

"That's the pine. My mother's been working on wreaths in the back all day. She actually just took a break to take the kiddos to the snow park up the hill to run off some energy. Which means I've got the shop to myself."

"I should leave you to it, then."

"No, no. I would love your company." She turned toward the counter and the project she'd been working on before Rachel stopped in. "Would you like to do an arrangement with me?"

"Only if you're sure I won't get in the way."

"Nonsense. I would love the chance for adult conversation. It seems most of my discussions revolve around superheroes and toy cars these days."

It was wonderful to see Trinity chasing her dream while also leading a life that fulfilled her as a wife and mother. Rachel wasn't sure when the idea that the two were mutually exclusive had come to her, but Trinity quickly shot that misconception down.

The woman handed off an apron, much like the one Rachel had donned at her parents' market the other day.

"What was it you said you were working on for work? A new project?" Handing Rachel a crimson vase, Trinity gestured toward the large floral cooler behind them. "Feel free to use anything you like. It's all yours."

"Thank you," Rachel said. "And for work, it's a prototype for an artificial mistletoe."

"Oh, yes, that's right. I remember you saying that now. What's got you hung up?"

"Everything." An insecure laugh slipped between Rachel's lips. "I can't really pinpoint it. For starters, I've been calling it Mistlefaux, but that wasn't received well in focus groups." At least not in a focus group made of one. She tried to keep the frown from forming when she thought of Holden's initial reaction. "My creative juices have run completely dry."

"It'll come to you."

Rachel hoped so. "It doesn't help that mistletoe isn't very pretty."

"Well, it is a disease on a plant. I suppose it shouldn't be a surprise that it's not beautiful. But the use of it is. Two people in love, sharing a sweet moment beneath its sprigs of green."

A sweet moment. Rachel liked the way Trinity phrased that, and as they stood side by side, each crafting their own floral holiday arrangement, the words inspired her.

An hour passed and Rachel would have continued whiling away the long afternoon in the shop had her ringing phone not interrupted her budding creativity.

"Your father needs help at the market." Her mother bypassed a formal greeting and got right down to it. "Everyone's going a little forecast crazy, stocking up on food and nonperishable goods. Any chance you could help him man the place until closing? There's a line out the door."

"I'm just around the corner, at Trinity Tillman's flower shop. I can be there in less than ten minutes."

Her mother sighed her relief through the phone. "That would be wonderful, sweetie. I know he would appreciate the help."

"Not a problem." She said her goodbyes to her mother and then to Trinity.

"Please take your arrangement with you," Trinity offered. "It's beautiful."

"I would if I were heading straight home, but I'm walking over to the market and don't want to drop it. Why don't you keep it here? Who knows? Maybe it will even sell."

"I'm certain it'll fly off the shelf to the next customer to walk through those doors."

Trinity's optimism was catching. Rachel clung to that encouragement as she traipsed down the street toward her father's market. The wind chill had her teeth chattering instantly. The scarf hanging loose around her neck couldn't ward off the cold the way it was currently looped, so she tugged the edges and tightened it up. Had she been confident that she wouldn't trip face-first on the icy pavement, she would've tucked her hands into her pockets.

Running her palms up and down her arms for friction, she picked up her pace. When she rounded the corner, that line her mother mentioned filtered into view. It wrapped all the way around the block, coiling lights and lamp posts like a strand of Christmas garland.

"Excuse me." Rachel pressed between the throng of patrons congesting the sidewalk. She slid her way through the shoppers filling up the entry doors. "Pardon me."

"Sugar Plum!" Stewart raised his voice and hands. "You're here!" He called her over to the register and passed off an apron. "And not a moment too soon."

"This is crazy." Rachel had never seen the store at full capacity like this. "What is everyone here for?"

"Supplies. We're running low on canned goods and are already completely out of bottled water. Flashlights and batteries are getting scarce too."

As a young cashier rang up a customer's items and read their total aloud, Stewart loaded the things into a paper bag. While composed on the outside, Rachel could read her father's internal stress level easily. He had a tell that was a dead giveaway: he would remove and polish his glasses with the hem of his shirt whenever his anxiety reached its peak. He'd done it twice already and Rachel had only been in the store for a few minutes.

"How big is this storm supposed to be?" She'd grown up on the mountain and lived through her share of winter weather. But she didn't remember this level of panic buying and prepping. It was as though the town expected the apocalypse.

"They're projecting up to three feet overnight with widespread outages and road closures."

Rachel shuddered. "What can I do?"

"It would be wonderful if you could restock the shelves with the remaining inventory we have in the back. Non-perishable goods being the priority, then whatever else can fit on the shelves."

"I'm on it," she said, giving her father a swift nod.

He removed his glasses again and forced a smile.

A hum of commotion pulsed about the market, and while noisy, neighbors remained friendly and surprisingly calm in composure. One customer helped another get a hard to reach item from the top shelf. Another patron in line offered to share his bounty with a woman looking for a specific item he had the last one of. There was camaraderie even amid the frenzy, something Rachel hadn't been a part of in years. It wasn't every man for himself. Rather, the townspeople worked together as one to ensure their fellow neighbor could ride out the storm in comfort and calm.

By five o'clock, the atmosphere dimmed, and it wasn't just the setting sun that darkened the skies.

Wind whipped at the exterior awning, flapping the

fabric like a tattered flag. Wet, slushy snow splattered against the windows.

Rachel glanced around the market. The only time she had ever seen the shelves this bare was right before their grand opening, when their store was brand new and their inventory not yet displayed.

"I think that's the last of them." Stewart removed his glasses and swiped them clean. "Now that it's dark, I doubt anyone will venture out on the roads. And even if they do, we have little left to sell them." He pressed his palms to the counter and took a breath that puffed his chest. He blew it out through his mouth. "Summit Superstore is open twenty-four hours. Access to that supermarket will be easier since the plows clear the more heavily trafficked roads first. I think we're safe to close down for the night. Thank you so much for your help, Sugar Plum. I don't know what I would've done without you."

Rachel didn't feel like she had been very helpful. Telling customers they were out of the items they so desperately sought was like being the bearer of bad news ten times over. But most people just nodded their understanding and moved along, many even wishing her family well and thanking them for staying open. One look up and down Main Street confirmed not all business establishments had.

After reconciling the register and straightening up what little items remained, Stewart flipped off the lights and locked up the building.

The biting wind from earlier now mixed with dense

snowdrops that marred Rachel's vision and coated her cheeks with slick moisture. They rushed toward her father's SUV in the back lot. Equipped with four-wheel drive and snow tires, they didn't need chains, but even with the windshield wipers on max, it was a white-knuckle kind of ride. Rachel had never been more grateful that her father knew these roads like the back of his hand. She was certain he could navigate them blindfolded, which wasn't far from their current visibility situation.

"Your mother's gathered all the candles, flashlights, and blankets. I called her about an hour ago. We still have power, but I don't hold a lot of hope that we will through the night. You bring some warm pajamas with you? I don't want you to get cold in that spare room. It tends to get drafty."

"I'll be fine, Dad. What can I help with when we get home?"

"We've got everything under control, Sugar Plum." With an abundance of caution, Stewart gently lowered his foot to the gas to make the incline up their street. Tires spun beneath them, trying to gain traction. "Come on, Betsy, you can do it." He rubbed a hand on the dashboard. "Just a little bit further, girl."

The wheels finally found purchase in fresh snow and gripped their way up the rest of the driveway and into the garage.

"Oh, good!" Paula had obviously rushed to the door to meet them. Her chest heaved with relief. "You two are finally home!"

"Everything okay around here?" Taking his wife into his arms for a hug, Stewart pressed a kiss to her cheek.

It was the most affection Rachel had seen her parents exchange in years.

"I've been holding down the fort just fine, Stew." Paula guided her family into the cabin like a hostess ushering guests in from the cold. She took her husband's coat from his shoulders first, then Rachel's. "Just threw a log on the fire and pulled a pecan pie from the oven. There's a candle burning in every room and a flashlight in every nightstand. I know the drill."

"And the tree? How's it fairing?" Stewart's glasses were in his hands again.

"As tall and sturdy as ever. These forests are built for the elements, Stewart. It'll be just fine."

CHAPTER 22

Holden guided the snowmobile up the ramp and into the truck bed before killing the engine.

"You got an extra tie-down?" Lance hollered from his pickup parked next to Holden's in the lot. "I'm one short."

"You know me; I always come prepared."

Holden lobbed a coiled strap toward his friend and got to work securing his own snowmobile. They had agreed they should each take one home in the off chance roads were closed and they needed a mode of transportation to check in on neighbors or trek into town for supplies.

This wasn't their first snowstorm rodeo.

Scout wove her way up one ramp and down the other as though playing a game. While some animals experienced anxiety during storms, they didn't faze Scout. In fact, it was fair to say she loved unpredictable weather. Out of the corner of his eye, Holden spotted her chomp in the air to catch snowflakes on her tongue, tail wagging full-force.

"Silly girl." He ratcheted down the strap and gave it a good tug. "I'm going to grab my headlamp out of my locker before I head out. You need anything, or is it safe to lock up?"

Lance jumped off his tailgate, landing in a pile of snow that swallowed him up to his shins. "I've got everything I need. You can close it down." He ran a gloved hand along his jaw. "You okay to ride out the storm alone at your place?"

"I've got a cord of firewood and a week's worth of food. And I won't be alone; I've got Scout."

"You holler if you need me, buddy."

"Will do. Drive safe. I'll reach out later on tonight."

He watched his friend start up the engine and angle out of the parking lot of Major Hart Mountain Sports. Lance's three-quarter-ton pickup had large, knobby tires that made easy work of driving in these conditions. It wasn't like watching travelers slip and slide on the highway, assuming their all-wheel-drive vehicles would get them to their destination safely, but unfamiliar with the genuine danger of it all.

When Lance's taillights were out of sight, Holden walked inside the shop. Scout followed. A crack of wind rattled the windows. A storm of this magnitude was epic anywhere in the High Sierra, but on the summit, it was downright colossal.

"Just need to grab one thing," he said to Scout.

While he had plenty of flashlights back at his cabin, a headlamp was a huge help when hauling in firewood or doing other tasks that involved the use of both hands. He moved toward the back of the store and yanked open the locker to retrieve the item. When he turned around, a paper on the break room table caught his eye.

Rachel's waiver.

Holden picked it up. With no real reason, he pulled out his phone and input her number.

It wasn't like he had plans to call her, and yet he couldn't keep himself from stowing the information away.

"Let's go, girl."

* * *

THE LIGHTS FLICKERED one too many times for his comfort. Holden knew he'd be lucky if the power stayed on another hour. He'd cranked the heat in his cabin full blast, nearly roasting himself out of the place. But if that power cut off like it threatened to, he'd be grateful for the residual heat. Come morning, the house would be an icebox.

He washed up his dishes from dinner along with Scout's food bowl and slipped his phone out of his pocket to check in with Lance.

"How you holding up?" he asked when his buddy answered on the second ring.

"Power's out here." Holden thought he almost heard

the guy's teeth chattering through the receiver. "Downed power line off of Alder Streams. I was thinking of heading over on the snowmobile to see if I could be of any help. I've already got some firewood tarped and loaded on the back."

The last place Holden wanted to be was out in the elements. He still had power...wait, no he didn't. As if giving him the necessary nudge to go help his friend, the lights flickered one final time before shutting off completely. Even the white-noise hum of the heater stopped.

"Need some help?" Holden asked. "Scout and I can be up the ridge in less than ten minutes."

"That would be aces. You two take the south road and I'll work my way up the north."

Holden nodded slowly. "I see what you did there."

"What?" Even though he feigned innocence, Lance's guilt was clear.

"Rachel lives on the south end of Alder Streams."

"Oh, does she really?" His voice pitched an octave. "I'd completely forgotten."

"Mm-hmm." Holden wasn't buying it, but now wasn't the time to argue. "I'll head that way as soon as I get my gear on. If you run into anything you need my help with, just shoot me a text."

"Roger that."

Holden clicked off the phone. Scout sat at his feet, awaiting her instructions.

"Want to go for a ride, girl?"

In a flash, they loaded up and strapped everything

in. Like Lance, Holden secured firewood to the back of his snowmobile, along with a case of water, extra flashlights, candles, and batteries, and several books of matches he had on hand for emergency situations. Stopping at each dark house along the route, he made sure the residents inside had the supplies they needed to hunker down for a cold, dark night.

Snow clumped on his goggles as he zipped from cabin to cabin. Scout had so much snow frozen to her long fur that she resembled an arctic wolf more than a happy-go-lucky golden retriever. It was wet, freezing work, but with each house he visited, he felt better about fulfilling his duty. It felt good to help, always had.

Holden had already handed out all of his water and flashlights. Everyone was thankful to see him, even more grateful for the items he offered. And the snuggles from Scout were an added bonus.

It wasn't a coincidence that Holden saved the Joy cabin for last.

From outside, he could make out the dancing flicker of candlelight in the front room, and he tracked the swishing movements of a flashlight as the person holding it worked their way around the house.

"Seems like they're doing just fine in there," Holden justified to Scout.

The dog barked, and that illuminating gaze swung out the window and straight onto Holden like a spotlight.

He groaned.

"Looks like we're doing this," he mumbled, maneuvering the still-running snowmobile up to the house before cutting the engine. "Come on, girl. Let's get it over with."

"What are you doing here?" Rachel had the door open before he'd even scaled the front steps.

"I'm just making the rounds over the mountain to make sure everyone is okay and has what they need to endure the storm."

She kept the floodlight on him. "What are you? Some sort of knight in shining snow gear?"

Holden gave an imperceptible shrug. "Just trying to be a good neighbor."

The woman actually snorted. "Sure, you are. Good neighbors go around sabotaging Christmas tree contests all the time."

"I didn't sabotage anything!" Holden's volume rose along with his blood pressure. He fought to reclaim both. "Are you good here, or do you need anything?"

She didn't respond right away, and Holden took that as his cue to leave. He turned to go.

"Wait."

He froze. "Yeah?"

"My mom and dad actually headed back to their store an hour ago to pick up batteries and more candles, but they're stuck there and have to wait it out for a bit." She looked around him. "So if you have either of those things, I guess I could use them."

"I've got both. Hang tight and I'll grab them for you."

Apparently Scout took that as an invitation to make herself at home because the dog suddenly loped into the house, shaking off her dense fur right in the entryway.

"Scout!" Holden scolded from the snowmobile. He ascended the front steps two at a time, but it was too late. Bits of snow dotted the walls like fresh spackle. "I'm so sorry." He let himself in when Rachel took a step back. "Do you have a towel I could use to get this cleaned up? I've never seen her do that before."

"She was probably uncomfortable riding on the back of that snowmobile in a blizzard. I don't blame her."

That wasn't it at all. Scout loved the snow, loved being covered in it head-to-toe. No, Holden had a feeling his dog was doing something else entirely. Could a canine actually play matchmaker?

"But to answer your question, yes, I do have a towel." Rachel moved further into the cabin, using the flashlight to illuminate the path. "Right over here in the linen closet."

In all the years they'd known one another, Holden had never set foot in the Joy's cabin. It felt a lot like his parents'—likely built in the same era. Long, wooden beams stretched across a high-pitched roof and pine cabinets and trim accented the beige walls. His gaze traveled the room, pausing on a massive, floor-to-ceiling stone hearth.

"Your fire's out."

"I know."

Holden tilted his head. "You plan to get that started? It's going to turn into a freezer in here if you don't get it lit soon."

"I'm working on it," Rachel said. "Or I *was* working on it before you came snooping around."

"I wasn't snooping around," he defended. "Not this time, at least."

Rachel's lips pinched tightly. "Do you have the candles and batteries?"

Holden dipped his hand into his jacket and pulled out a set of four taper candles, along with pairs of batteries ranging from AA to D. "This should cover things." He settled the items on the table.

"Great, then you can be on your way." She practically shooed him out the door.

"You don't know how to start a fire, do you?"

Her mouth dropped open. "Of course, I know how to start a fire."

One look at the ash in the fireplace refuted that. There weren't even embers. The fire had dwindled long ago. And evidently, Rachel hadn't been successful in getting it going again.

"I can start it for you."

She looked at him like he'd offered to build her a condo, not merely get a fire ignited. "I said I know how to start a fire."

"I don't doubt that."

"It's fine. My dad will be back soon and he can do it then. You can be on your way."

Like a bee had stung her, Rachel jumped. She withdrew her phone from her back pocket and read the incoming text that made her leap out of her skin. "You've got to be kidding me."

Holden didn't know if it was even safe to ask, but he couldn't keep his curiosity contained. "Everything okay?"

"No, everything's *not* okay." Her chin trembled. While that often indicated tears, in this instance, it was aggravation that had Rachel's entire jaw ticking. "My parents are staying the night at the market. They said all the roads are closed and they can't make it back up the hill."

"Will they be okay there?"

She nodded. "They have a generator and sleeping bags. They've done it before."

"So it sounds like your dad won't be back to help with that fire, then."

Rachel's eyes narrowed. "I will figure it out."

"You'd really rather spend a night shivering than let me help you?"

She loosened her arms previously crossed in defiance. "Fine. You can help start the fire. But you'll leave right after that. I can take care of myself."

Holden was sure she could. After all, surviving on her own in a city of close to one million people wasn't for the timid. Rachel was a capable woman.

And an unbelievably stubborn one, too.

CHAPTER 23

"Do you have some dry logs around here?"

"On the east wall of the house. You can go out through the side door in the garage." Rachel moved a hand to stroke the top of Scout's head. "She can stay here."

Holden didn't argue, which was good because Rachel didn't have a comeback. She wasn't sure why she wanted Scout to remain with her, but the thought of being alone in the dark house didn't sit well with her.

But neither did being in the dark house with Holden.

"Maybe he'll get lost out there," Rachel mused. Scout's chocolate eyes flicked up. "Oh. That's right. Sort of your job to make sure he doesn't, huh?"

He'd been right about the fire. She would never admit it out loud, but starting a fire in her apartment consisted of flipping on a switch. She'd tried for a good half hour to get the kindling and logs in the fireplace to ignite, but by the end of it she'd used up all of her matches and just as much determination.

Cozying up beneath a thick blanket and warm layers would just have to suffice.

But not with Holden around. He needed to go as soon as there was a roaring fire in that hearth. She still hadn't forgiven him for sneaking around their property. And here he was, a *second* time, right outside her door.

Try as she might to be upset by that now, she couldn't cling to that obstinate resolve. It wasn't a lie to say she was a little grateful to see his snowmobile. Her parents had been gone longer than they'd predicted, the temperature within the cabin was easily dropping by several degrees per hour, and the candles placed throughout the house made creepy, elongated shadows dance on the walls. She wasn't afraid of the dark, but her eyes played tricks on her.

And maybe Holden was to blame for that. The thought of someone sneaking around their property wasn't one she'd entertained before, but after seeing that video footage of the noble fir fugitives, her mind filled with eerie thoughts.

As though sensing her suddenly elevated heart rate, Scout gently licked along Rachel's palm, then nudged her head on her leg. Rachel scratched right behind the dog's ears. "You really like all of this snow?"

Scout obviously didn't answer, but when Rachel heard the door from the garage squeal open on its hinges, she was grateful for the interruption. She must really be off her rocker if talking to a dog was her form of keeping calm.

Holden moved into the room, a piercing beam of light strapped to the middle of his forehead like a third eye. Rachel squinted against the glare.

"Sorry." He bundled the logs under one arm and lifted a free hand to switch the headlamp off. "Didn't mean to blind you."

"You didn't. It's fine."

"Come on over." Large boots padded across the room. He crouched down in front of the fireplace, arranging the logs in a stacked triangle to the left of it. "I'm going to show you how to do this."

"I told you—"

"Right, right. That you know how to start a fire. But this one doesn't have a remote, so it works a little differently."

She would have scowled had the shock of being found out not pulled her mouth into a straight line. "What makes you think I don't have a wood fireplace?"

"At your apartment? In the city? Oh, I don't know. You can't get a tree up to your place. I'm assuming logs are in the same boat."

Rachel didn't answer. She sat back on her heels and waited for the tutorial.

"I'll need those matches," Holden instructed.

He probably couldn't see her eye roll in the dark, but the accompanying huff that indicated her frustration needed no highlighting. Searching her way with her hands, she skirted the couch and gathered the matchbook Holden had placed onto the table earlier. On her way back, her foot caught a corner of the floor rug. She launched headfirst toward Holden like a stone from a slingshot.

Thankfully, she regained her footing mere moments before stumbling into his crouched form. That was close.

"You alright there, Mittens?" he called over his shoulder, not even bothering to turn around to investigate the commotion.

"We're not back on that again, are we?"

"I don't know." He tossed a single log into the fireplace. "You seemed to like me a lot better as Buddy. I was trying to see if I liked you better as Mittens."

"Hilarious." She passed him the matches, her cold fingers grazing over his large, warm hand. How were his hands so warm when he'd been outside collecting firewood? She shuddered.

"So, what you want to do is arrange two logs on the grate first, then stack the third so there is plenty of room for air to circulate around them. Then you stuff your tinder into place. I found some newspapers in the recycling bin in the garage that we can use." He balled up a page. "And we'll use the metal prod to stoke the fire when the flames fade."

"We?"

"Or you will. Once I leave." One look outside made the thought of venturing out in the elements about as appealing as eating stale fruitcake.

"You can warm up for a few minutes in front of the fire before you leave to check on the rest of the neighbors," Rachel acquiesced. It wasn't generous since Holden would be the one responsible for starting the fire, but it was the only olive branch she had on hand.

"You were the last cabin."

She bristled. "I see. Saved the best for last, huh?" Why on earth did those words come out?

"I saved the one I was most scared of for last." With a match between his thumb and index finger, Holden scraped along the rough strip and a bright orange flame sprung to life.

"You were scared to come over here?"

Holden moved the lit match over the crumpled pieces of newspaper, waiting for the flame to catch and grow. "You're a little scary, Rachel. Not gonna lie."

The fire spread quickly over the logs, and a golden glow swathed the room.

He sat back on the hardwood, knees drawn to his chest, arms wrapped around them like a hug. "You don't think you're scary?"

"No, I don't think I'm scary." She couldn't understand this sudden assertion.

"Fine. Maybe scary isn't the word." Holden clasped one wrist and his ear met his shoulder as he contemplated. "Intimidating."

"Why would I intimidate you?"

"Why wouldn't you?" His chin drew back. "You're smart. Opinionated. Beautiful."

He might've added to the list, but Rachel stopped

hearing it. Her thoughts snagged on that third word he'd uttered, unable to compute anything else.

"And you're a little mean," he tacked on.

"What?" She shoved him with the flat of her hand and with the way he was sitting—all balled up in an unsteady bundle—Holden almost tipped completely over.

"Case and point." He lifted himself back up and stretched out his long legs in front of the fire. "You just pushed me."

"I didn't push you. I nudged you."

With one wide shoulder, Holden gently bumped hers. "That's a nudge."

He wasn't wrong, but the way her pulse skittered out of rhythm from the contact felt all kinds of wrong. She inhaled deeply to clear her head. Was it possible the smoke was already getting to her?

"Like I said," he continued as if he didn't even notice her falter, "You're intimidating. Always have been."

"Oh, please. There was nothing intimidating about the skinny, freckly, brace-faced kid I was in high school. I was a nerd to the one-hundredth degree."

"Nerds are intimidating!" Holden's voice lifted. "You were always so smart, Rachel. So creative. You were the only person better than me at practically everything. You think that's not intimidating?"

"Everything I did, you tried to do better," she said firmly. "You just wanted to show me up."

"I just wanted to *keep* up," he corrected. "There's a difference."

Just then, a spark from the fireplace shot out of the hearth and landed on the brick ledge in front of it. The embers fizzled almost immediately, but Rachel's pulse didn't readjust as quickly.

"What is this? Some sort of campfire confession?" She forced the joke.

"I don't think I'm confessing anything. It was public knowledge that we were rivals," he said. "I guess we still are."

Is that what they were? Rivals? Because it didn't feel like that now, sitting side by side in front of a crackling, cozy fire. It wasn't friendship, but there was something there. Acquaintances weren't this casual.

"I'm not your rival, Holden." She smirked. "Our Christmas tree is just going to annihilate yours."

"Is that so?"

Scout began to yap in her sleep from her curled up position next to them. Her little paws stretched, racing in place while she likely dreamed of gallivanting over snow-covered hills. Rachel ran her hand over the dog's soft coat.

"You measured the tree yourself," she said.

"I did. And it's exactly the same height as ours."

Her throat scratched. "There's no way they are exactly the same height."

"But they are."

"My dad is going to lose his mind." Rachel bit her lip.

"If he's anything like mine, it's already lost. They are really into it, aren't they?"

She laughed. "Do you think that's our fault?"

"That they're obsessed with this whole homegrown Christmas tree thing? How would that be our fault?"

"Because we've set the tone with all of our competitiveness over the years. They don't know how to view one another as anything but family rivals."

Holden wobbled his head. "There might be some of that. But I also know it's really important for my parents to have their tree selected. My dad's sixtieth is coming up and when his dad turned sixty, they chose his tree for the lighting," he carried on. "My dad's really big on tradition and legacy. It's part of the reason he wanted me to follow in his footsteps and become a firefighter."

"But you'd rather build fires than put them out?" she teased, her gaze meandering over to the steady flames in front of them.

"I thought about firefighting, but it wasn't for me. I also thought about becoming a doctor. I figured something in the medical field would make him equally proud," Holden explained. "But that wasn't in the cards, either."

"And why was that? Your grades were certainly good enough."

"The money wasn't there," he admitted freely. "And neither was the passion. I need to be outside. Up on this mountain. Out on those slopes." He looked out the windows next to them. "Do you ever miss it? This place?"

"Miss the summit?"

"Yeah. I mean, it's fair to say Snowdrift couldn't be further from the city, landscape-wise. But are you satisfied with your concrete jungle?"

She didn't know how to answer. "It was always my goal to get there. Me and Bethany—that's what we were going to do. Grow up, move out, and live together in the bay, achieving our dreams side by side."

Holden's features softened. She hadn't meant to bring up her sister, and the sudden turn the conversation took surprised even her.

"I'm so sorry you had to go through that, Rachel. Losing a sister." His eyes found hers, and nothing but compassion filled his green gaze. "I don't know what I would do without Sarah. That must have been devastating."

"It was," she said on a shallow breath. "But I threw myself into academics, focused on my grades, and got to live out those dreams all on my own."

Holden just nodded, but she knew he could sense the uncertainty in her tone.

"And believe it or not, competing with you all of those years was a good distraction. It's hard to find time to grieve when you spend every waking moment trying to prove you're better than Holden Hart."

CHAPTER 24

❄

Her words gutted him.

How had he never realized there was more to Rachel's motivation to succeed than just one-upping him? Had he really been that inwardly focused? That dense?

Hearing this revelation, the history somehow played out differently. It wasn't just about defeating Holden. It was about Rachel choosing to carry on when her sister could not. It was about putting one foot in front of the other, taking life one day at a time.

Sensing the seriousness that had descended upon their conversation, Rachel let out a laugh that Holden knew was every bit artificial. "How has it been living with the knowledge that you were bested by a girl?"

"Easy, because I wasn't bested by a girl. We were tied."

"No, our last competition was the Christmas Contest our senior year. Don't you remember all of those elaborate challenges I came up with? Gingerbread house decorating? That sledding race down Holiday Hill? The snowman making contest? There were twenty-four contests in all. One for every date in December leading up to Christmas day." She lifted to her feet. "I still have the ornaments I made as trophies."

That didn't surprise him one bit. In fairness, he still had his tally of paper rings.

"I'm sure you do," he said, chuckling. "And if you look, you'll probably see that you have twelve ornaments. I have the other twelve."

"There's no way. I know for a fact there are thirteen in that box."

She withdrew a brown packing box from behind the dimmed Christmas tree and picked it up to bring over to the fire. She set it down between them and lifted the lid. Holden would've looked inside, but he couldn't wrench his gaze from her haughty mouth all curved up in defiance.

With determination in her movements, she thrust a hand into the box and pulled out each ornament one by one, lining them up on the floor like toy soldiers.

Ten, eleven, twelve...

Her eyes bulged. "It must be missing."

Holden leaned closer. "What must be missing?" he asked, purely for entertainment's sake.

"The thirteenth ornament. It must be misplaced or something, because I *know* I beat you."

"If you beat me, then why do you think I spent the following year planning the ski race down the summit?

That was the tiebreaker, Rachel. The competition to end all competitions."

Unfortunately, the event broke more than just the tie. Poor Lance was still feeling the repercussions of that disaster.

"I don't remember competing in that."

"Correct. Because you didn't. You didn't even come home for Christmas your first year of college."

Her expression fell. "I had just gotten my internship with December Décor. I couldn't leave. It was a big break for me."

"I know. I get it," Holden assured. "I think I just didn't expect things to be over between us." His throat bobbed with a swallow. "I mean, with competing and all."

Rachel's blue eyes held Holden's and didn't release, even when he cleared his throat.

He pulled the steel fire poker from its hook and jammed it into a log. Cinders popped and hissed. Was he the only one currently burning up? His face flamed with the instant regret that he'd said too much.

"Looks like this is going pretty steadily," he said of the fire. "It's probably safe for me to head out now."

Rachel's eyes lingered on him a moment more before switching to the window. The panes rattled as wind howled across the frame and wet snowdrops smattered the glass. "It's anything but safe out there, Holden." She drew her focus back to him. "You should stay."

* * *

Watching Rachel Joy sleep was at the very top of the list of things Holden figured he would never do. It had never even crossed his mind that he'd be in this kind of scenario. But as the evening wore on, and the storm picked up in intensity and duration, Holden knew he didn't have any other option.

It was downright hostile outside.

He knew this mountain well, but not perfectly. Whiteout conditions would make navigating through the terrain fuzzy. Volunteering with Search and Rescue had prepared him for riding out in inclement weather, but it had also prepared him in another way. He saw what happened when people placed themselves in the path of danger. And he saw how tragically something like that could end.

Around nine o'clock, and prompted by a series of continued yawns, Rachel admitted she should head to bed. And that would have been fine, if the spare bedroom where she slept wasn't an igloo. She'd suggested Holden take the couch, but he wasn't about to do that. This was her cabin and that was her fire, even if he could take a little credit for getting it going.

No, Rachel would sleep on the couch and Holden would be perfectly fine in the recliner tucked into the corner of the room. He didn't plan on sleeping much, anyway. Someone had to add logs to the flames when it started to go out. While he'd given her a brief lesson on building a fire, he was pretty positive she hadn't been paying much attention.

But all Holden could pay attention to now was the way her full lips parted as she breathed softly. How her long, flaxen hair spilled around her face on the pillow. How his heart quickened every time she stirred.

What was happening to him?

Was Lance right? Was the line between love and hate really so thin that it could be crossed that easily? Because Holden felt nothing but warmth when he looked at Rachel now. And when his thoughts traveled back to their conversation—to her confession about her sister and the real reason for her competitive nature—an empathy that bordered on pain coursed through his veins.

He'd been a punk kid. He couldn't believe all he'd put her through. Sure, she'd admitted she needed the competition—needed something to drive her. Only, he'd never realized the true reason.

Holden supposed he wasn't a *complete* jerk. After all, his decision to pull out of the running for the college scholarship had more to do with wanting Rachel to succeed than he'd ever admitted to himself. Until now.

He hadn't been disqualified. No, he'd withdrawn his application.

Even now, he remembered stopping into Main Street Market near closing one day and overhearing a private discussion between Paula and Stewart Joy. Holden had been an aisle over while they counted out the money in the till. Even the candy aisle—all stocked with its packaged promise of a sugar rush—couldn't distract him. He'd heard them loud and clear.

Their business would go under if Rachel couldn't secure some financial assistance. They'd be forced to foot the entire bill of her education. They hadn't said it begrudgingly; it was just a matter-of-fact statement that didn't come with a choice. They would do anything necessary to let Rachel fulfill her big city dreams.

And Holden knew he held the key to making sure that happened.

One scholarship shouldn't make or break a college career, but this had been a big one. It covered nearly half a year's tuition, along with room and board. It allowed its recipient to dream bigger, hope brighter.

He might not have even won had he stayed in the running, but that was something Holden would never know. And that was just fine with him.

Around eleven, Scout rustled. She rarely needed to be let out past sundown, but Holden hadn't taken her to do her business before bed. It was just too blustery.

Her head lifted and those bleary, blinking puppy eyes found Holden's. Immediately, her tail wagged.

"You need to stretch your legs, girl?" Holden whispered.

He collected a flashlight and slipped his feet into his boots by the front door, not bothering to tie up the laces. In two large bounds, Scout was out in the yard, bounding over the powdered terrain like a child set loose on a playground.

Wind cut across Holden's upper half. He shivered.

"Make it quick, Scout!" he whisper-yelled.

The moon was full, swathing the landscape in silvery-white light. It was beautiful, the night even clearer without the power on. Streetlamps and porch lights no longer competed with the galaxies overhead. Stars shone more brilliantly. The landscape almost appeared to glisten.

He inhaled a frigid breath that seared his lungs but was invigorating all the same.

Scout trotted back to stand by his side on the porch. "Wipe your paws," he reminded. "And if you need to shake off, do it out here and not inside."

The dog gave a little wiggle, knocking bits of clumped snow from her underbelly and shaking it free from her tail.

"Good girl."

Holden pushed on the handle to the front door. It didn't budge.

With more force, he leaned into the wooden door and tried again. Still nothing.

"This isn't good."

He tried once more with the same result. Even Scout standing on her back legs with her front paws pressed to the door did nothing, but Holden appreciated her effort.

"I really don't want to do this." He pulled his cell phone from his back pocket.

Another cold whip of air drew his shoulders clear

up to his ears. He shivered so hard it looked like a ridiculous dance move.

Scrolling until he found her number, he was grateful something had prompted him to store it in his phone earlier. But he wasn't grateful for waking her. There had to be another way. A quick pass over the porch came up empty. No hidden key. He thought about going around to the garage, but distinctly remembered locking it behind him when he returned with the firewood that evening.

If they were going to get back inside, they would need to be let in.

"I'm sorry. I'm so sorry," he recited as he pressed his finger and the phone dialed her number. He could hear it ringing even from outside. It would be a startling, unwelcome alarm, to say the least.

"Hello?" Rachel's voice cracked from sleep.

"I'm locked out."

"Who is this?" The gravel worked its way out of her tone. He could see her figure lift from the couch and into an upright position.

"It's Holden. I stayed over to wait out the storm, remember? I needed to let Scout out, and it appears the door locked behind us."

Holden heard her footfalls over the hardwood, and when she came up to the window with her phone pressed to her ear, they locked eyes. A small smile curled the corner of her mouth.

The lock turned over. "Get in here. It's freezing."

Scout jumped up and left a kiss on Rachel's cheek.

"Down, girl," Holden scolded, but Rachel didn't seem to mind.

They moved to the family room where Holden quickly put another log on the fire. He bent down and opened his palms to the flames. He'd only been outside a few minutes, but he didn't think to bring his jacket and his flannel shirt provided little protection against the elements. Even with the crackling warmth from the hearth, it would take a good half hour before his temperature got back to normal. Chills iced up his spine again.

He didn't anticipate the sudden weight of a blanket draped over his shoulders, nor the kind, caring gaze Rachel gave when he lifted his head to meet her eyes.

"Take this," she offered. "It'll help you warm up faster."

It was the wool blanket she'd been tucked under the last few hours, sleeping soundly on the nearby couch. Her perfume permeated the fibers with rich notes of vanilla and mint, and Holden inhaled deeply, nearly drowning in the intoxicating mixture. Had she always smelled this good? He didn't know if he'd ever gotten close enough to tell.

"Thank you," he said. "I appreciate it."

She lowered to his level, tucking her legs beneath her. "Of course. And I don't know if I said it earlier, but thank you for stopping by." The smile that challenged her lips earlier spread into a full grin. "And thank you for the fire."

"You're welcome," Holden replied quietly.

She hadn't said thank you before. No, she'd said he'd been sneaking around the property again and that she was fully capable of starting her own fire. But Holden didn't throw those words back at her, and that was a restraint he'd never exercised in the past.

She shuddered. Her hands cuffed her arms and rubbed for friction.

Holden wouldn't hog all the warmth for himself. Without saying a word, he lifted his arm and the corner of the blanket, altogether surprised when she easily slid under it. No hesitation, no biting remark.

He settled the fabric around her and held her close to his side.

Maybe she wasn't fully awake. Maybe this was some prolonged bout of sleepwalking and she would suddenly come to, horrified to be so close to him.

He didn't really believe that, but he also couldn't believe she would voluntarily share this blanket. This proximity. This moment.

"It's a nice fire." Her voice was gentle, peaceful. "You did a good job."

"I try."

"I know." He felt her head nod against his chest. "You've always tried with me, Holden. Tried to be nice when I was nothing but immature and overconfident."

"I wouldn't say I was all that nice."

"You asked me to the Winter Ball in eighth grade. That's a pretty nice thing to do."

"Sure." He lifted a sulky shoulder. "But then you

never gave me an answer and went with that Cody kid instead. I couldn't get your attention."

He'd been trying to ever since.

Angling to look up at him through thick lashes, she asked, "Would you believe me if I told you I didn't know you were the one asking me?"

"Probably not."

"I'm serious." She straightened. "I thought it was Cody. I thought he made the cookies and left them for me to unscramble. It wasn't until last week that my mom told me it had been you this entire time."

"For such a smart cookie, you didn't do a great job figuring that out."

She laughed at his joke. "I didn't think someone like you would want to go to a dance with someone like me."

"You mean someone with two left feet who barely weighed a hundred pounds soaking wet? Because that's the only way to describe me back then."

Nestling back under his arm, she moved a hand to his chest. "We were both late bloomers. Like, *really* late bloomers."

"Isn't that the truth?" He worried she could feel his heart hammering beneath her open palm. Its kick drum beat made his ribcage ache. What was happening between them? Was it the late hour and the winter storm that had brought on this sudden storm of emotion too? Holden couldn't make sense of any of it.

"You are almost unrecognizable," she confessed.

"Almost? So you're saying there was a piece of you that recognized me, Mittens?"

A breathy giggle released from her lips. "I recognized your spirit. Your quick wit and playful jabs." She paused and looked forward, as though searching for the words in the flames that danced in front of them. "Honestly, I think I didn't want it to be you. I put blinders on to the possibility that it was."

"Why's that?" He smoothed down a strand of her hair that caught on the blanket and kept his hand on the crown of her head, holding her close.

"Because I'm in San Francisco and you're in Snowdrift," she conceded. "And I'm Rachel Joy and you're Holden Hart."

"Sworn enemies." His chest lifted with a laugh.

"Something like that." Her fingers fiddled with a button on his flannel shirt.

Of its own volition, his hand covered hers.

Her head tilted back again, hooded eyes meeting his own.

He moved his hand up to her chin, taking it between his fingers. "Rachel," he spoke softly.

He brushed his thumb along her cheek and her eyes drifted shut when he cupped her jaw with his hand. Her skin was smooth, her expression so devastatingly beautiful.

He pressed closer.

Her eyes remained shut. Holden closed his too.

CHAPTER 25

❄

Holden Hart was going to kiss her.

And she *wanted* him to. What was happening?

She knew the storm had shut off the power to the house, but at that moment, it was as though the power to her brain was completely gone too.

This couldn't happen. It wouldn't be good for anyone. What about the tree competition? What would happen when their parents found out their child was fraternizing with the enemy?

Her thoughts swirled more vigorously than the snow flurries outside.

And yet, she wanted to be kissed by Holden. To be held in his powerful arms. To stay wrapped in his protective embrace.

He seemed to want it too, evidenced in the way he curled his arm around her back and pulled her to him, his hand still on her cheek. He was so gentle, so tender.

The opposite of the boy she remembered from her past who would do anything to challenge her. Right now, the only challenge Rachel had was to keep her heart from skittering right out of her chest. Its pulse rang in her ears, thrummed feverishly fast along her neck.

"Rachel." He spoke her name on a breath. His mouth came only an inch from hers.

She met him the rest of the way, pausing only before their lips were about to touch.

Scout barked sharply.

Holden's eyes flashed instantly open, but they didn't waver from Rachel's.

"Quiet, girl." He shooed his dog with a fluttering hand behind him.

Scout barked again.

"Scout, calm down." He pulled back.

A growl as low as thunder rumbled behind bared teeth, and then Scout was off like a shot toward the front door.

Remorse flashed across Holden's gaze. Rachel gave a single nod. He tossed the blanket from his shoulders and met his dog in the entryway. Her barks echoed, bouncing off the vaulted ceiling.

Rachel blew out a massive breath.

She wasn't thankful for the interruption, but maybe it was what needed to happen. Would it really be wise to kiss Holden? All signs pointed to no, but her heart challenged that logic.

She raked a hand through her hair, bringing her

fingers to the ends and twisting them. Why did everything have to be so complicated?

As suddenly as it had started, Scout's growl completely cut off, and Rachel heard the telltale jingle of the dog's collar as she danced with excitement.

The happy canine rushed back into the room, the voices of two men filtering in behind her.

"If it's not your partner in crime," Rachel said, standing. She gathered the discarded blanket, folded it into a small square, then draped it over her forearm.

Lance Major's gaze ping-ponged over the room. "Did I interrupt something?" He scratched along his scruffy jaw.

"Nope," Rachel answered. "Not at all."

He didn't believe her. His side-eye look silently showed his doubt, but he carried on all the same. "I was headed home and saw Holden's snowmobile parked out front. Just wanted to make sure everything was okay in here."

"You've been out this entire time?" Holden's arms crossed over his chest.

"The Hendersons lost a huge fir. Took out half their deck. I helped Roger cut it up and haul it out. Then I stopped by Miss Patty's and you know that woman. Wouldn't let me go without a cup of tea—albeit cold—and a good, long story about the colossal snowstorm of 1962."

"Let me guess, this is nothing compared to that historical blizzard," Rachel surmised.

"Believe it or not, she actually admitted this was

worse." Lance gave a shrug. "And according to the news, there's more to come. Apparently, this is just a small break before it starts dumping again."

"Then I should probably take advantage of that and head out while I can." Holden's eyes found Rachel's in the candlelit room. "Will you be okay here by yourself for the rest of the night?"

She would be fine physically. She had watched him keep the fire going all evening and knew what to do. But her heart...the thought of their moment from earlier not having the chance to unfurl made it squeeze with disappointment.

There would be no *to-be-continued*. Morning would come and shine a light on their foolishness. It had been a vulnerable moment, but not one they would reenact.

No, the stars, the snowflakes, and the storm had perfectly aligned, and the chances of that happening again were woefully slim.

Rachel couldn't keep the disheartened sigh from escaping.

"I'll be fine."

Holden's eyes lingered before he gave a long nod. "You'll call me if you need anything?" He moved like he was going in for a hug, but then stopped short, aware of Lance gaping at his side. "You should have my number in your phone now. Please feel free to use it."

"I'll be just fine, Holden. You don't need to give me a second thought."

Whatever made him hesitate earlier was no longer an issue, because Holden pressed in close and took her swiftly into his arms. His words tickled her ear as he said, "That's going to be sort of impossible."

And then he was gone. All three of them, out the door and loaded up on their snowmobiles.

Rachel stood a moment on the porch, catching her breath and rallying her heart, wondering why it suddenly felt whisked away on that snowmobile too.

* * *

Rachel was rarely aware of the sunrise. It wasn't as if she didn't know it took place every morning. It was just that she never really relied on its rays to wake her. Alarm clocks, programmed coffee makers, and email notifications typically did that.

But the power was still out, and that meant it was solely Mother Nature's job to illuminate the day.

The fire was entirely gone. She'd done her best to keep it ignited, even setting an alarm on her phone to wake her every couple of hours to check on it and add a log or two. But by four in the morning, she hit the snooze. She was dog tired and another blanket would have to suffice.

As she curled up on the couch beneath several layers of heavy fabric, she couldn't help but feel as though she was missing something. Or someone. Being held in Holden's arms felt like a dream. Had it all been one? Had she dreamt up the moment between them? Contrived the connection that had her heart quickening within her chest and knees going weak every time she replayed the tender scene?

And what had he meant when he said he was trying to get her attention all of those years ago by asking her to the dance? Had he been trying to get her attention ever since? She had always viewed Holden as a potential roadblock to her success, never as a person who had real, tangible feelings.

A person who seemed—against all odds—to have feelings for *her*.

She didn't know what to do with that.

Rubbing the sleep from her eyes, she yawned and stretched her arms above her head. She thought it was a ringing in her ears, but when she dropped her hands back down and the jingling continued, her eyes landed on the vibrating phone. She scooped it from the coffee table.

Hope nosedived when she saw it wasn't Holden, but lifted once she heard her mother's voice on the other end.

"Mom! How are you and Dad? Is everything okay?"

"We're fine, sweetie. The market's fine too. In fact, we're thinking of opening up today, on the off chance customers can make it into town for supplies. Since we have to stay put, might as well make the most of it."

"Do you think anyone will?" If her parents couldn't get out, she doubted anyone could get in.

"The highway is down to one lane, but it's passable. It's just when you head further up the summit that things get dicey," Paula said. "I just wanted to call to make sure you knew to stay put. Roads by the cabins haven't been plowed and likely won't be for some time."

"I know. I don't plan to go anywhere," Rachel answered. "You sure you guys don't need anything?"

"Like I said, we have all we need here. How about you? How's the cabin holding up?"

"So far, so good." She left out the part about Holden coming to her rescue with matches, batteries, and his solid arms that wrapped around her and made her lose her mind. "I'm fine here."

"How's the tree?"

Still on the line, Rachel moved to the back of the house to peer out the frosted windows. Like a beacon on a hill, their noble stood proud amongst an ocean of white. "It's perfect."

"Good to hear. Sounds like that's not the case for everyone."

"I heard the Hendersons lost a big one. Who else?"

Rachel could hear the store's bell chiming in the background, along with her father's cheerful greeting. Sure, having a customer could make him that happy, but apprehension snaked through her gut that something else entirely was the cause of his mood.

"Rumor has it the Hart tree sustained some significant damage," Paula said, her voice purposefully low. "Obviously, this isn't how we wanted to win, but it looks like our humble little tree is finally going to have its day on the square."

CHAPTER 26

❄

*H*olden could hear the wailing before he even reached the front door, and he had a feeling it wasn't his niece doing the crying.

"Enter at your own risk," Sarah warned as she passed through the foyer, happy baby bouncing in her arms. "I'm going to put this little one down for a nap. But it sounds like there's another grumpy pants in this house who could use one too."

Holden gave his precious niece a kiss on the cheek before his sister carted her off.

He hesitated in the entryway. Even Scout's typical spring in her step slowed to a hesitant crawl as they made their way into the cabin and toward the commotion.

His father's lamenting continued. "This can't be happening! Why is this happening? This was our year!"

"Zeke, it's just a tree," Jill countered.

Ouch. That would not help. It was the equivalent of

telling someone to calm down amid a major breakdown—it would only add to the frustration.

"Maybe there's a way to salvage it?" Holden's mother offered.

"Do you honestly think there's a way to salvage *that*?"

Until then, Holden hadn't had a clear view of the noble fir in question. But when he came up behind his parents—their noses practically pressed against the glass window like children peering into a toy store—the source of his father's theatrical sorrow was on full display.

In the middle of the property was that giant tree—still standing, in fact—but leaning against it like a crutch was another, smaller fir. It was good news that it hadn't taken out the potential Christmas tree entirely. Less good that on the felled tree's way down, it had swiped a third of the noble's lower branches, making the skirt noticeably lopsided and uneven.

"Oh," Holden groaned. "Yikes."

"Yikes, is right." His father spun around, smacking his walking boot on every corner of furniture as he fumbled his way to the couch. He dropped onto the sofa like a sack of potatoes.

"Maybe Mom's right?" Holden proposed. "Maybe there's a way we can salvage it. I can take the chainsaw to it this afternoon and see about bringing the rest of the lower branches up. Who knows?" he continued to suggest hopefully. "It might even look better. Some of those branches were hanging pretty low. Maybe all it needs is a good haircut."

Jill's compassionate eyes met her son's. "That's a great idea, Holden." She turned to Zeke. "Isn't that a great idea, dear?"

"It never occurred to me that something like this could happen," Zeke mused into the void.

"Mother Nature's an unpredictable beast."

Zeke winced as he lifted his injured ankle to the coffee table. Holden assisted him by placing a fluffy pillow beneath his lower leg. "How's that, Dad?"

"I don't even feel the pain anymore." In the most dramatic fashion, Zeke pressed his hand to his chest. "I only feel it in here."

"Speaking of pain, it's time for your meds." Jill came to her husband's side with a small cup of water and a handful of pills. "Take these and get some rest, Zeke. You were up all night with that storm and the doctor said the best thing for you is to stay off that foot and relax."

Holden's father grumbled, but took the medicine and lowered his head to the couch cushion. In true Zeke Hart fashion, he was snoring within less than a minute.

"Why don't we step out on the deck for a moment while there's a break in the storm? Both the one inside and the one outside." Jill led the way. "Let's leave him to sleep off some of that grumpiness."

Clear skies greeted them, yesterday's blizzard only

evidenced in the single toppled tree and the fresh coat of white that draped the hillside behind the cabin.

"I like your idea of trimming it up a little. That was an excellent suggestion," Jill encouraged. "But I think your father should accept the fact that it's just not in the cards for our tree to represent the town." She rubbed her forehead. "I can't imagine many other trees fared any better."

Holden knew she referred to the Joy tree, and it felt almost wrong to keep his knowledge to himself.

"It might not be what you want to hear, but the Joy's tree is still standing."

Jill's mouth lifted into a little grin. "I'm actually *very* glad to hear that. Our town needs a tree. It's good that there are still options." She glanced over at their marred evergreen and sighed. "Do you mind me asking how you know that? Please don't tell me your father sent you over there again. I wasn't comfortable with the first covert mission he begged you to execute."

"No, I went all on my own. And not to check on the tree," Holden said. "To check on Rachel."

Jill's surprised eyes swung back to her son. "Oh, really? And how is she?"

"Without power, like the rest of the mountain. But I got a fire going."

Huffing a laugh, Jill almost smirked. "Holden, there's been a fire going between you two for longer than I can recall."

Holden bristled. "What?"

"You and Rachel. That fire between you. It's always been there."

"I'm not entirely sure what you're talking about, Mom." He challenged her with a serious expression.

"I know there's been a competition with you two all these years, but did it ever occur to you that you were competing for more than just a winning title? Did you ever think maybe you were competing for her heart?"

"No." Holden whipped his head in a shake. "I hadn't thought of that."

Not until last night, at least.

"I don't know why you've had such a difficult time just admitting your feelings for her." Jill's hand came down on her son's shoulder in a motherly gesture. "Or admitting that she's the reason you've never been able to settle down. Why you have little interest in relationships. Why you can't seem to find your perfect partner to share your life and your adventures with."

"Do you have some sort of emotion-detecting goggles I don't? Because honestly, none of this ever crossed my mind."

"I'm a mother and I know my son." Her hand squeezed. "And I know when something brings you joy. That look when you're on your snowmobile, speeding down the mountain. Or when you're training Scout. Your entire being lights up," she said. "It's the same look you always had around Rachel. She's been your adventure too."

* * *

He didn't have the guts to call her. It wasn't as though Rachel had been privy to Holden's conversation with his mother, but having that revelation brought to light exposed him. He still needed to process it.

In truth, he needed to process what had happened between them the night before too.

Had Scout not interrupted them, Holden would've kissed Rachel. Everything within him wanted to. And he sensed everything within her did as well.

Was his mother right? Were these emotions Holden suddenly let himself feel truly there all along? Latent under the surface, just waiting for the opportunity to rise to the top?

When he'd asked her to the Winter Ball as a kid, he'd had a crush on her. He could admit that much. But she'd rejected him. No, not so much rejected as flat-out ignored. And he'd made it his subconscious mission that she wouldn't be able to ignore him after that. Somehow, he always stayed in her periphery and she in his, until the point their paths diverged.

The summit was Holden's home, and she'd made one elsewhere. He couldn't fault her for that. The only person he could fault was himself, and that was over the fact that he'd wasted all these years overlooking his true feelings.

But it was too late now. Feelings aside, they were on different journeys, heading toward different goals.

He left his parents' after lunch. Scout hopped onto the back of the snowmobile and they wove their way through the mountain neighborhoods. Sunny skies had added a few more degrees to the temperature and made going without power a lot more manageable.

He was going to text her, but the battery on his phone was running precariously low. Maybe he should just swing by her place really quick. Just to make sure she was managing okay. He'd do it for any other neighbor, wouldn't he?

As if needing some sort of justification, Holden took a slight detour and swung by the Henderson's first. A brief check-in proved all was well there. And now he wasn't just singling Rachel out. He was being neighborly with more than just her.

But the way his heart gave a tight squeeze when his snowmobile shot up the hill toward her cabin refuted that thin defense. It hadn't done that with the Hendersons. No, it was the thought of seeing Rachel that had him dizzied with anticipation.

Even Scout sensed it. That dog could always read him. She stood up on all fours as he drove the snowmobile up to the porch, and she jumped off and bounded up the steps before Holden had even hiked his leg over the vehicle. Holden wasn't the only one excited by the reunion.

But what was he hoping for? That they would pick up right where they left off? That wasn't about to happen. They had an entire night and the clarity of day standing between that memory and today's reality. He wasn't even sure he had the confidence to bring it up.

It had been late. Their guards were down, and their emotions primed. Romance practically infiltrated the air, setting up the intimate scene with candlelight, cozy blankets, and a fire that ignited flames of an entirely different kind.

Today would be different.

He gave the door two solid knocks, bolstered by that assurance. He wouldn't think about kissing her. That fleeting opportunity was over and done with. He would ask her if she needed any supplies, maybe check on her fire, and be on his merry way.

But when Rachel's silhouette came into view through the side window, Holden's resolve slipped, and his throat went dry.

How was he not going to think of kissing her when she was carrying a handful of mistletoe?

CHAPTER 27

❄

*O*f course, she would have a visitor at the exact moment she'd glued her fingers to that silly sprig of mistletoe. She shook her hands about, but the frustrating greenery stayed put. It was enough to make her want to rake her hands through her hair in aggravation, but she feared the leaves and stems would get entirely tangled.

"It's always something, isn't it?" she bemoaned as she paced toward the door.

Her parents hadn't mentioned company, and when she glimpsed Holden's form on the other side of the threshold, her face heated with the warmth of a thousand Christmas candles.

This was not good.

Maybe she could run away and hide in the bedroom until he left.

Nope, not possible. He'd already seen her through

the side window next to the door. Why had her parents thought those were even a good idea? A simple peephole would suffice, not to mention give her the opportunity to pretend she wasn't home.

But she'd been found out. Shoving her hand behind her back, she took hold of the doorknob with her other hand and twisted.

"Holden! What are you doing here?"

Scout snuck past and immediately sniffed behind Rachel's back, like maybe there was a hidden tennis ball ready for a game of fetch.

"Sorry, girl. I don't have anything for you."

"Do you have anything for me?" The spark in Holden's emerald eyes made Rachel's stomach dip.

"Nope." She eyed him. "Should I?"

He scrunched his broad shoulders against his neck. "I don't know. I thought I saw you carrying a little something when you were walking up to the door. Maybe my eyes are playing tricks on me."

His eyes weren't, and the ridiculous trick she'd tried to pull off wasn't working. Heaving a sigh, she moved her hand around and held it up between them. "I'm in a bit of a predicament."

"Is the predicament that you have mistletoe and no one to kiss beneath it?"

Her heart catapulted into her throat. "What? No!" she shouted. "I'm glued to it!"

The flirtatious grin plastered to Holden's mouth faltered and his expression went slack. Genuine concern crept into his gaze. "You *glued* your hand to mistletoe?"

"More accurately, to my fingers. But yes." She stepped back. "Come on in, by the way. It's too cold out there and this story is too long to tell on the porch."

He trailed her into the cabin, and when she sat down at the kitchen table slash mistletoe craft station, he took the seat immediately next to her. Even Scout walked in one small circle and then dropped into a curled ball beneath Rachel's chair. It sure was sweet how quickly that dog had taken a liking to her. A hot blush crept up Rachel's neck at the hope that Scout's owner might have taken a similar liking to her too.

"Since I'm a little cabin-bound today, I thought it would be a good opportunity to do some brainstorming for my Mistlefaux campaign."

Holden winced.

"I know. The name's awful. I'm working on it." She surveyed the table littered with festive greenery, ribbons, and glitter. "I stopped by Trinity's floral shop yesterday to work on some holiday arrangements, and it gave me an idea. She'd said something about mistletoe being sweet. Or at least the use for it being sweet. That got me thinking of sweets, which got me thinking of sugar." She glanced toward a container on the table filled with the stuff. "And I wondered to myself, maybe sugared mistletoe could be a thing? You know, like flocked Christmas trees?"

If he followed along, his face didn't convey it. Holden's look was as empty as a recently raided Christmas cookie jar.

"I thought I could make a quick prototype," she carried on. "My dad had some spray adhesive in the garage and my mom had sugar in the cupboard."

"And now you've got a sugar-covered, artificial mistletoe sprig glued to your fingers."

"Bingo." She waved her hand in the air, which just so happened to be directly at eye level. Lightning fast, she yanked it back down.

Holden angled back coolly in his chair, ankles crossing. "You know? I've never had a woman so boldly dangle mistletoe in front of me like this. If you want to kiss me, all you have to do is ask."

"I don't want to kiss you!" She tugged on the fake greenery, her skin burning as the glue pulled taut.

"You sure about that?"

She would not answer that. "I need to get this unglued." Before *she* came unglued.

"What have you tried so far?" He pressed back toward the table, elbows perched on the ledge, suddenly interested in helping her.

"Other than praying? Nothing."

"You haven't run it under hot water?"

"Seeing that the power is out and our hot water heater isn't working, I haven't."

"Right." He thumbed his chin. "Good point. What about lemon juice? I've heard that works. Do you have any lemons lying around?"

"Sadly, no lemons." She was just going to have to come to terms with the fact that she was Snowdrift Summit's holiday version of Edward Scissorhands.

"We need to get these mistlefingers off of you," Holden deadpanned.

She blinked. "Excuse me?"

"I tried to make a joke, but evidently, it didn't translate. But you get it, right?" His brows shot clear into his hairline and a mischievous grin lifted his cheeks. "Mistle*fingers*? Like mistle*toe*?"

"Holden, that is even worse than Mistlefaux. And that's saying a lot."

"I hear you. And this isn't really a joking matter." He feigned seriousness and forced a neutral expression. "I think this needs to go in our Search and Rescue training book. Right up there with how to tourniquet an artery in the field."

Rachel gave a maddened look. "Ha, *ha*." She punctuated each word. "What did you come by for again?"

"To check on you and make sure everything was okay," he answered in a rush. "And as it turns out, it's a good thing I did. Looks like you could really use my help."

"Right, if jokes and witty banter were super-glue solvent."

He bristled. "I'm sorry. I really do want to help. What about vegetable oil? The oil might work to loosen the glue. It's worth a try."

Honestly, she'd try just about anything. That stupid

piece of mistletoe was a glaring reminder of their almost-kiss from the night before. A leafy, sugar-covered elephant in the room.

"Where might I find vegetable oil?" He was already on his feet, moving about the kitchen.

"First cabinet to the left of the fridge. Top shelf."

She would have to climb onto the counter in order to reach the bottle, a feat made infinitely more difficult one-handed. Holden didn't even have to stretch. His tall stature and long arms made quick work of pulling the bottle down easily. He spun the nearby paper towel holder and tore off a few sheets.

"Okay, let's take a look at the damage." Dragging a chair closer to Rachel's, he flipped it around and straddled the seat. "How long have you had these magical powers?"

"What?"

"The ability to grow mistletoe from your hands?"

The awful joke elicited a throaty groan. "Can we please cut the *funny* business and get straight *down* to business? I'd really like the use of my hand again."

"Sorry." He lifted her right hand and took it into his. "Jokes are my method of choice when combating nerves."

"What do you have to be nervous about? You don't have a plant for a hand."

"No, and thank goodness for that." He grinned smugly. "But to answer your question, *you* make me nervous."

"Right, to go along with the whole intimidation thing."

"You make me nervous in a butterflies-in-my-stomach sort of way."

She didn't know how to respond. "Well, butterflies don't belong there, just like this mistletoe doesn't belong *here*." She gave the offending artificial greenery a pointed look.

If Holden's coping mechanism was humor, hers was absolute diversion.

Luckily, Holden didn't elaborate and instead lifted the bottle of vegetable oil, unscrewed the cap, and sprinkled a small amount over Rachel's hand like a chef adding salt to his cuisine. Most of the oil got on the mistletoe, not in the space where it was secured to her fingers.

"Is that supposed to magically dissolve it or something?" she challenged.

This was going to require more precise work, and Holden knew it.

He pulled her hand closer, dragging her arm over the table between them, and doused a good amount directly onto her hand where the glue heavily coated her fingers. It required a decent amount of elbow grease, but after a few minutes of working it free, the mistletoe finally detached.

Rachel gasped her relief. "Oh my goodness, thank you!"

"Sure thing," Holden said. He gathered the remains

of the sugary, oily greenery mess and carted them to the kitchen trash. "I've got you."

Even though the water ran ice cold, Rachel spent time at the sink freeing the remaining bits of glue from her skin. Her fingers were tender. She ran a towel over them and pulsed her hand open and closed to ease the ache.

"Here. Let me see." Holden gestured toward her hand with a wave.

With a lump the size of a snowball in her throat, Rachel slipped it into his.

He rotated it, turning it over slowly. She wasn't sure what he was examining in particular, and when he threaded his fingers into hers, her own swarm of butterflies released in her belly.

His strong fingers curled around her hand. "Seems like it's working just fine." His words were a shallow whisper.

Had they not been face to face, Rachel would've looked elsewhere, not directly into the captivating green eyes that fastened onto hers. The intensity was enough to heat the entire room; she could feel it. She began to sweat.

He took their threaded fingers and pulled their hands to his chest, tugging Rachel closer. Her neck craned to hold his gaze.

"Rachel…"

"Too bad I'm all out of mistletoe," she said stupidly.

He chuckled, and then his voice lowered. "We don't need mistletoe."

"We're back!" Her parents' sudden greeting from the hallway severed the moment like a snapped wishbone. Because she had been wishing for him to kiss her, hadn't she?

Rachel shot back. She jammed the hand previously in Holden's into her pocket.

Holden speared his fingers through his hair and paced across the kitchen, chest ballooning with a sizable breath.

"In the kitchen!" Rachel shouted her location. Her volume dropped to a whispering hiss. "Go out the backdoor," she instructed Holden. She grabbed his shoulders and spun. "Go, go!" Pushing against his muscled back, she walked him to the door with a shove. Having her hands on him did nothing to convince those butterflies to leave. Nope, they were everywhere now, fluttering around her head and all the way down to her tingling toes.

He zipped up his jacket and moved quickly.

She threw the door open, but before he crossed the threshold, he spun back and pressed a quick kiss to her cheek.

She all but slammed the door in his face.

"There you are, Sugar Plum."

Stewart and Paula entered the kitchen, their gazes sweeping the scene.

"Goodness." Paula's hands clasped in front of her. "It looks like a tornado went off in here."

Rachel pressed her backside to the counter's ledge and clumsily wove her arms over her chest. "I was just working on that mistletoe project for December Décor. Sorry I made such a mess. I'll clean it up." She strode across the hardwood, taking a trash bag with her. Jamming the many failed attempts into the bag, she forced some calm into her breathing. She was going to hyperventilate if she didn't get a hold of herself. And Holden was going to freeze if her parents didn't leave the room quickly.

"Did you make any progress?" Paula asked.

"A little." Rachel's shoulders trembled in a nervous wobble.

Because she had made progress, right? Just not with the thing they were referring to. Only two days ago, she and Holden were lifelong adversaries. And only moments ago, he'd kissed her on the cheek. If that wasn't progress, Rachel didn't know what was.

"My heavens!" Paula practically jumped. "There's a dog in here!"

How had Rachel forgotten? That dog slumbered so silently beneath the kitchen table that she'd nearly made herself invisible. *Nearly.*

"Wait…is that Holden's dog?" Paula stepped closer and bent low, about to investigate the ownership tag attached to Scout's collar.

Rachel couldn't lie her way out of this. "It is. I'm dog-sitting."

With her hands on her knees to help push her back up, Paula straightened. "You're dog-sitting Holden Hart's dog?"

Stranger things had happened, right? Like that

moment when Holden kissed her cheek—that took the cake.

"I am."

"And why are you watching his dog?"

While Paula interrogated her daughter, Stewart slowly moved about the room like a detective scanning for out-of-place evidence.

"He was out checking on neighbors and came by. His dog seemed cold. I offered for her to stay here while he finished up."

"She was cold? I thought she was training to be an Avalanche Rescue Dog."

"Right. Sure," Rachel stammered. "She is, but even rescue dogs deserve a cozy place to nap. Plus, I've been thinking about getting a golden retriever, so this is good practice." The lies strung together like a chain of paper snowflakes.

"You're thinking of getting a dog of this size? To live with you in your six-hundred square-foot apartment?" Paula gave her daughter a dubious look. "I thought your landlord didn't allow pets."

"It's more of a suggestion than a hard and fast rule."

After circling the kitchen, Stewart came to a stop in front of his wife and daughter. "Then I *suggest* you think twice about it. Dogs are a big responsibility, Rachel. And if you get that promotion, you won't have much time for one. That's not fair to you, and it's really not fair to the dog." He moved closer to Rachel. "And it's also not fair to leave Holden outside in below-freezing temperatures."

"What?"

Stewart walked across the small kitchen and flung open the backdoor. There stood Holden—stock-still—directly on the other side.

"Oh!" Rachel went into an acting mode she didn't even know she possessed. "Hey there, Holden! I didn't realize you were back already. Scout's been a great girl. Thanks again for letting me dog-sit her."

She would not get any Oscar nominations for this sorry performance.

"Right." Holden's chin lowered in a nod as he caught on. "Yes. Thank you for watching my dog. How much do I owe you?" He moved for his wallet.

"On the house." She waved him away. "She's been a great girl. Hardly even noticed she was there."

Wasn't that the truth?

"I really appreciate it. Mr. Joy." He tipped his chin toward Rachel's father. "Mrs. Joy."

"Nice to see you, Holden," Paula reciprocated his greeting. "And thank you for checking in on the cabin and Rachel. We appreciate it."

"Of course. Happy to."

His gaze snagged on Rachel's before he clapped his hand against his thigh to call his dog over. "Come on, Scout. Let's get going, girl."

Stewart saw them out, but Rachel remained immovable, like that superglue had suddenly secured the tread of her shoes to the hardwood too.

It didn't help that Paula's glare also pinned Rachel in place.

"What's really going on here?"

"I told you. Holden came by while he was doing the rounds. He was just checking in."

With her mouth pinched, Paula narrowed her eyes at her daughter. Suddenly, all tension on her face faded. "Well, I'm glad he did. I've been worried about you all alone in this cold house. Your father and I headed back up the mountain as soon as it was plowed. We're just making a pit stop to change our clothes before we go back to the store. You sure you're alright here?"

"I'm fine, Mom. Promise."

Paula took her daughter's chin between her fingers. "Sometimes, I forget you're a grown woman who can take care of herself. You've been doing it for over a decade in that big city. But you'll always be my little girl. And I'll always worry about you, like it's my job."

"You don't need to worry about me."

"I know I don't *need* to, but I do." Her mother's hand slipped, and she tilted her head, regarding Rachel with the most maternal gaze. "I also sometimes worry that you've made a decision you feel forced to stand by. Sweetheart, do you still love your job?"

It should have been a simple answer, but Rachel couldn't locate the words. Did she love working at December Décor? No, it wasn't love. But she was motivated, and she knew if she could work her way up the corporate ladder, she'd certainly love the view from the top.

Wouldn't she?

"It pays well and it's challenging. What more could I ask for?"

"Oh, I don't know. Maybe that it would be fulfilling and fun too."

Rachel gave a little shrug. "It sometimes is."

"Life is too short to be satisfied with 'sometimes'. You deserve to love every bit of it. Every precious bit."

CHAPTER 28

Holden wasn't prone to panic attacks, but being buried in the snow was a surefire way to bring one on. He knew the statistics—the more rapidly you breathed, the quicker you went through your oxygen supply. He didn't need to stay in the cave long. Scout would find him.

Or at least, he prayed she would.

It was the final test in getting her Avalanche Rescue Dog validation. She'd passed the first round with flying colors. But finding a human was an entirely different thing than locating and digging out a piece of fabric. The stakes were higher, the timeline shorter.

Holden knew fully that if things went south, someone would get him to safety. There was an entire team waiting in the wings. He wouldn't be left to freeze below the packed surface, and that knowledge was a mollifying comfort that tempered his nerves and slowed his heart rate. His breathing too.

That hadn't been the case for Lance all of those years ago. How long had he been buried beneath the snow? It likely wasn't more than five minutes, but they must have been the most terrifying minutes of his life.

And Holden knew he was to blame.

The ski race had been a stupid idea. After all, the one person he had wanted to beat down the hill hadn't even shown up. It was with that disappointment that Holden had set out the markers that fateful morning, delineating the path skiers would take in their race to the finish. It had been shoddy, hasty work, and it almost cost his best friend his very life.

Not that Lance would ever admit that. No, he'd been 'just fine'. Veering off-course and falling into the tree well was an adrenaline rush, he'd claim. That's how he would go on to tell the story. But when Holden saw Lance's scattered ski poles and skis snapped free from their boots, each landing several yards away from the spruce trap, Holden had never been more terrified in his life.

It took him much too long to dig Lance out. His hands had forgotten how to work, forgotten how to scoop and shovel to clear away the snow. They trembled with terror. Finally, Holden had resorted to using his own helmet to dig down and locate his friend.

Lance had been knocked out, which made Holden fear the absolute worst. He didn't answer Holden once wrenched free, just laid there lifeless. Holden jostled him about, not realizing at the time that Lance's knee was completely dislocated too, making his leg bend unnaturally.

A few minutes of desperate prayer and a smack on the cheek brought Lance back to consciousness. All the other skiers had already zoomed by and made it safely down the hill, which left Holden and Lance alone on the mountainside.

But Holden had to get his buddy out of there.

So he did what he had to do. He hoisted up Lance—who was easily fifty pounds heavier than Holden at the time—and skied them down the slopes and to the medics waiting in the off-chance something of this horrific nature occurred.

Holden had been labeled a hero. Everyone praised him, most of all Lance. Bitter Cold Coffee Bar even named his favorite drink after him.

In the eyes of his friends and neighbors, Holden had not only saved the day, but likely his best friend's life.

But Holden knew better.

He'd been the reason for the accident, his poor attention to detail nearly costing Lance everything.

It was hard not to let those guilt-ridden thoughts plague his mind now as he hunkered in the shallow cave. In truth, that accident had been a motivating factor when Holden signed up to volunteer with Search and Rescue. And over the years, he learned that having a dog like Scout was an even better, more effective tool. What he wouldn't have given for her kind of help way back then.

But today was a new day, and past regret shouldn't

put a damper on things. Scout was about to get her certification. Holden crossed his fingers that she would succeed.

"Come on, girl," he murmured, knowing she couldn't hear him beneath the snowpack but saying the encouraging words still.

Silent moments passed, and then the first few bits of snow shook free, then larger clumps that landed on his goggles as he peered up toward the covered opening. More and more bits trickled in until two furiously digging paws broke through the slushy surface.

And there was Scout, peering down at him, silhouetted by golden winter rays that resembled the halo she so deserved.

"Good girl, Scout!" Tears brimmed Holden's eyes. "You did it! I'm so proud of you!"

Climbing out of the cave, Holden struggled to stand and fought hard to harness the pride that welled within him. He had trouble collecting himself, but Scout had done her job, and her reward was in order.

Lance came over with her favorite rope toy in his grasp. "Mind if I do the honors?"

"I can't think of a better person." Holden brushed the snow from his chest and gave his buddy a solid hug. "If I haven't told you lately, I love you, man."

Lance stumbled back from the unexpected display of brotherly affection, but returned the embrace heartily. They clapped each other on the back.

Crouching down, Holden looped his arms around Scout's neck and nuzzled into her furry cheek. "And I love you, girl. Congratulations on your big achievement!"

The happy pup gave him a lick before bounding off for her promised game of tug-of-war.

Holden watched his two best friends whip back and forth, not knowing who was having more fun, dog or human. And even though he'd been buried in a snow cave only minutes earlier, his entire body filled with inexplicable warmth as he observed their game at the periphery.

As Holden stood there, the head of the validation committee tracked over, boots crunching over the snow in a determined stride.

"Congratulations are in order for you too, handler." The man passed Holden a piece of official looking paper. "You and that dog make an outstanding team, and we're more than grateful to finally have you both on ours."

"Thank you, sir," Holden said. He slid the certificate into his jacket. "It's a pretty big day for us."

"One that deserves to be celebrated. I think a steak dinner is in the cards for you and your lady."

Holden knew he meant Scout, but not for the first time that day, his heart and thoughts couldn't help but travel to Rachel.

* * *

THAT SECOND EXPECTED storm wave never came through. Meteorologists said it had dissipated somewhere over the Pacific, never making landfall. Temperatures remained low, so the snow didn't melt, but it gave the plows and crews an opportunity to clear the roads without another storm cycle to hinder them.

Neighbors emerged from their cabins. The power came back on. Main Street bustled again, those few missed shopping days more than made up for, as evidenced by the customers lining the streets with overflowing bags and ready wallets.

All that was missing was the town square tree.

Thankfully, Zeke Hart's disappointment dissipated just like the storm. It made little sense to get so riled up over something you couldn't change. And it wasn't as though the town would go without; the Joy's tree would be the perfect substitute.

On Monday, Holden went into work early. Like the small town shops, they'd closed Major Hart Mountain Sports during the peak of the storm. Today would be their first full day back in operation. In truth, the conditions were primed for an epic snowmobile ride down the slopes. Lance was already out with their first customers: a pair of newlyweds visiting the Sierra Nevada for their honeymoon. Like everyone else, they'd also been cabin-bound for the last several days. But neither seemed to mind, and Holden knew why.

It was beyond romantic to be snowed in with the one you loved—or in Holden's case, the one he maybe, sort of liked. He even wondered if the heightened drama and forced proximity had been the true reason for his heightened feelings. Would that attraction be the same now that life and routine slipped back into place?

On his end, he figured it would. He'd already admitted to himself that his feelings toward Rachel weren't what he once thought they were. It was something else entirely. *She* was someone else entirely.

But he didn't know what that meant for their future. Not that they even had a future. Sure, they had their individual futures, but a big mountain and a Golden Gate Bridge separated them.

When he thought about that, his mood went downhill faster than his highest-powered snowmobile. He would not go there. They still had the holidays together. She'd go back after the new year and Holden would figure out his feelings from there.

He found himself staring out the store's window, admiring the pristine landscape that resembled a winter painting. The view couldn't be beat. It was as if the storm made the scene even more beautiful, and Holden hadn't thought that possible.

Around noon, another vehicle slowed into the parking lot. He scanned their appointment schedule. Nothing on the books for another hour. Taking a closer look, he suddenly recognized the SUV.

What were they doing here?

He rushed through the store. "Mom?"

"Hi, Holden, sweetheart." Jill Hart got out of the vehicle and moved to help her husband around the passenger's side. She steadied Zeke as he gingerly slunk onto the pavement, his grip on the bar above his head for balance. Holden came to assist them.

"What are you two doing here?"

"Dad needed a change of scenery." Holden's mother gave a pointed look.

"They're cutting down the tree today and your mother doesn't think I can handle being there when it all comes crashing down."

Holden had to agree. "Probably a good call."

"I was hoping the two of you might be able to hang out for a few hours." Jill ushered her husband inside the store while Holden held the door open for his parents. "Sarah and Laney and I are doing some holiday baking and could use some—"

"Peace and quiet?" Holden guessed. Not that a chainsaw would give them that, but it was likely less jarring than his father's lamenting.

She just smiled her answer.

"That's not a problem at all. I'd love to have you here, Dad."

Jill gave her son a squeeze around his shoulders. "Thank you, Holden. And Zeke, don't do anything to aggravate that foot of yours. I expect to pick you up in the same condition I'm leaving you."

Zeke batted her instructions away. "I'll be fine, Jillybean. Holden will take good care of me."

His mother hadn't been out the door for two seconds when Zeke turned to Holden, eyes twinkling with mirth. "Which snowmobile are we gonna take out?"

"Dad, Mom gave pretty clear instructions that you don't injure yourself again."

"Who said anything about injuring? Sure, maybe on skis I could, but on the back of a snowmobile with the safest tour guide I know at the helm? I have a better chance of falling off the couch and hurting myself."

Holden gave his dad an unconvinced look.

"I need to get out, son."

"I know being laid up isn't ideal—"

"It's not just that." His dad cut him off and his gaze turned serious. "Ever since retiring, I've felt like I'm floundering. There's no daily excitement. Don't get me wrong, I love spending more time with your mother. That has been an absolute gift. But I miss the firehouse. I miss the calls and the rush of adrenaline."

Holden got it. Even the few days off from mountain tours had made him itch to experience that thrill again. Oddly enough, he'd felt a different form of it around Rachel. Adrenaline rushes and nervous excitement weren't all that different when it came down to it.

He glanced toward his dad's bulky boot. "You promise not to do anything silly out there? Nothing that could hurt your foot and get me in trouble with Mom?"

"I'll be on my best behavior." Zeke lifted a hand in pledge. "Now let's get out there and carve up some mountain!"

CHAPTER 29

❄

"I sold it!" Trinity met Rachel at the entrance of the flower shop, a massive smile spread on her lips. She did a little hop of excitement. "Right before I closed down for the storm, a couple came in and purchased your arrangement. I'm telling you, Rachel, you're a natural. They didn't even bother looking at the others."

Rachel couldn't make sense of the satisfaction that expanded within her chest. It was just a simple floral arrangement, and yet she'd never experienced that same pride regarding her creations with December Décor. Sure, her prototypes held a special place in her heart, but the assembly line productions that weren't much more than carbon copies—those didn't make her feel like this. She couldn't understand it.

"Do you remember who purchased it?"

"A pair of honeymooners." Trinity beamed. "They

were the sweetest couple. Said it reminded them of her bouquet from the wedding."

Rachel grinned and inhaled fully. The shop smelled every bit as delightful as Rachel had remembered it from the other day. That unique combination of pine and roses, holiday splendor mixed with a hint of romance. Rachel almost wished she could bottle it up.

"So, what are we working on today?" She removed an apron from a hook on the wall and joined Trinity at the long counter. As she took in the array of wires and greenery, she had a strong hunch she already knew the answer.

"My Mom's home with the little ones and she usually works on the wreaths, so I thought we could step in and help with those. It's crunch time. They're literally flying off the walls." Trinity giggled to herself. "*And* flying off doors from that gusty storm."

"I do have a little wreath making experience."

"Isn't that the truth? I almost worried you might be tired of making them. Do you know I own one of your cow shaped ones from your farmhouse line? I keep it up year round in our kitchen and switch out the bow around its neck to match the seasons."

"Well, that's a great idea." Rachel wondered why she'd never thought to do that. But after all, the company was called *December* Décor. They didn't give much thought to the remaining eleven calendar months.

"You sure you're not wreathed out?" Trinity suggested.

"Tired of making wreaths? No way. But to be fair, I don't think I could say the same if today's project involved mistletoe."

Rachel took a pair of shears when Trinity passed them off. The florist pulled a set of gloves from a drawer and fit them onto her hands before giving Rachel a pair to do the same. "How's that going?"

"It's not. I keep reminding myself that I have time until the presentation, but the ideas just aren't coming. I'm really stuck." She bit back the ironic laugh that wanted to accompany that very literal statement. Her sore fingers still felt the aftermath of that predicament.

"If it's meant to be, it will come to you. And if not, then something else will."

Rachel couldn't interpret the full meaning of that phrase. If she didn't come up with a mistletoe prototype, she'd be up a creek without a paddle. Or more accurately, out the door without a job. That wasn't an option.

The two women worked side by side for hours, weaving branches of leafy evergreen onto wire frames and embellishing them with berries, pinecones, and ribbons. Rachel's hands were stained green and the woodsy aroma permeated her gloves, her clothes, the entire store. It was a lush forest of holiday sights and smells.

She was just about to begin working on a new wreath—her fifth of the day—when her phone vibrated within the front pocket of her apron. She tugged it out.

Cathryn Marlin, her boss.

A shudder climbed its way up her spine. She connected her gaze with Trinity and mouthed, 'One moment,' as she threaded her way through the shop and stepped out onto the sidewalk. The mountain air was cold, but the winter sun kissed her skin with an unexpected warmth. She felt a similar dichotomy within her, the sense of anticipation and dread filling her gut equally.

"Cathryn," she began as soon as she clicked to answer. "How are you doing?"

"I'm well, Rachel." Her boss's voice was the same practiced monotone Rachel had remembered, giving absolutely nothing away. "I take it you're still in Snowdrift?"

"I am. Through Christmas."

"That's actually what I wanted to discuss with you." Still no indicating inflection. "We've moved your meeting up to December twentieth. Roger is heading to Colorado through the new year, so we had to slide things around a bit. I hope that's not a problem."

A lump wedged squarely in Rachel's throat. She could barely force the words around it. "December twentieth?"

"Yes. We figured that would still give everyone time to make their travel plans and head home for the holidays. We're looking forward to meeting with you on the twentieth. We will see you then."

The click of the line at the end of the conversation was the only punctuated part of Cathryn's discussion. Everything else fell flat. Just like Rachel's spirit.

She stared at the phone in her palm for a beat before stowing it back into her pocket. What was she going to do? She wasn't any more prepared now than she had been the last time. Arguably, she was even *less* prepared.

"Everything okay?" Trinity easily read Rachel's crestfallen expression when she came back into the shop.

"They've moved my Mistlefaux presentation up to the twentieth."

A concerned sigh dropped Trinity's shoulders. "Oh no. That doesn't give you much time, does it?"

"No, it doesn't."

"I'm so sorry to hear that. You're welcome to head out if you need to." She dipped her chin toward the door in an encouraging nod. "I can take care of the rest of these wreaths. You've already been such a tremendous help. I honestly can't thank you enough."

Rachel knew she should leave—should pore over her mistletoe campaign until revelation dawned and she had a worthy product—but she didn't want to. She picked up a wire frame and gave Trinity a smile.

"You know what? I think I'd like to stay here, if you'll have me."

"You are always welcome, Rachel." Trinity returned the full grin. "And please know, that's a standing invitation."

* * *

STEWART JOY WAS BESIDE HIMSELF. Mayor Thornton would come by the house today to measure their noble fir and crown it the official town square tree. Fifteen years, twenty-feet, and constant doting and affection was all it took to earn that prestigious title.

That, and the demise of their competitor's tree.

Rachel tried not to dwell on that little piece of information.

She couldn't really dwell on much, other than that in a few short days, she'd be back in San Francisco with zero changes made to her original Mistlefaux product. Maybe they wouldn't notice if she gave the same presentation. After all, she was pretty convinced a few of the executives had dozed off a time or two the first go around.

She shook her head. Who was she kidding? This had career sabotage written all over it.

"Is he here yet?" Stewart bounded down the stairs with all the exuberance of a child awaiting a holiday visit from Saint Nick.

"Not yet, Dad. But I promise I'll let you know as soon as he arrives."

Stewart pressed his nose to the glass window by the door. "I'll just wait here so I don't miss him. Wouldn't want the man to wait out in the cold."

Rachel didn't bring up the fact that they would have to brave the cold to measure the tree. "Sounds like a good plan, Dad."

Luckily, Mayor Thornton was a prompt man, arriving at twelve o'clock on the nose. And not a moment too soon. Stewart flung the door open and sang, "O' Christmas tree, O' Christmas tree!" in the most booming greeting.

The mayor humored him with resounding applause as he walked up the porch and into the foyer, a single clap in time with each step. "I can't say I've had a more celebratory welcome. It's good to see you, Stewart."

"And you, as well." Stewart gave a little bow. "Are you ready?"

"That, I am. I hear your tree is a true sight to behold."

"It is. The most gorgeous noble fir this side of the mountain. And it'll be even more beautiful decked out and lit up in the center of town. It's the perfect homegrown Christmas tree."

"I don't doubt that." Mayor Thornton tipped the edge of his plaid newsboy cap.

The two gentlemen moved through the house, toward the back door. Rachel thought about joining them outside, but she had a perfectly good vantage point from her workplace at the kitchen table. And in truth, she wanted to give her father a little privacy in his big moment.

Mistletoe mocked her from every angle. She deflated with a sigh. The only solid plan she currently had was to tell the execs that she *didn't* have one—no plan, no prototype, no passion.

It wasn't like her to throw in the towel like this, but it seemed inevitable.

For the first time in her life, Rachel faced the

genuine possibility that she just might lose. It tugged on her stomach like a heavy weight.

Sliding her gaze from the discouraging mess in front of her, she peered out the window. The men had already finished measuring the tree, and the exchanged handshake indicated the Joy's success.

Her father was going to be on cloud nine.

They were in mid conversation when they came back into the house.

"I'll be honest, Stew," the mayor said as they passed back through the galley kitchen. "It's getting harder and harder to cut these trees down each year. They're such a beautiful part of the landscape that it feels almost wrong to remove them from it."

Stewart gave a tight nod. "I can understand that. But if it's any comfort, we planted this tree for this very purpose. We consider it the highest honor to harvest it for our community to enjoy."

One more friendly handshake and Mayor Thornton was on his way.

Stewart paused behind the closed door, his palm still lingering on the wood.

"You okay, Dad?" Rachel called out from the kitchen. When he didn't answer, she checked on him. "Everything good?"

He turned slowly. "That last thing the mayor said." He shook his index finger as he recalled the words. "About it getting harder and harder to cut down the trees."

"I can imagine it must be," Rachel agreed. "It takes

years to grow trees that large. I see what he means about them being almost permanent fixtures in the landscape."

"I never really gave much thought to the tree *not* being right outside the window each morning when I come downstairs for my cup of coffee. Or no longer seeing the moon reflected on its branches each night when I close up the house. It's always been there."

Rachel touched her father's forearm. "It's just a tree, Dad," she tried to console, but the words tasted false as they left her mouth.

"Is it, though?" A mist clouded his steel-gray eyes as he added, "Because there's a little piece of each of us in that tree. And there's a piece of your sister too. Even your grandma. We all dropped that sapling into the ground together…as a family. I don't want to cut that out."

"You can't cut out the memories. Those will always be there."

Rallying his composure, Stewart straightened his spine and bobbed his head in an agreeing nod that was only half convincing. "Thank you, Sugar Plum." He moved to kiss the crown of her hair. "That's exactly what I needed to hear."

CHAPTER 30

Holden loaded another heaping armful of freshly cut boughs into the bed of his truck and swiped his hands on his pant legs to brush off the stray needles. It was good to know the tree wouldn't go entirely to waste. His sister had mentioned running into Trinity Tillman the other day on Main Street, recalling that the woman owned the local floral shop. A quick phone call confirmed Trinity would be overjoyed to receive the extra trimmings from their failed town square tree.

Zeke's approval was really the only one that mattered. Thankfully, he was delighted about the opportunity to donate portions of his tree to become wreaths that would ultimately adorn cabin doors throughout the summit.

That impromptu snowmobile ride the other day provided more than just an opportunity to stretch their legs. It provided Holden with the real reason his father had been so passionate about winning.

When they had taken a break near one of Holden's favorite lookouts, appreciating the sloping valleys and cresting peaks of Snowdrift over a Thermos of hot chocolate, Zeke had admitted to more than Holden could ever have pieced together on his own.

"I really wanted to give our town that tree, Holden," Zeke had confessed. His brow was drawn tight in what Holden acknowledged as an intentional effort to keep the tears from brimming. "For so many years, it was my job to take care of those people. To help them in their darkest hours. To let them know everything was going to be okay, and that help was on the way. Having our tree selected for the annual lighting felt like one last time I could be there for our town. And this time, for something much brighter."

Holden had never thought of it that way. What he'd coined as crazy was just his father wanting to give back. It made guilt settle in his chest, but only briefly. Knowing their tree could serve another, equal purpose was the opportunity they all needed.

The drive into town was faster than usual. Roads were clear and the holiday jingles cranked up loud on the radio perked up Holden's spirit.

He perked up even more when he strode into the floral shop—a cheerful spring in his step and hope in his heart—and he glimpsed Rachel at Trinity's side behind the counter.

"You're here!" Trinity rushed over to greet him.

"And not a moment too soon. We just used up the last of our trimmings."

"Well, I'm glad we could be of service. I have the branches out in the truck. Let me grab them for you."

Rachel skirted the counter. "I'll join you."

He'd hoped she would say that, but she also looked knee-deep in a project and he hadn't wanted to interrupt.

"I'm really sorry this was the fate of your family's tree, Holden." She peered into the truck bed and it dawned on Holden that this was the first time Rachel hadn't reacted with arrogance about a win. And she had every right to. The Joy's tree won, fair and square.

"You know? I thought my dad would be more upset than he is, but it turns out having the tree made into wreaths is a close second…maybe even a tie." He gathered several long branches and pushed the tailgate into place.

"I wouldn't go that far." There was that spirit he liked so much. A playful challenge swept over her lake blue eyes, and it made Holden's heart kick up in tempo. Then, just as quickly as it appeared, her expression went slack. "Hey, there's something I've been wanting to talk to you about."

"Oh, yeah?"

"Any chance you're free tonight?"

"Rachel Joy, are you asking me out on a date?" Shuffling the branches from one arm to the other, Holden propped open the flower shop door and let her pass through first. She didn't answer. Not the time for jokes, apparently. "I am free. How about this? You come to my place around seven and I'll cook dinner. Maybe we can even finish decorating that tree if you're up for it?"

"That sounds perfect."

Holden agreed, but he couldn't shake the feeling that things wouldn't stay that way for long.

* * *

Béarnaise was a temperamental sauce. Those were just the facts. He wasn't sure why he'd selected a recipe that required so much whisking. He had stirred the mixture for what felt like all evening, and based on the remaining steps to go, he wasn't even close to done.

As he stared into the saucepan, his mind wandered back to that afternoon. Rachel's tone had turned serious when she'd asked to meet. He couldn't pinpoint why. Things with their parents seemed surprisingly fine. Holden even overheard his father call Stewart Joy, congratulating him on their tree's selection with a maturity that had been absent in recent weeks. If that wasn't an improvement, Holden didn't know what was.

For the first time in decades, the Hart/Joy feud seemed put to rest with things settled in a manner that left everyone pleased.

So why didn't Rachel appear that way?

Scout heard her knock first. The dog dashed to the front door and Holden followed. He hadn't bothered to remove his apron or even discard the wooden spoon.

He brought them all with him, looking his domestic best.

It wasn't often he had company to cook for, but it was something he took great pride in. Which was why he kept the greeting short and scurried back to his finicky steak sauce. They'd come this far—he wasn't about to let the recipe fail now.

"I didn't know you were such a chef."

Rachel slipped her ski jacket from her shoulders and settled it over a barstool. She looked gorgeous in a powder blue sweater with slim fit jeans paired with leather booties. Her hair pulled into a low ponytail at her neck and framed her face in feminine wisps.

Holden drew in a breath. "You look gorgeous."

A flicker of embarrassment sprinted over her face before she reconciled it with a smile. "Thank you, Holden. You look—"

"Like I've been in the kitchen all day, which would be a fair assessment. This béarnaise sauce is no joke. I think I've spent more time whisking this than I did working up a business plan for our rental company. And I spent a year on that!"

"I've heard it's a fairly difficult sauce to make. But oh so yummy." She rubbed her stomach and glanced toward the steaks on the counter. "And I'm starving. This smells so wonderful."

They made more small talk in the kitchen, and despite the cramp in his hand, Holden was actually a little grateful the meal took so long to prepare. It put off whatever Rachel really wanted to discuss. Holden wasn't sure he was ready for that. It had only been a couple of days that things had been normal between them. Hopeful, even. He wanted to sit in that space and enjoy that feeling for as long as he could.

"You're probably not going to want to hear this," she said after taking the last bite of her meal. She lowered her fork to the plate with a little clink.

Holden ran his cloth napkin over his mouth. She was right. He didn't want to hear whatever she was going to say. How else could he delay the inevitable? Maybe the meal should've been more courses—that would've drawn things out even longer.

"This is the best béarnaise sauce I've ever eaten," she finally finished the thought she'd left hanging in the air. "I know it's time consuming to make, but I think you should add this to your repertoire of go-to sauces. It's a real winner."

That was the bad news? Holden knew it wasn't. There was still more waiting in the wings.

"I think I'll keep this one on reserve for special occasions only."

"Is that what this is?" She lifted her wineglass to her mouth, her brilliant smile even more dazzling behind the crystal. "A special occasion?"

"Considering our history, I would say so." Lifting the bottle of white wine from the ice bucket on the table, Holden topped off her glass and then refilled his own. "It's a special occasion when Rachel Joy and Holden Hart can be civil for an entire meal," he teased.

"I think we can be more than civil." She chased the

flirtatious words with a sip of wine and a wink that had Holden almost choking.

Maybe he didn't need that second glass. His head already spun like he'd had a few too many as he tried to interpret that unexpected gesture.

"We should get to work on that tree." Rachel scooted back from the table. She stacked their plates and collected their utensils.

"You don't need to do that," he insisted. "I'll take care of all that later."

"You made me dinner. I'm not going to leave you with a sink filled with dishes. What kind of date would that make me?"

So, it *was* a date. The confirming hint wedged sneakily into her sentence made Holden's heart do a little skip. He'd wanted it to be one, but a looming apprehension wouldn't let his heart fully settle into that hope.

"How about we do them together?" He met her halfway.

Washing dishes with a woman had never been on his list of first date ideas, but there was something satisfying about the way they worked as a team. She scrubbed while he dried, and now and then their hands would meet beneath the water. Her fingers happened to graze his more than necessary, and one time when he dipped his hand beneath the soapy suds, he grabbed ahold of hers completely.

She gave a little startle, then threaded her fingers between his.

It was a brief exchange, but it had Holden's pulse tapping against his neck double-time.

Once they'd cleaned up the kitchen, they moved to the tree. It didn't look bare, but didn't appear to be completed either. There were gaps in the decorations and areas where the tinsel needed to be separated and spread out more evenly. Holden had one box of decorations left. He removed the lid and pulled out an ornament resting gently on top.

It was a set of skis that crossed in the middle like an X. His mother had gotten it for him the year he put on that botched skiing competition. He hesitated to hang it on the tree and instead let it dangle from his finger by the hook, the memory stalling his movements.

"Is that one meaningful?" Rachel asked, noticing his deliberate pause.

"In a way. It's from the year I planned that downhill ski race."

"The one I didn't make it home for." Something resembling an apology crowded her gaze. "I'm so sorry about that, Holden. I had no idea it meant so much."

He shook his head and stowed the ornament away. Lance had forgiven him years ago, and now, even Rachel seemed to ask for forgiveness, although she had no blame in the matter.

Maybe it was finally time for Holden to forgive himself.

"I think we're good on ornaments." He returned the lid to the box. "You know what this tree needs? Popcorn."

"Popcorn?"

"Popcorn garland," he elaborated, marching toward the kitchen to gather the jar of kernels, tinfoil, and a pan. "You know how to make it?"

"Do *I* know how to make popcorn garland? Holden, I'll have you know you're looking at the Joy Family Popcorn Garland Queen. I once strung twenty feet in under an hour."

Of course she had. A bemused grin lifted his lips. "I had no idea I was in the presence of royalty. So what do you say? Are you up for one more Christmas contest challenge, Mittens?"

"That's Your Majesty, Queen Mittens to you."

CHAPTER 31

Her thumb felt like a pincushion, but that didn't slow her. Rachel punctured the piece of popcorn with the tip of the needle and threaded it onto the fishing line. She had coiled her strand next to her like a snake about to strike. And that's how she felt. She couldn't wait for the timer to ring out at the one-hour mark, making her the victor. And for once, it would all be in good fun.

Holden cozied next to her on the couch, working so furiously sweat formed along his brow. He'd dropped more pieces of popcorn into the couch cushions and onto the floor than he'd secured on the strand, but sloppiness aside, his garland was impressive. It would be close.

They bumped hands as they reached into the shared bowl.

He pretended to cut her off, jamming his hand directly in front of hers.

"Interference!" she yelped. She pointed the tip of the needle at him.

"Someone's a little feisty."

"Are you at all surprised?" Her fingers swatted his and dove into the bowl for another handful.

Holden tossed a single piece of popcorn into his open mouth, looking cooler than ever. "Not one little bit."

Rachel crammed another dozen pieces onto her garland before she glanced up again. "How much time do we have left?" They must be getting close.

He peered toward the phone. "Three…two…"

"Hands up!" Rachel dropped her supplies and shot her hands into the air like a chef on a cable network cooking competition. "All done!"

Holden did the same, but much less dramatically. "Shall we crown the winner?"

He stood from the sofa and took the end of his garland between his fingers. Stretching it to its full length, the rope of popcorn came in just shy of his six-foot, three-inch stature.

Rachel easily had that beat. Prematurely celebrating her victory, she jumped up and flung the strand into the air, lifting her arm clear above her head. Even more garland remained coiled on the floor, but she wouldn't need it. That was all extra. She whooped in delight.

"Looks like you get to keep your title, Your Royal Highness." Holden gave a theatrical bow.

"That was really fun."

"Well, of course it was. It's always fun to win, isn't it?" he asked in jest.

"It's fun just being with you." She rolled the garland into a big popcorn ball and left it on the coffee table.

She had put the conversation off all night, and time was running out. She was like Cinderella awaiting the ominous stroke of midnight when reality would come crashing down. It was a countdown she nearly dreaded.

After their garland making session, they watched *It's a Wonderful Life* and shared the rest of the bottle of wine, along with stories from their past that translated differently with the new lens of hindsight and maturity to view them through.

What would her teenage self think if she could see her now, snuggled at the side of her sworn adversary? Rachel decided she didn't even care. What mattered now was this moment, and she would cling to it for as long as she could.

Later on, the credits rolled on the movie and the cabin swathed in darkness, save for the tree that twinkled with a holiday glow. Holden removed his arm from Rachel's shoulders and reached for the remote. "Are you up for another? I hear *Elf* is on next. Might be fun to watch my namesake in action."

"Holden, there's something I've been meaning to talk to you about."

Here goes nothing, she mused, her stomach knotted like a pretzel.

"I know." He clicked off the television and brought

his leg up onto the couch to face her straight on. "I was just hoping I could distract you until you forgot what it was you originally came here for."

"I came here for you." Sure, she'd had something she needed to tell him, but she'd also wanted to be with him. Wanted to share this beautiful December evening. Enjoy his company and amazing food. She knew they wouldn't have the opportunity for more nights like this very one, and she wanted to savor it for all it was worth.

She felt the full intensity of his piercing, attentive gaze. A flush bloomed on her cheeks and the fine hairs along the back of her neck tingled.

It also made her heart feel like it could split right in two.

"My boss called yesterday."

Widened eyes and a dip of his head wordlessly encouraged her to continue.

"They've moved up my Mistlefaux presentation to the twentieth."

He produced a frown. "And you're not ready?"

"I'm not," she admitted. "But more than not being ready for my presentation, I'm not ready for this." She waved her hand in between them. "I'm not ready to start something with you, knowing in two days' time, I'll be back in San Francisco and you'll still be here in Snowdrift."

He didn't say anything.

"Maybe I'm being presumptuous," she continued, needing to fill the space his absence of a response created. "It's not like we're dating or that we would even start a relationship—"

"Rachel," he cut off her sentence midway. "If you lived here, or I was there, we would absolutely start something. It's fair to say, I think we already have."

She knew it too, and it hadn't just happened during this recent trip home. It had built over the course of their entire lives. Was this really where it all ended for good?

She found her courage in a large breath and said, "I just don't think it's possible for us to continue this when I live in—"

He cut her off a second time, but this time, it wasn't with words. Holden's mouth met hers in a kiss that had the twinkle lights on the tree blurring into one dazzling glow, had her heart zigzagging within her chest, had her fuzzy head spinning as she tried to process the reality of his lips suddenly upon hers.

She was kissing her lifelong rival. And yet, the only challenge she currently faced was an inner battle that pulled her in two opposing directions. In all aspects of her life, she let her head take the lead. This time, she decided to give her heart that chance.

She melted into his strong embrace. Holden kissed her like a man falling in love, and she let herself be that woman. Because she was. Their romance had been a whirlwind; a tornado of emotion. But it had placed them solidly in this moment, and that wasn't something she was about to overlook.

She let herself fall too.

Finally, Holden pulled back, his tender eyes opening slowly as they found hers. He leaned back in and pressed his forehead to hers when he said on the lightest laugh, "So, it looks like you don't need that mistletoe after all."

* * *

Rachel woke the next morning with a lump in her throat that made the backs of her eyes scratch with unspent tears. It wasn't just Holden she was sad to leave. Going year after year without so much as a visit home had hardened her in a way. Sure, the physical distance separated her from her hometown, but it also enabled her to distance herself emotionally. And that hadn't been healing, nor healthy.

For the first time in years, the thought of spending Christmas anywhere other than Snowdrift produced an ache in her chest. But she knew she couldn't make it back in time. If, for some miraculous reason, December Décor decided to move forward with Mistlefaux, she would need to stay put. Clock in hours. Put in the hard work of launching a brand new campaign.

And if it failed? Then she'd really need to put her nose to the grindstone.

How would it look for her to flit off to the summit yet again? The executives were gracious enough to let her have another opportunity at bat. When would that grace run out?

She wasn't about to test it.

She sat up from the pullout couch and pushed a fist to her eyes to rub away the remnants of sleep. Her bleary gaze landed on a framed photo at the edge of her father's desk.

It was an image of Rachel and Bethany. They couldn't have been more than five and eight-years-old respectively, the ages when Santa Claus was still real and Christmas wishes came true. In the photograph, they each sat upon the jolly man's knee. Rachel remembered the moment well. Grandma Birdie had taken just the sisters to San Francisco for a day of holiday shopping, more sugar than two young girls could ever need, and memories that—as Rachel noted even now—would last an entire lifetime.

"What did you wish for?" Rachel remembered asking her older sister the moment they had hopped down from Santa's lap. She had taken her grandmother's hand in one, her sister's in the other.

"I can't tell you, or else it won't come true." Bethany had swung their joined hands like a jump rope as they walked around Union Square.

Grandma Birdie had an answer for everything. It was no surprise she had a solution for Rachel's inquisitive nature too. She'd known full well her youngest granddaughter wouldn't relent until Bethany fessed up.

"Most people don't know this,"—the older woman had leaned in close to her granddaughters and lowered her volume to a whisper—*"but you can tell your wish to someone if you both wished for the same thing. It doubles the chances it will come true."*

How would Rachel know if she and her sister had wished the same thing unless they told each other? It made no sense.

Rachel had been close to protesting when Grandma Birdie had glanced down and given her the slyest of winks. Her false lashes had crinkled around her gleaming, mischievous eyes. *"Why don't you go first, Bethany, and we'll see if it's the same as your sister's?"*

Bethany hadn't been as easily convinced, but both Grandma Birdie and Rachel had pinned her with an expectant stare until she'd caved.

"Did you wish we could stay in this city forever?" She had released Rachel's hand and spun around in a circle, pirouetting so fully her sparkling holiday skirt twirled around her like a flurry of falling snowflakes. She had looked so magical with the city lights dancing behind her, almost ethereal. *"Because that was my wish. That you and I will live out our dreams, right here, side by side."* She'd hugged herself. *"And I just know it will come true."*

It hadn't been Rachel's original wish. She'd wished for a puppy. But in that moment, her heart had latched onto Bethany's like it was her very own.

And until now, it never thought of letting go.

CHAPTER 32

❄

He knew she would leave again. That wasn't a secret. But he thought he had at least two more weeks, not two days.

Rubbing his temples, Holden groaned.

"You okay there, buddy?" Lance waltzed over to the register and rapped his hands on the counter.

"Just trying to figure out how to cram an entire relationship into forty-eight hours."

"You're going to have to explain that one," Lance said. He fiddled with the display of sunglasses next to the cash register, rearranging the women's from the men's and lining them up by color.

Holden didn't know how much he should divulge. Of course, he had hoped last night would end in a kiss, but he hadn't let himself believe it actually would. Everything about the evening had pointed toward it, though. From the way Rachel had looked at him under fluttering lashes, to how his heart had quickened each time his fingers grazed hers. That part was all on purpose. He didn't just-so-happen to need another piece of popcorn at the exact moment she did. Every. Single. Time.

She had kissed him back, which was the biggest gift in it all. Holden considered himself pretty perceptive when it came to women, but Rachel was an entirely different book. He couldn't always read her. He didn't think she would pull away, but he also didn't think she would curl into him the way she had, meeting his mouth with eager expectation.

It had been perfect.

And within the span of two days, it would all be over.

"You gonna fill me in? Or do I need to become a mind reader?" Lance pressed his fingertips to his forehead and shut his eyes, as though attempting to pull Holden's thoughts into his own brain.

"I kissed Rachel last night."

Lance slapped the countertop. "I knew it!" He hit his palm on the surface again and smirked. "I *knew* you two were sneaking around. You said you weren't, but I know you better than that. I knew you had feelings for her."

"We're not sneaking around," Holden corrected. "This hasn't been going on long."

"I beg to differ, my friend. This thing with Rachel has been going on just shy of two decades. I think that's probably the longest courtship on Snowdrift Summit record."

"I'm not courting her. I'm barely dating her," Holden insisted. "And I only have two days to do that."

Squinting at his buddy rather than rallying another comeback, Lance said, "Then you better plan something pretty epic."

"That's what I'm trying to do. But everything I come up with seems so dumb. It's like I don't even know how to date her."

"I bet it's hard to plan a date for a woman you're only used to competing with."

The light bulb in Holden's mind flashed on, sudden and bright. "That's it!" Reaching across the counter, Holden grabbed Lance by his shoulders and shook him wildly. "Thank you! You just gave me an idea."

* * *

Holden had their entire day planned, starting with a trip to Bitter Cold Coffee Bar.

He had picked her up from her parents' place early, surprised to find her already waiting on the porch, admiring the dawn as it crested over the ridge. She appeared cold with a reddened nose and watering eyes, but couldn't seem to pull herself away from the scene.

Holden couldn't blame her—the morning was spectacular with a watercolor sunrise that painted the skies in a delicate wash of yellows, oranges, and pinks. It was almost enough to keep Holden in bed that morning, his vantage point from the loft the best seat in the house.

But the thought of spending the entire day with

Rachel was even more spectacular than that showy sunrise. It filled him with more warmth, at least. And when he glimpsed her as he pulled into the driveway, he would argue she was even more lovely.

Rachel's beauty rivaled that of Mother Nature, and if pressed to give an answer, Holden would declare Rachel the winner.

She was breathtaking in every way.

They talked the whole way into town. Not about anything earth-shattering, just small talk that came easy and felt comfortable.

And she beamed when the truck drove up and settled in front of Bitter Cold.

"I would say we're back where it all started," she spoke over the engine that hissed as it cooled. "But I think that was actually in Mr. Matteo's eighth grade class. And the thought of setting foot on that middle school campus has my anxiety shooting through the roof."

A chuckle passed through Holden's lips. He unclipped his lap belt and regarded her from his seat. "I'm good with not doing that. Junior high was rough. Let's just say this is where it all *re*started. Rachel and Holden 2.0."

"I like that," she agreed with a single nod.

Holden jogged around the back of the truck to reach Rachel's side before she opened the door first, careful to avoid the slick ice on the sidewalks. If this was going to be a true date, he would treat it like one. And that meant pulling out all the stops.

With his hand pressed gently to her lower back, Holden guided her into the coffee shop. Carols played over the speakers. Several baristas joined in, their melodic voices filling the space with holiday cheer. Even the workers who weren't singing danced along, bells strung around their necks and on their hats jingling merrily in time.

Holden loved this, loved the holidays in a small town.

He could tell Rachel did too, the evidence in the beautiful smile lifting her cheeks to her eyes.

They slipped past a mother wrangling a crew of little ones, all bundled and dressed for a day of snow play. They looked like puffy marshmallows with legs as they bounced off of one another. All of those layers made them waddle and teeter unsteadily. Holden smiled at the sweet sight.

A new carol came on and the café workers cheered their recognition. It was clearly a favorite, as it should be. Who didn't like "All I Want for Christmas is You"? It was practically Christmas carol royalty.

"Do they do this in the city?" Holden turned to ask Rachel. He kept his hand loose at her waist. "The free song and dance routine with a cup of coffee?"

"I really wouldn't know," she admitted as they moved up in line. "I typically get my coffee from a cart pushed around the office by an intern."

That surprised him, considering the amount of time she'd spent in Bitter Cold since returning home. "You don't go to coffee shops to get your daily fix?"

"Honestly, I don't get out a whole lot. If I couldn't see the city from my apartment window, I think I'd sometimes forget I lived in it. It's to the office and then home for me every weekday. Even some weekends."

"What's the draw of living in the city when you don't even get to explore it?"

"That's a fair question," she said with a hint of resignation in her tone and in the breath that lifted the strands of blonde fringing her face. "One I don't think I have an answer for anymore."

He left it at that. It had helped that the music track was an inherently bubbly tune that encouraged dancing along to the beat. Even in line, Holden found his foot tapping and head bobbing in time, despite the melancholy that had unexpectedly slipped into their conversation.

"What'll it be, big guy?" Holden's favorite barista, Perry, aimed finger guns at him. "The usual?"

"You know? I think I'm in the mood for something different. Surprise me."

"Up for a little adventure." Perry nodded beneath his colorful beanie. "I like it. I'll come up with something good." He transferred his attention to Rachel. "What about you, miss? What can we get started for you?"

Rachel thumbed her chin as she peered up at the illustrated menu. "How is the Gingerbread Breve?"

"My current favorite on our seasonal menu," Perry answered emphatically. "You can't go wrong with that one. It's like an entire gingerbread house in a cup. Magical."

Holden pulled his wallet from his back pocket. "How about you make it two?"

"Righty-o. Two Gingerbread Breves coming right up."

Inserting his card into the reader, Holden waited for the beep before returning it to his billfold. "Thanks, Perry. And Merry Christmas."

"Same to you, boss."

They found a table near the back—the one Rachel usually claimed as her own—and waited while the baristas crafted their holiday drink order. Rachel unwound the scarf from her neck and piled it onto the table in a knit coil of reds and greens. She was always beautiful, but something was different today. Holden wondered if the thought of their kiss drew the pink blush to her cheeks. If it set the smile on her mouth and the shimmer in her eye.

He knew being in love changed people from the inside out, and her magnified beauty verified that tenfold.

But they weren't in love. Not yet. Time was not on their side when it came down to it. You couldn't fall in love with someone in forty-eight hours. And yet, Holden wasn't going to let that stop him.

She stood quickly when the barista called out the drinks, making a move to collect them before Holden had the chance.

"Thank you." He took the proffered cup from her

grip when she returned. "It's fitting we would order this particular drink since gingerbread house making is on today's agenda."

Her gaze filled with delight as she reclaimed her seat across the table. She cupped her hands around the specialty drink. "Is it, really?"

"Yep, along with sledding and snowman building."

"This is beginning to sound a little familiar." She cocked her head slightly, deciphering his plan.

"It should. Those were all challenges in your Christmas Competition. Only now, instead of vying with one another for the title, we'll be working as a team."

"Probably something we should have done all along."

"Probably so," Holden agreed. "But better late than never, right?"

She didn't answer. The question might have sounded rhetorical, but Holden hadn't intended it to be. He wanted her reciprocation. Some confirmation that it was okay to invest his heart in this.

In the end, it didn't matter. Who was he kidding? He was already invested, whether or not that was wise.

"What's the order of events?" She removed the lid from her drink and blew across the caramel-colored surface. Her lips pressed together and her beautiful cupid's bow pursed as steam rose around her in wispy curls.

He wanted to kiss her right then and there, and if a table hadn't separated them, he very well might have.

He cleared his throat. "I was thinking sledding, then snowman building. And then we'll finish up with gingerbread decorating at my parents' place, if that's okay with you."

It was a bold suggestion received much better than expected.

"Sounds like the perfect day." She refitted the lid and took a sip. "But are you sure your parents will be okay with that? I don't think they're big fans of me."

"It was actually my mom's suggestion. Plus, you'll get to spend time with Laney, and that's a treat in itself."

Her brow arched to a point. "Laney?"

"My niece. The baby I had with me at the store the other day. She's my sister's daughter and the most precious little girl in the entire world. Though I might be a little biased."

Rachel's eyes softened, and she sank a little into her chair, smiling sweetly. It was the same look most women got when they saw Holden out and about with Scout at his side. What was it about men with puppies and babies that turned women into balls of mush?

"You know? She was the only reason I didn't lose my temper with you that day," Rachel said.

"That was you *not* losing your temper?" He hid behind his cup, ready to dodge the comeback.

Instead, she just laughed. "I was upset. I'll give you that. But goodness, that sweet baby is adorable. Do you realize how hard it is to be mad at a guy holding a baby? It's like some weird sort of maternal kryptonite."

"Noted." He nodded for emphasis. "So I just need to borrow a baby for all of our tough conversations in the future?"

"I wouldn't worry about that. I think we've proven we can get through the tough things all on our own, Holden."

That was true. He just prayed there would be a future between them to even worry about.

CHAPTER 33

Sledding was exceptionally more terrifying than snowmobiling. Why hadn't Rachel remembered that? At least with a snowmobile, there was a way to adjust the speed with the throttle, or even come to a full and complete stop by cutting the engine.

Not so on a sled. It accelerated all on its own and stopping mid-race wasn't an option unless you bailed into a snowbank or completely jumped ship. Two things Rachel had no intention of doing.

It didn't help that she was in the sled's front with Holden seated immediately behind her. She hadn't wanted to take the helm, but he'd explained she wouldn't be able to see around him. His large body would block the view. But at this moment, she preferred that scenario. She would rather have his broad shoulders impeding her view of the trees that rushed toward her and then darted past her periphery. It was like a computer game where the player had to dodge incoming objects hurled from all angles. Somehow, Holden maneuvered their sled around rocks and berms with finesse. All while Rachel screamed until her lungs ached.

It was only a handful of minutes, but she saw her entire life flash before her eyes as they plunged down the hill.

Leaning sharply to the right, Holden curved the sled to a stop once on flatter ground. Slushy bits of snow marred Rachel's vision. She lifted her ski goggles and sucked in a breath.

"Okay. So that takes the lead as the scariest thing I've ever done."

She could feel his chest rise against her back with a hearty chuckle. "Scarier than snowmobiling?"

"Infinitely more so. We were totally out of control, Holden."

"Nah. I had control over this thing the entire time. You were completely safe with me. I've got you."

Truth was, she did feel safe with him, even when barreling down an icy hillside seated on thin slats of wood. His strong arms bound around her with all the protection of a seatbelt, securing her in place.

Maybe her heightened heart rate could be blamed equally on that. The rush of adrenaline and flush of attraction were twin emotions.

Holden kept his arm coiled around her. He hugged her to him with a little squeeze. "Want to go again?"

"Not a chance."

She scooted forward on the sled and struggled to

stand on the compacted snow, even when he aided her with a small push. Sunshine and higher temperatures had melted the powdery layer, leaving a more solid, slippery surface beneath. Her boots shuffled like ice skates, seeking stability.

Holden pushed up from the sled next, but his feet were just as uncoordinated. Rachel reached down to give him a hand.

She tried to pull him up to her level, but with the precarious sleet and nothing for their boot tread to cling to, both ended up like toddlers learning to walk. Suddenly, Holden's entire left foot slipped out from under him, and he landed squarely on his back. Absent any amount of grace, Rachel lost her footing and tumbled directly on top of him.

A loud "Oomph!" whooshed between her lips. Sprawled across his chest, she lifted her head. "Are you okay?"

His knuckle raised to graze her forehead, and he tucked a wayward strand of hair behind her ear, eyes narrowed and unreadable.

Rachel flung back and scurried in an uncoordinated crabwalk over the snow. She sprung to her feet. This time, her shoes gripped the ice firmly, but it didn't keep her from feeling like she was still spinning. Still struggling to find up and down.

Holden bobbled back to a standing position too. He lifted the large sled and held it vertically; the edge jammed into the snow as he peered at her over it. "You surprise me."

"How so?" She smoothed her palms over her static-coated hair and swept it into a ponytail. She figured she looked like she had stuck her finger in a socket. She sort of felt like she had. All of this electricity between them charged the air, their energy, her nerves.

"You're really fun."

"And you didn't think I was fun before?" She fit a hair tie around a loose bun and moved her hands to her hips.

"If I'm being totally honest, you weren't all that fun in high school. You never came out to any of the games or parties. Never spent time with any of your classmates outside of school projects. The only time I got to see you was when we were competing in something."

He was right. She hadn't gotten out much. But she hadn't realized her absence from those events had even been noticed. "I had a goal, and it didn't allow time for much else."

"And what's your goal now?"

To keep myself from falling for you was the answer waiting on the tip of her tongue. Instead, she offered, "For us to build the best snowman Snowdrift Summit has ever seen."

He bought her fib and laughed. "I think that's something we can coordinate."

There wasn't an official medal for the snowman to win, but had there been one, theirs would've secured first place. And the best part of it all was the creation was equal parts Rachel and Holden. The snowman sported Rachel's holiday scarf, along with Holden's wool beanie. She supplied false lashes and buttons for eyes while Holden borrowed a carrot from his fridge for the nose and found a piece of red licorice for a mouth. For arms, he pulled a few branches left from the Hart family tree that were still in the back of his pickup, and Rachel donated her fingerless gloves to the project.

"Now there's no chance his hands will get cold," Holden had teased, and instead of annoyance, she finally found the humor in it. She'd lightheartedly nudged him in the side and he scooped her into his arms in a hug that had her wishing they didn't have to leave for the Hart's cabin. In that moment, curling up on the couch with cocoa and a movie sounded like the perfect end to their lovely day.

Holden assured her that could still happen, but only after they visited his parents.

She hadn't been anxious at the start of the day, but as the minutes ticked down, apprehension swelled within her. Holden explained that Zeke Hart was fine with the way things shook out over the whole Christmas tree thing. Rachel just prayed there wasn't any residual animosity regarding the outcome, or for the many years she had put their son through the ringer. Her own mother had a tendency to switch into Mama Bear mode when it came to her daughter. She doubted Jill Hart was any different regarding her only son.

But Holden—of all people—had detected the change in Rachel. Would his parents be as perceptive? Or forgiving?

"I don't like showing up empty-handed," she confessed on the ride over. Why hadn't she thought to toss a bottle of red wine into her bag? Or taken the time to bake a fresh batch of cookies? Goodness, she could have even stopped by her parents' store to grab a quick, prepackaged item. "I should have brought something with me," she groused.

"That's not expected," Holden assured. From the small back seat of the cab, Scout pressed her face in between them.

Rachel leaned around the pup. "I know it's not expected, but it's still a nice gesture."

"If you'd like, we can swing by the store, but that might make us late. I'm happy to stop, but it's up to you."

That wasn't the better option, so Rachel let it rest. "You sure they're okay with me tagging along?"

"First of all, you're not tagging along. You're my date. And second, my mother lives for this. Any opportunity to cook for guests is better than Christmas for her."

Rachel noticed another truck as they inclined into the driveway, but couldn't pinpoint where she'd seen it before. She hadn't anticipated an entire house full of company.

"That's Lance's." Holden noted her gazing toward

the additional vehicle. "He's always here. More often than I am."

Lance was harmless, but still a loose cannon. And after their strange interaction the other night, when he'd caught Holden at her place during the storm, she wasn't sure what to expect out of him. She felt her guard rising already.

It turned out he was much more preoccupied with getting someone else's attention than he was in drawing attention to the situation between Rachel and Holden.

"How long has Lance liked your sister?" Rachel asked later when they were alone at the kitchen island, a spread of charcuterie arranged in holiday shapes and colors on culinary display.

Holden coughed. "What?" He pounded his chest with a fist.

"Lance." She nudged the tip of a baby carrot toward Sarah, Lance, and Laney, all huddled on the floor playing with a stuffed reindeer that sang when they pressed an antler. "How long has he been interested in your sister?"

"Lance isn't interested in my sister." He plunged a piece of broccoli into a dish of ranch, nearly drowning the poor vegetable. "That's crazy."

"Is it?" She directed her eyes to the trio and his followed. Holden's sister stared adoringly at her baby while Lance wore a matching expression. Only his was directed at Sarah.

"There's no way Lance likes my sister." Holden snapped the floret between his front teeth. "Right?"

"You can tell yourself that all you like, but it won't suddenly make it true," she replied with a knowing smirk.

He picked up another veggie from the platter, still scrutinizing the scene unfolding in the family room. "You know? I'm beginning to think I'm not as perceptive as I once believed. I mean, I didn't even realize that the woman I'd been pining over all of those adolescent years was sitting *right* next to me. How's that for clueless?"

Rachel could say the same. But the confession that he'd had feelings for her other than bitterness still took her by surprise. She laughed at the thought. "Given our history, it's almost comical that we were reunited at a place called Bitter Cold."

"It sure is," he agreed, his eyes sparking with something that made her belly dip. "I definitely don't feel cold toward you right now. And there's no bitterness anywhere to be detected." He snaked an arm around her waist and drew her close. "The opposite."

Her breath was shallow and her pulse erratic. "And what would the opposite be?"

"Joy," he said softly before pressing his nose to hers and then lifting his lips to her forehead in a chaste kiss. "Rachel Joy, that's all you bring me now."

CHAPTER 34

❄

*H*e knew it wasn't, but everything about the evening felt like a familiar family get together. Rachel wove herself into the evening seamlessly. She'd offered to help Holden's mother with the tasks in the kitchen, chatted with Zeke about a football game Holden didn't even know anything about, and read a stack of board books to Laney—once all the way through and then again when the baby cried with glee for more.

It was everything Holden had hoped for in bringing a date home to introduce to his family. Or in this instance, *re*introduce.

So the ache that tightened his chest felt unpleasantly out of place. And yet, it had every right to be there.

It was like unwrapping the most precious present, only to have to return it the next day. Holden tried his best to appreciate the evening for what it was, but all it did was make him want more nights exactly like this.

Minus the part where Lance flirted with Sarah at every turn, trying to engage her in conversation. That part Holden could do without. What he could do without even more was his sister's flirtatious reciprocation. It set Holden so far off-kilter he nearly toppled over each time he spied them exchanging coquettish grins and longing glances.

How had he not picked up on this before? And why hadn't Lance said anything?

Maybe for the same reason Holden had said nothing about his feelings for Rachel. It was risky to expose yourself when your heart was on the line. Riskier when the person it beat for might not even want it.

After they cleared dinner, Holden and Lance set up the ingredients and prepared the kitchen table for gingerbread house making. Sarah and Rachel entertained a sleepy Laney with block toys, while Zeke and Jill stole a sweet moment together on the couch with two glasses of tawny port.

Holden poured a package of peppermint candies into a glass dish and caught Lance's attention. "How come you've never said anything to me?"

"'Bout what, buddy?" In true Lance fashion, he funneled more candies into his mouth than into their designated bowls.

"That you like my sister."

Lance's eyes rounded as wide as holiday wreaths. "Listen, man, if it's too weird or if it makes you uncomfortable—"

Holden fiddled with the cellophane wrapper on a candy cane. He twisted it in his grip. "Does she like you back?"

The typically overconfident friend Holden was so used to suddenly vanished, replaced by the likes of a nervous schoolboy. "I think so." Lance gave a guarded shrug. "At least, I hope so."

Hauling his buddy into a bear hug that transformed into a playful headlock, Holden rubbed a fist over Lance's hair and said, "Then I couldn't be happier."

Lance went rigid with surprise. "Really?" He stepped out from Holden's grasp.

"Why wouldn't I want the two people most important to me to find happiness with one another? Heaven knows you both deserve it."

Usually readied with a quick comeback or witty remark, Lance stood there wordlessly. But his relief about Holden's approval was easily interpreted in the relaxed smile that transformed his entire posture.

"But," Holden had to add on, "if you break her heart, I'll break your other leg."

Lance chuckled and dumped a bag of gumdrops into a dish. "Fair enough."

Once the ingredients were all organized, the two men called the rest of the crew into the kitchen. They split into three teams: Rachel and Holden, Zeke and Jill, and Lance and Sarah with Laney.

He tried not to read into the symbolism of it all—constructing a house with the woman he wanted nothing more than to construct a future with—but it was there. There in the way he piped the icing while she pressed the candies into it. In the way she chose the frosting color for the roof and he slathered in on. In the way she fashioned a wreath with the candies he slid her direction. They were a well-oiled machine, finishing their house well before everyone else.

Of course, Laney's grabby hands slowed down Team Lance-Sarah. Working with a baby tossed a monkey wrench into productivity, but what an adorable little distraction she was.

Holden's parents cuddled close as they decorated. Holden always knew they loved one another, but rarely displayed it so freely. His heart clenched when his father snuck a quick kiss. Jill blushed and waggled her shoulders, and Zeke went in for another.

Enduring love was something to celebrate. Holden knew that, and in that moment, he wanted it more than anything in the world.

He didn't want to cut short his opportunity to experience that.

Sarah excused herself from the festivities first to put an overtired Laney to bed. The poor little girl had been rubbing her eyes for the last half hour, coating her cheeks with sticky sugar and frosting.

"Night, Laney girl." Holden gave his niece a kiss and squeezed her tightly.

"Say goodnight to everyone." Sarah took her daughter's tiny hand into hers and mimicked a wave. "I'll be down after I get this little beauty bathed and put to bed."

Once Sarah retreated upstairs, Jill let out a sigh. "I sure wish she would move back home," she said wistfully.

"Now, Jillybean, we've said before that we will support whatever she decides to do. And if that decision is to stay in Sacramento, then she has our full blessing," Zeke said.

"She moved there for Darren, and then *he* moved across the country," Jill interjected with an edge to her voice Holden didn't often hear.

"I understand what Mom's saying." Holden came to his mother's support. "It sure would be nice to get to be a bigger part of Laney's life. And to be able to help Sarah." He shot a look over at his buddy. "And I'm sure it would make Lance pretty happy to have her around more."

Lance's face turned a darker red than the cinnamon candies in his hand.

Zeke just carried on. "In my humble opinion, there's no better place on this planet than Snowdrift Summit. And there's no other people I'd rather have around me than family."

Holden looked over at Rachel. Her expression was indecipherable, but her focus remained on readjusting the small shingles she'd constructed out of licorice bits. She fiddled with one, then moved on to another.

Holden didn't want her to have guilt over leaving. For choosing to live elsewhere, away from her family. She had every right to make that decision. He moved a hand to her knee and squeezed reassuringly before letting go. Her eyes flicked up to his.

"You ready to go soon?" He spoke only to her as he flipped his wrist over to look at his watch. "We've had a big day."

"We can stay a little longer."

They waited until Sarah returned and then commenced with voting for the best gingerbread house.

Sarah and Lance's won, and Holden knew it was the baby handprint placed directly on the snowy front yard that sealed the deal. It looked like a snow angel pressed into coconut shavings and it was the perfect finishing touch.

And, as creativity would have it, both Jill and Zeke and Rachel and Holden had crafted twin Christmas trees on their displays, towering nobles made from upside-down ice cream cones slathered with green frosting. They decided not to measure them this time.

Holden and Rachel ducked out first. While Rachel was in the foyer zipping up her jacket and gathering her purse with Scout waiting patiently at her side, Jill took her son by the elbow and steered him out of earshot.

"Don't let this one get away," she said pointedly. "Again."

Holden didn't answer, only smiled, because if he spoke in that moment, he wasn't sure what would come out. He had more emotion bottled inside than he knew what to do with.

The truck was cold. Holden cranked the dial on the heater all the way up. Frigid air gradually turned warm and swirled about the cabin, but he still gave Rachel his scarf to ward off the chill. She twisted it around her slender neck and pulled the fabric up to her chin, breathing deep.

There had been an introspective quiet that settled between them throughout the last portion of the evening.

It wasn't for lack of things to say. Holden had an entire novel of words he wanted to confess. A whole love story. But he couldn't. It wasn't fair to try to convince Rachel to stay when he'd always known she had to go.

He could kick himself for all the wasted years.

"What's your plan for tomorrow?" He turned down the heater a few degrees and the white noise filtered out.

"I'll be spending the morning with my dad at the store and then helping my mom with some Christmas wrapping."

"Any chance I might steal you away in the evening?" *And forever after that?*

"I think that could be arranged." Her fingers twirled around the fringe on his scarf. "Your family is wonderful, Holden."

"Eh. They're alright."

"I'm serious." Her tone indicated that clearly. "They were so warm and welcoming. I'd had it in my head all of this time that they were these impossible people who only cared about their son succeeding. But they are all so lovely. I wish I had given them a chance before. Given *you* a chance."

"But you are now." He stole a look in her direction.

She didn't answer.

"Can you tell me what you're thinking?" he asked. They were only a few minutes out from her parents' cabin, and he felt the opportunity slipping through his fingers like sand.

"I'm thinking about a lot of things." She dropped the ends of the scarf. "I go back and forth between wishing I never reconnected with you and being over the moon that I did."

That was a sucker punch to his gut. He winced. "Oh."

"And I don't mean to say that to hurt you at all. It's just…" Her gaze trailed out the passenger window, not latching onto anything in particular. "It would make leaving again easier if I still thought you were this annoying guy who had it out for me."

A quiet laugh came to his lips. "That might be true, but you need to think of it like this. When you were little, did you believe in Santa?"

Her attention swung back to him. "Of course, I did."

"And when you found out he wasn't real, did you

wish you'd always known that? Or were you grateful for the experience of getting to believe?"

"I suppose I was grateful for the experience."

"Then let yourself do that now. Let yourself experience the magic between us, even if it's only temporary," he said. "Because at the end of the day, it's still a gift."

CHAPTER 35

"Hey, Dad? What's your honest opinion of the Harts?"

Stewart paused, a can of cranberry sauce in his grip still halfway from the shelf. "The Harts? Oh, gosh, I don't know."

He placed the can down and turned to his daughter by his side, helping him restock a new delivery of items. The store was finally filling back up after being completely depleted during the blizzard. Trucks could make it back up the highway, and along with them came all the essential items that had flown off the shelves earlier in the week.

"I'd say they're a hard-working family that does what they can to make sure their children are taken care of and have the best lives possible."

"So not all that different from you and Mom?" Rachel passed off another can and her father placed it on the shelf in a row of similar products.

"Not all that different, I suppose." He gave her a look. "What brings this up?"

"Have you ever thought something was one way your entire life, only to realize it's the opposite?"

He thought on that while he emptied the box and moved on to a crate of canned peas. He paused and took a single can into his palm. "I used to think I didn't like peas until I finally gave them a chance. Turns out, they're not so bad."

Rachel laughed. It wasn't a perfect analogy, but it would do.

"I think I might have feelings for Holden Hart."

The can slipped from her father's grasp, but he recovered quickly and snagged it with his other hand before it hit the ground. "Oh." He put the item down, then swiped his glasses from his face and rubbed them with the hem of his apron. "Is that so?"

"He's a great guy, Dad. I think he always has been; I just never took the time to get to know him for the man he truly is."

"And are you getting to know him now?" Stewart refit his bifocals onto his nose and lowered an inquisitive gaze.

"That's the entire problem. I'm going back to San Francisco tomorrow and he's here, in Snowdrift." She twisted the fabric of her own apron in her fists. "I just don't know that it's worth starting something that has no potential for a future."

"Long-distance relationships can work," Stewart suggested, much to her surprise.

She knew they could, but that was typically when there was an end in sight to the separation. Not when the two people lived in different cities, permanently.

"I'm just not sure what the right thing to do is."

Removing a box cutter from his apron pocket, Stewart sliced into the tape on the next package. "You'll figure it out, Sugar Plum. You've always been a great problem solver."

When it came to numbers and figures, she had been. But this was a bigger problem than she'd ever tackled, and matters of the heart weren't solved so easily.

The day went by quickly, and part of that was a relief. It was an understatement to say she looked forward to her evening with Holden. But saying goodbye to her parents would be difficult, and she was grateful to spend one last day with them before heading down the mountain. At least with them, she knew exactly where she stood. She knew whenever she returned—if she decided to return—they would welcome her with open, loving arms. That wasn't the case when it came to Holden. Their relationship—though long-lasting in its own strange way—wasn't unconditional.

She sat on the family room floor that afternoon with her mother, slicing through Christmas-patterned sheets of paper and wrapping presents for neighbors and friends. The room finally felt festive, with the tree fully decked with ornaments on its branches and gifts beneath its leafy boughs.

"How come you and Dad waited so long to put up a tree this year?"

Paula's hand stilled. The scissors in her grip caught on the paper. "We weren't planning to put one up at all. But then you said you were coming home, and we decided it wouldn't feel like a family Christmas without one."

"And now I'm leaving again before we even have the chance to celebrate. I'm sorry, Mom."

"Don't you apologize." Paula slid the scissors the rest of the way. "There's more to it than that." She dropped her hands into her lap and gave Rachel a look that made her insides knot more than the decorative bows on the packages. "Things between your father and I haven't been great lately, sweetheart."

That knot tightened.

"Until recently, we weren't even sure we would spend Christmas together."

"Oh, Mom. I'm so sorry." Rachel stretched out a hand to her mother's arm. "I had no idea."

"How could you? We didn't tell you, and you hadn't been home in a while to notice the change."

"Did something happen?"

Paula shook her head tightly. "No. We just lost our way for a bit. Forgot to put the other person first. Forgot all the many reasons we fell in love to begin with." She cupped her daughter's hand and gave a little grin. "But we're good now, sweetheart. I don't want you to worry about that."

"What changed?"

"Oddly enough, the storm brought us closer. Working at the store together and then having to stay the night there, just the two of us. It took us back to a time when we really had to rely on one another to get by. Back when we found joy in getting through the tough things together, as a team. When it comes down to it, there's no teammate I'd rather have on my side."

Rachel's chest constricted. She'd found her teammate too, and yet she was going to walk away from him. It made no sense.

Around six o'clock, her phone buzzed with a text. It was from Holden. He gave her instructions to wear her warmest attire, even suggesting gloves with full fingers. She'd smiled at that.

A half hour later, his truck rounded into the driveway. She watched him jog up the porch steps, a certain golden-haired beauty missing from his side.

"No Scout?" Rachel asked when she opened the door. She closed it behind her, locking it in place.

"She's with Lance," Holden said. "And Sarah and Laney. Not something I thought I'd ever say." His hand met her lower back as she made her way down the steps. Even with so many layers, the light connection still made her toes tingle. "Plus, I want you all to myself tonight. Scout sometimes has a way of being an attention hog."

"An absolutely adorable attention hog."

"I'll give her that." He held her door open, then skirted the vehicle to find his seat.

In the space between them was a picnic basket,

resting on a pair of neatly folded, wool blankets patterned in green, white, and red plaids.

"Are we going on a picnic?" She had to admit, the frigid weather outside didn't match the activity.

"Sort of." He winked. "You'll see."

The drive was familiar and within no time they arrived in the parking lot of Major Hart Mountain Sports. But instead of parking in front of the building, Holden drove the truck around to the back. The sweeping view of the saw-toothed ridge, dotted with evergreens and capped in snow, was nothing short of breathtaking. Indigo skies with silver stars encased a moon so brilliant it rivaled the sun's illuminating glow.

Holden swung the vehicle around and backed up to the edge, stopping just a few feet from a drop off that had Rachel's stomach going weightless.

"Take my hand?" he asked when he met her at her side.

He didn't need to ask. Of course, she'd wanted to hold his hand for a myriad of reasons. But at the moment, it was to make sure she didn't lose her footing and tumble down the precarious cliff. He guided her to the truck bed and helped her up onto it, then went back to the front for the basket and blankets.

"Here, put this one down first." He passed her the top blanket.

She spread it over the cold metal, then lowered to sit. Hiking a leg up, Holden lifted into the back and found his place beside her. He took the corner of the remaining blanket and moved the hefty fabric over her shoulders, then curled next to her beneath it.

"You good?"

She nodded.

"Warm enough?"

"Yes, Holden. Thank you."

He flipped open the latch on the basket and withdrew a Thermos and two aluminum mugs. The moment he twisted off the lid, she sensed the aroma of rich chocolate, spiced with chili powder and a hint of sea salt. Her tongue watered in anticipation.

He poured her a cup first, then one for himself.

Rachel cradled the mug in her hands. "This really is incredible."

"It's a good recipe," he agreed.

"Yes, it is. But I was referring to this."

She nudged her chin toward the landscape ahead of them. She'd always known Snowdrift was a special place, but right now she realized it was truly one of a kind. And so was the man sitting beside her.

"You know? I remember now why I thought this place looked familiar." She took a slow sip of the hot cocoa and let the warmth slide down to her stomach.

"Oh, yeah?"

She lifted her head in a nod. "I came here once, all by myself, and parked pretty close to where we're parked right now." She took another drink as the memory came filtering to the forefront of her thoughts. "It was right after I'd turned in my application for the scholarship. Believe it or not, I was still torn about whether I should actually go to the city."

Holden's brow furrowed. "Was it ever a question?"

"Not one I ever spoke aloud," she confessed. "But in my heart, I was pulled in two directions. I came up here one night and made a wish. It seemed appropriate because it was a wish my sister once made that even led me to San Francisco in the first place. But that day, I made my own. On a star. I wished that the decision would be made clear, one way or another." She blew out a breath that suspended in front of her mouth in a frosty cloud. "And the next day, I found out the scholarship was mine."

Holden discarded his mug to the rail of the truck and drew his knees to his chest. He wrapped his arms around them, his prominent brow strained as though in pain.

She thought she heard a small groan. "Are you okay?" She settled her own mug in front of her.

"I can't help but think I'm the reason your wish came true."

"What do you mean?" The blanket slipped from her shoulder. She tugged it tighter.

"I wasn't disqualified. I pulled my application."

"Why would you do that?" Her fingers stiffened on the fabric.

"Because I knew you needed that scholarship. I overheard your parents talking about it once in their store."

Rachel's throat felt like she'd swallowed sand. "I don't understand."

"I eliminated myself from the competition."

"Why, Holden?"

"Because forfeiting my chance felt like the right thing to do so you could live out your dream."

How had she never known? And why hadn't he told her this sooner?

His eyes remained fixed ahead.

"Why would you give up so much for me?" Her voice shook with emotion.

"Because I loved you," he said simply. "I didn't know that's what it was back then. I just knew that you deserved to win without me challenging you on it." His eyes pulled toward hers. "For once."

The only thing she cared about right now was winning the heart of the man next to her. And yet, she knew she didn't deserve it. Holden deserved someone who would stay by his side, no matter what. Not someone who latched onto dreams that would likely never come true.

Had Holden really been her dream come true all of this time? Her answered wish? The searing pain it brought to her chest was almost unbearable.

"I don't even know what to say."

"I'd love for you to say you're not going to leave this time, but I think that would also break my heart in two."

He slid his arm around her back and drew her to him. She lowered her head to his shoulder.

"So I'm not going to let you say that, even if you want to."

She wanted to say that and so much more. But she didn't, not only because he'd asked her not to, but because his lips landing on hers in a kiss stopped the words from falling. Stopped the thoughts from forming. All it did was draw her heart even closer to his.

He'd said it would break his heart if she stayed, but she knew it would break hers if she left.

Either way, it would end in heartache.

And for the first time, there would be no winner at all.

CHAPTER 36

❄

His running shoes crunched the ground as he jogged down the trail. Scout kept up so effortlessly, she seemed to float over the snow. It was barely above freezing outside, but Holden was heated with anger. Not toward Rachel. No, he was angry at himself for letting her walk away. A second time.

And not just letting her, but encouraging her. In fact, he'd given her no other option.

But that was how it had to be. Just as he couldn't be the reason for Rachel missing her opportunity in the city the first time around, he couldn't let himself be another roadblock to her goals. She deserved everything she ever wanted out of life.

He'd hoped that was him. And a piece of him knew it was. But a bigger piece knew her plan, and he just couldn't see how he could fit into it.

After clocking five miles and soaking through his thermal undershirt, Holden called it quits on the run and headed back to the rental shop. He had a guided tour in thirty minutes, and while that was plenty of time to freshen up before he was needed on the back of a snowmobile, he also hoped to grab a snack.

That leftover béarnaise sauce was just as delicious as the first time he'd eaten it. But maybe it was the memories that made it so good. The company he'd shared it with.

He couldn't escape her, even with her gone.

"What's up, buddy?" Lance looked happier than ever. His date with Sarah the night before might've had a little to do with that. "Good run?"

Holden's heart rate decelerated with his pace, but it still pounded in his ears. "Yeah. Just needed to clear my head."

"A run is always good for that," Lance said. "How's the rest of you?" He tapped right above his heart and gave a pouty face.

Holden chuckled. "I'm fine, Lance."

"Are you, though? Because your eyes are sadder than a puppy dog's." He shot his gaze down to Scout. "No offense, girl. You know I love those beautiful browns of yours."

Holden fixed on a false smile. "Maybe I'm not completely fine yet, but I'll get there. It'll just take time."

"Which you actually don't have a lot of at the

moment." Lance looked at the computer. "Your one o'clock is coming in early." The jingle from the door cut him off. "Speaking of…"

Stewart and Paula Joy walked through the entrance, outfitted in cold weather clothing that had them looking prepared for a day on the slopes.

"They're not…" Holden started.

"They are. Requested you specifically."

Acid crept up Holden's throat. As if it wasn't hard enough being without Rachel, now he had to paste on a grin and spend the afternoon with her parents? How could he go on pretending he wasn't absolutely in pieces over losing their daughter a second time?

He could be sick. Maybe that wasn't such a bad idea. If he feigned illness, would it get him out of his expedition duties?

Too late for that. They spied him instantly and waved in unison.

"Holden." Stewart came up for a handshake. "Good to see you."

"Likewise." Holden grasped firmly. "I didn't realize I had you two on the calendar today."

"It was a last-minute decision," Stewart said. "Can you believe we've lived here all these years and the two of us have never done this?"

He knew their schedules were busy with the market. He also didn't think this sort of activity was up their alley. But if he'd learned anything, it was that the Joys were constantly surprising him.

He gave them the rundown and passed off their helmets. They decided to each take a snowmobile, another surprising decision. Holden figured they would want to share, and that thought had his memory hanging on the time he and Rachel rode together just a week earlier.

The expedition was nothing short of epic. Stewart's words, actually. They raced up and down the mountain, hooting and hollering louder than customers half their age. When they took a break at one of the lookout points, Holden saw Stewart sneakily pack a handful of snow into a ball and tuck it behind his back.

He'd lifted his finger to his mouth, instructing Holden to keep quiet while he lobbed the snowball at his unsuspecting wife.

That started an all out war, one Holden tried not to get in the middle of, but couldn't resist when Paula Joy smacked him between the shoulder blades. Bits of snow splattered everywhere. It was more fun than he'd had during a snowmobile tour in a long time. And exactly what his heart needed.

As they were about to pack up their snacks and get back on their snowmobiles, Stewart came over to Holden.

"Thank you." He clamped a gloved hand on Holden's shoulder.

"Of course. This was a lot of fun."

"I mean, for what you did for Rachel all of those years ago. She mentioned you finally told her last night."

Holden's lungs burned with a large breath. "It was nothing."

"Maybe to you. But to her, it was everything." He lifted his hand. "You're a good man, Holden Hart."

It took the entire ride back up the hill before the compliment fully settled. Stewart Joy's approval meant so much to him, but he didn't know what to do with it. He didn't know what to do with anything—his emotions, his time, himself in general—which was likely why he found himself at his parent's door later that evening.

"You have room for one more?"

"Always." Jill Hart backed up and welcomed her son into the cabin.

"You're seriously already here?" Holden peered around his mother to see Lance giving Laney a shoulder ride. The baby squealed and cooed from her high perch.

"He's been here all evening," his mother whispered.

Sarah came up and tickled Lance's side, which made both Lance and Laney erupt into a fit of giggles.

"Did Rachel head back to San Francisco?" Jill asked her son.

Holden scratched the back of his neck. "This morning."

"And how are you holding up?"

He tried to take a full breath, but it caught in his chest. "Not so great."

"Come here, sweetie." Jill drew Holden into an embrace, and Lance followed suit. Sarah wrapped her arms around them all, and even Scout jumped up to get in on the massive sandwich hug.

"There, there." Lance ran a hand over Holden's hair. "It'll be okay, buddy."

"You're suffocating me, guys."

One by one, they peeled away from Holden, finally giving him room to breathe.

"It'll get easier," Sarah confessed as they moved from the entryway into the cabin. "The pain of breaking up. It won't always be this bad."

That was just it, though. Could it even be considered a breakup if they were never really together to begin with? Compared to the pain Sarah had gone through, it felt selfish to wallow. Because that's exactly what he was doing, right? Wallowing in his pitiful misery?

This was the season of joy. Hope. If he'd learned anything, it was that what-ifs only broke your heart, never healed it.

But family. That had always been Holden's place of healing. And he let them be that for him that night through the carols they sang around the piano, to the holiday fudge they made in the kitchen, to the wreath they hung on the door, constructed from their very own noble tree scraps.

The love and laughter was almost enough to distract him from his situation. If only each activity didn't make him long for the one person who wasn't there. The one person he wanted to share it all with.

The one person he wanted his family to fall in love with just as much as he already had.

Of all the gifts he could possibly get that Christmas, having Rachel by his side was the only one he wanted.

And his heart shattered all over again, knowing it would never be his.

CHAPTER 37

❄

"*Turns out, you don't even need mistletoe.*"

Holden's words from a few days back rang in Rachel's ears throughout the elevator ride up to the offices of December Décor. Of course, you didn't need mistletoe to initiate a Christmas kiss. But sometimes that sweet sprig was a nudge of encouragement. A bold prompt to muster up bravery and just go for it.

In a way, it was fair to say mistletoe actually brought Rachel and Holden together. Had he not teased her about her failed product back at Bitter Cold Coffee Bar, and then taken her down the mountain to scout for some of their own, she wasn't sure where they would be.

But he was right. The magic wasn't in the mistletoe. The magic was in the person you wanted to meet beneath it.

She pulled her shoulder bag close to her body as the

elevator doors yawned open and she slid her way through the workers continuing on to higher floors.

The December Décor level buzzed with palpable energy and it wasn't even eight o'clock.

"Morning, Rachel." Teddy, the coffee cart intern, bowed his head as he scooted his cart past.

Rachel made sure to give him a wide berth today. She already had enough nerves jumbling through her; she didn't need the addition of caffeine and she certainly didn't need the anxiety that accompanied being doused in hot coffee. She'd learned that lesson weeks ago.

"Good morning, Teddy."

On her way to her office, she smiled at several coworkers. Throughout the weeks leading up to Christmas, most everyone at the company donned silly holiday hats or wore necklaces made of bright lights that flashed on and off with a little switch. It was fitting, after all, since they specialized in holiday decorations. It made sense to decorate oneself too.

While not over the top with festiveness, Rachel had decked herself in a fitted red blazer, paired with a charcoal pencil skirt that fell just above her knees, and a pair of black kitten heels. And in a last-minute wardrobe decision, she'd fastened the crocheted mistletoe sprig she'd made with her mother at In Stitches directly to her lapel. The perfect finishing touch.

She slipped into her office. A half an hour until go-time. Pulling in a breath, she felt her phone rattle within her purse on the exhale.

Her father's image blipped across the screen.

"Dad," she answered with a swipe of her finger. She placed the phone on speaker and settled it on her desk.

"Good morning, Sugar Plum. I promise I'm not calling for a song request this time."

She laughed at that. Even if he had been, Rachel probably would have obliged. For some reason, it all didn't seem so silly now.

"Do you have a few minutes to chat?" he asked. "I know your big meeting is this morning."

"I do have some time." She lowered to the swivel chair at her desk. Based on her father's tone, she had an odd hunch she should be sitting down for this conversation. "What's going on, Dad?"

"It's the tree."

Her heart dove to her stomach.

She'd kept her eye on the weather when traveling back to the city and hadn't been aware of any storm fronts moving through the area. It wouldn't make sense for the tree to have sustained any damage or harm. Last she'd seen, it was still standing, tall and proud as ever.

"Is it okay?"

"It's perfect," her father said. "And that's the entire problem." A space of several breaths passed before he added, "I don't think I can cut it down, Rachel."

Her chest tightened. She'd never heard her father's voice like this. So unsure and unsteady. Even though she couldn't see him, she knew he'd removed his glasses and nervously wiped them clean.

"I'm so sorry, Sugar Plum," he added.

She detected a slight quiver in his tone and wished in that moment that she could reach through the phone and hug him. She'd often looked to him for comfort over the years, but now it felt as if the roles were reversed.

"I know you planted that tree all those years ago hoping it would be in the town square," he continued. "So I'm sure this comes as such a disappointment. But I just can't do it. That tree has so much of our family in those branches. And I don't think I'm ready to cut that out."

She blinked back tears. Why hadn't she thought to put on waterproof mascara that morning? She'd certainly needed it the day before when she'd said her goodbyes to Holden. She'd hoped today would be a new day with a sunnier outlook, but things weren't looking good.

"I'm not disappointed, Dad," she said. And she wasn't. Not an ounce of disappointment filled her being. "Honestly, I'm relieved."

"You are?"

Hope caught in her chest and bloomed. "Yes, I am."

"You're really not upset that it won't have its day on the square?"

"Not even a little. It will have a life with our family, and that's what that beautiful tree deserves. And it's what you and mom deserve too. To be able to look out at it every day, knowing it's not going anywhere."

They finished their conversation with an exchange of *I-love-you's* and a final reassurance that this was the right move. Unfortunately, it left Main Street without a proper tree for the lighting on Christmas Eve, but she knew there was a solution to that somewhere. If the people of Snowdrift were anything, they were resourceful and resilient. They had a long legacy that beautifully proved that point.

Rachel set up in the conference room early. When Cathryn and the other executives filtered in and took their seats at the intimidatingly long table, whatever nerves Rachel had had during the previous presentation were surprisingly nowhere to be found. She was calm. Composed. It was like she was a different person.

And in a way, she supposed she was.

She wasn't the same woman standing before her superiors now. She was different, and she knew she had Snowdrift Summit and Holden Hart to blame.

Or maybe, to thank.

"We appreciate you moving things around so we could get this out of the way before the holidays," Cathryn said, likely completely unaware of the insult slid right into her words.

"Of course." Rachel rose to greet them and fastened a placating smile onto her lips.

That's exactly what she was going to do. Get out of the way.

"I've spent the last week going over the Mistlefaux

product, trying to explore ways I can improve upon the original design—"

Cathryn lifted a halting hand. "Rachel, I'm going to stop you right there. We're not here for a presentation. This isn't public knowledge yet, but we're in negotiations with a global company that has an interest in buying out December Décor. If things go through with the proposed deal, we will no longer be focusing on creating and manufacturing holiday decorations."

Rachel stifled a laugh and played it off as a sneeze.

"Bless you?" Cathryn offered as a question, not convinced by Rachel's effort to disguise her ill-placed laughter. "Either way, we will be eliminating your position after the new year. I'm so sorry to have to be the bearer of this news right before the holidays, but as the saying goes, it's not personal, just business."

Rachel was shocked by how impersonal the entire exchange seemed, and even more surprised how little this unforeseen news bothered her.

"Of course," Cathryn carried on while Rachel registered the previous information, "We have a robust severance package for you, along with your usual holiday bonus. You've been an asset to our team for many years now, and we'd like you to know how appreciative we are of your hard work and dedication. I'm sure this isn't the news you were hoping for, but unfortunately, it's the news we have to deliver."

Rachel didn't even bother masking the giggle that passed through her lips. It flew from her mouth full-force.

"Is everything okay, Miss Joy?" Cathryn's penciled brow arched on her forehead.

"Yes." Rachel attempted to collect herself, then decided not to bother. "More than okay." She stuffed her Mistlefaux in her tote, feeling like an even better place was in the garbage. "I just have one request."

"And what is that?"

"For my holiday bonus, are you open to suggestions?"

* * *

Cold air skated over her shoulders as she turned the humming street corner toward her downtown apartment. She often took regional transportation to and from work, but today she opted to walk home. She wanted to take in the holiday sights and sounds of the city one last time.

One week earlier, if someone had told her she would be fired from the job she had planned to one-day retire from, it would have devastated her. It would have collapsed her carefully constructed life from the top down. But today, the thought of rebuilding was anything but daunting. The opposite. And she knew exactly where she wanted to lay the foundation, and who she wanted to do that with.

Her step was light, her mood even lighter as her feet led her to her high-rise apartment. George, the building's doorman, usually greeted her each time she passed through the entrance. He was a constant, so when Rachel had to pull on the handle to let herself in, her heart held a beat. Maybe he'd gone home for the holidays. No one would argue against the man deserving a break.

Instead, it surprised her to find him near the elevator with a broom and dustpan, head swinging in an irritated shake.

"Everything okay here, George?" Rachel removed her mittens and fit them in her pocket.

Funny, she had more concern over George's disgruntled mood than the fact that she'd just been fired from her place of employment. Perspective was an interesting thing.

"There's a reason the landlord doesn't encourage real trees. Just look at this mess!" He shoved the dustpan loaded with needles toward her. Immediately, the smell transported her home. And this time, it wasn't to her upstairs apartment, but to Snowdrift.

The elevator doors stretched open and George went back to his grumbling. She left him to it.

But she had to disagree. Having a real, homegrown Christmas tree was worth the little mess it created.

Punching the number to her twenty-fifth floor on the elevator button, she took the quiet ride to absorb the day's events.

Starting January first, she would no longer be employed by December Décor. She knew there were a myriad of opportunities available for her in the city. Cathryn even emphasized that she would gladly provide a reference, should Rachel need one.

But Rachel didn't want to start on the bottom rung in another corporate machine, only to be spit out again when a bigger, hungrier business swallowed it whole.

In truth, she didn't mind starting over. That didn't scare her. There was excitement attached to the thought of creating a new life for herself. A new start, as blank as freshly fallen snow.

The elevator lurched to a stop on her floor.

As the doors parted, she peered down the hall. She could almost understand the fuss George had made about the pine needles now. They coated the entire walkway toward her apartment like an evergreen version of a breadcrumb trail.

When she made the turn down the long hallway, she had to blink twice.

There, standing just outside her apartment door, was Holden, with the most glorious Christmas tree she'd ever laid eyes on.

"Holden." His name caught on the emotion clogging her throat. It had only been a day, but her whole being ached to see him again. She rushed over. "What are you doing here?"

"I couldn't bear the thought of you spending Christmas without a proper tree." He moved his eyes toward the fir in his grip. "Not when we had this perfectly good one to share."

"I don't understand." She came up to the door and slipped her key into the lock, then swung her gaze back over her shoulder.

"You don't recognize it?" He trailed her inside,

bringing the tree along with him like it was a shopping bag.

Rachel placed her keys on the counter. "Should I?" She turned to survey the tree.

"It's the top of our family's noble fir. When the trimmers came out to cut it down, I'd asked that they save the upper portion. Wouldn't you know? It looks like it was always meant to be this size." He crossed the small apartment and placed the tree in the middle of the window frame. Even without strands of lights adorning its branches, the backdrop of the lit-up city made it twinkle. "And if you ask me, it looks like it was always meant to be right here."

She could feel the tears collecting in her eyes. She blinked them back. "Holden, this is so thoughtful of you. But—"

"I understand, Rachel. I know there's not a future between us, and I'm not here to convince you otherwise. I just couldn't let this tree go to waste. Not when there was a perfect home for it."

"But this isn't the perfect home."

Without a proper stand to place it into, Holden propped the tree along the glass. He crossed his arms over his chest and rotated to face her. "Why not? If it's the pine needles, I promised the doorman I'd clean all of that up. I was just in a hurry to get up here and I shook more loose than I intended."

"That's not the reason." She moved a step closer. "This isn't the perfect home because this isn't *my* home anymore. Or at least, it won't be after January first."

His arms came unbound and his shoulders sagged. "Oh, Rachel. I'm so sorry. I didn't even ask how the presentation went. I'm guessing not all that great?"

"Not great. In fact, before I could even get started, they fired me."

He drew her into his arms so quickly she stumbled. His immediate response to comfort her made her knees unbuckle, and she was grateful for his steadying hold, locking her in place. But it wasn't disappointment that weakened her. It was the man who held her so tightly she could hardly breathe that overwhelmed her with emotion.

"They fired you?" he whispered into her hair. "Right before Christmas? How could they do that?"

"Turns out they're not really focusing on Christmas at all anymore," she said. "But honestly, Holden. I'm okay. *More* than okay."

He cupped the back of her head and gently tilted her gaze up to his. "You're okay with losing your dream job?"

"I am, because I had plans to quit."

Confusion knit his brows together. His eyes roved over her face for an answer. "You were going to quit? Since when?"

"Since I decided I didn't want to be stuck in a job I didn't love when it kept me away from the man that I do love."

Those tears Rachel struggled to suppress now welled in Holden's jade green ones too.

"What did you say?" Holden's voice broke with emotion.

"That I didn't want to be stuck at December Décor."

His thumb moved over her cheek. "No, after that."

"That I love you."

As he had a way of doing, Holden cut her off with a kiss. But this time, there was no hint of goodbye.

Only the promise of a future even brighter than those city lights.

CHAPTER 38

❄

Holden wasn't sure how they were going to pull it off. It was Christmas Eve and there wasn't a tree in the square. But the buzz about town was that the annual lighting would still occur and for everyone to be there by six o'clock sharp. The holiday show would, in fact, go on.

Skepticism aside, Holden looked forward to the event. Either way, it would be good to spend time with the people from his community. There would be open fires with roasted chestnuts, holiday caroling from Miss Morgenstern's first grade class, and, of course, complimentary hot chocolate served by Bitter Cold Coffee Bar. Even Trinity would have a little tent set up to sell the rest of her Christmas wreaths. The people of Snowdrift Summit would come together to celebrate the season the best way they knew how, tree or no tree.

Holden had learned it wasn't even about the actual

tree, but the people who gathered around it that truly mattered.

Plus, Rachel would be there. That was the biggest present of all.

When he'd trekked into the city with the half-tree in the back of his truck, he thought it would be a drop and go sort of thing. That's what he had prepared for, at least. He had planned to leave it outside her door. But he hadn't accounted for the traffic that held him up on the freeway, depositing him in San Francisco after she'd already gotten off work. He had tried to rush out, but he'd gotten caught.

They'd already had their lengthy goodbye. He couldn't imagine doing that all over again.

But in the end, he wouldn't have to. Just a bye-for-now.

She still had to wrap a few things up in the city, but promised to make it home in time for the lighting. Holden could hardly wait.

It helped that he had his own work to occupy his mind and time. Major Hart Mountain Sports was remarkably busy, but not with scheduled snowmobile expeditions. Last-minute shoppers crammed the store, loading their arms with sweaters, scarves, beanies. You name it. Items flew off the shelves. The steady hum of the cash register continued throughout the day, and just when they got control over the checkout line, more customers would arrive.

Mayor Thornton was one of those customers. He

stepped up and dipped his cap toward Holden, passing off a large stack of items to purchase.

Holden slid the articles of clothing across the counter toward their new employee, Brady. They'd thrown him on the register that morning, hoping he was up for training under pressure. So far, so good.

"Merry Christmas Eve, Mayor," Holden said while Brady found the tags and started to scan.

"Same to you, Holden." He wrapped his knuckles on the surface between them. Holden couldn't help but sense the man's quiet impatience.

The mayor looked at his watch.

"We'll get you out of here soon," Holden promised.

"Sorry," Brady apologized. "It's my first day working the cash register. I'm a little slow."

"Oh, it's not that. You're doing just fine. I just got a call that our tree is finally here and I'm eager to organize things with the decorators."

Brady read the total and began folding the items into a paper bag bearing the store's logo.

"So, there is going to be a tree after all?" Holden asked.

"Believe it or not, we were able to secure one last minute."

"That's great news!"

Brady took the man's credit card.

"Miracles come in all shapes and sizes," Mayor Thornton said. "But in this case, in the shape of a giant Christmas tree."

Holden grinned and wished him well, his heart even

more at ease knowing the annual tradition would continue.

By four that afternoon, customers began to trickle out, most likely heading home to get ready for the night's festivities. Holden figured he should do the same.

"You think we can close up?" Brady asked. He wiped his brow with the back of his hand and blew out a breath.

They'd thrown him into the fire, no question about that. But he did great. After all, they were an extreme sports establishment. Might as well make a sport out of cashier work too.

"I think that would probably be fine." Holden hollered at Lance, lost somewhere in the racks rehanging snowboard pants. "What do you think?"

He popped out from a particularly disheveled display. "I think I have a hot date that I'd love to have some extra time to get ready for."

Holden scowled. "Please don't ever refer to my sister as a hot date again."

"Sorry, buddy." He clipped the waistband of a pair of pants onto the hanger and jammed it into place on the stand. "Noted."

They made quick work of straightening up the store and locked up within half an hour. Even Scout seemed to vibrate with anticipation over the night's events, as though she could also sense the magic in the air.

It was definitely there, as if the wind sweeping over the summit was filled with holiday stardust.

Back at home, Holden spent longer than normal getting ready. He picked a cable-knit forest green sweater with a plaid flannel shirt underneath so the collar and cuffs peeked out like holiday trim. He slipped on a pair of khaki corduroy pants and his dressier boots. He even took time to shave the two-day scruff from his face and splashed a bit of cologne on his neck before bundling it up with a classic gray scarf.

Before he hopped in the truck to head to the square, he wrapped a bright red bow around Scout's neck. She looked as pretty as a present.

"Ready to go, girl?"

By the time they arrived on Main Street, the crowds had already collected, the celebration in full swing. Scout sniffed a few friendly dogs as they threaded through the masses, and Holden greeted his friends and neighbors with handshakes and hugs.

He could glimpse the tree at the far end of the square, but without lights to illuminate it, the dark silhouette almost faded into the shadows.

"How are they selling?" he asked as he came up to Trinity's pop-up tent. Only a handful of wreaths hung from the poles.

"I'm down to just a dozen left," she answered. "I think I'll be sold out before the lighting even happens."

"That would be fantastic." Holden touched the branches on a beautiful wreath with a houndstooth bow at the top. "Then you won't have to worry about sales and can just enjoy your evening."

"I think I would enjoy this evening even if I didn't sell a single one. It's pretty perfect, if you ask me."

Almost perfect, Holden thought. Once Rachel arrived, it would be.

He found his mother near the local candle maker's tent, her nose in a small jar that—based on the label—smelled of vanilla and cloves. Her eyes drifted shut as she inhaled softly.

"Is that one a winner?"

Jill's eyes flit open. She returned the candle to the folding table. "You know I love the ones that smell like food." She gave the candle maker a smile and moved from the tent. "Plus, candles calm me, and after the day I've had with your father…"

"His foot acting up again?"

"Oh, no. The foot's fine. He's just been all worked up over his job tonight."

Holden didn't follow. "What job?" Scout stretched on her leash, and Holden gave a gentle tug to keep her in place.

"They asked him to do the honors of placing the star on the top of the tree. The guys from the station brought the engine and your father's going up on the ladder."

"Is that safe to do with his boot?"

Jill shrugged. "Probably not, but he's assured me all of Snowdrift's finest first responders will already be onsite, so I shouldn't worry."

"He must be over the moon."

"Oh, son, he's more excited about this than he was at the opportunity to have our tree on the square. Funny how things always seem to work out."

Holden grinned at his mother. That smile slipped from his face as his mouth went slack and his jaw unhinged. His gaze trailed across the crowd and landed on the one woman he hoped to pick out of it. She stood in a sea of people, but all Holden could focus on was her. A deep cranberry peacoat hugged her small frame, and a cream-colored scarf and matching gloves accented her outfit, along with a slouchy beret that cocked to one side. The sight of her took his very breath away.

Rachel's eyes met Holden's and his heart gave a tight squeeze.

Her beauty doubled when her entire face lit up with a beaming smile of recognition.

"I'll check back in with you in a bit, Mom." Holden hugged his mother and then made determined strides toward Rachel in the middle of the square.

"You look incredible," he whispered near her ear when he pulled her into a hug.

"So do you," she echoed. "For a mountain man, you sure clean up well."

Is that what he was? A mountain man? He supposed so and chuckled a little at the new label.

"Is it silly if I say I've missed you?" he asked.

"Not at all, because I feel the same." She took his

hand in hers. "I almost didn't think I would make it in time. Traffic coming up the hill was crazy."

"I think everyone wants to be here for the lighting. It's supposed to be a really special one."

She pulled him forward. "One we should try to get a front-row seat to, if we can."

"I think that can be arranged." Holden nudged Scout. "Go on, girl. Lead the way."

It was amazing how an adorable dog could part a throng of jam-packed people. Sure, everyone wanted to stop and give her a pat or a squeeze, but in time, the trio made their way closer to the base of the tree. Lance and Sarah already had their spots reserved, along with cups of cocoa in their hands and expressions too lovey-dovey for Holden's liking on their faces. Laney snoozed from her stroller, all bundled up like a Christmas cherub.

"Welcome back, Rachel." Lance took her into his embrace. "I'm glad to see you back in town for many reasons, but mostly because I won't have to deal with this lovesick puppy anymore." He jabbed Holden with his elbow.

"It's good to be home," she said. The telling words weren't lost on Holden.

"If I can have your attention, please." Mayor Thornton's voice crackled through the speakers. A hush descended upon the crowd, the deafening roar of excitement dwindling to a murmur of anticipation. "If you all can find your places, we will begin shortly."

"Are you guys sad neither of your trees ended up

being chosen?" Lance asked. He lifted his cup of hot chocolate to his mouth for a drink.

"I'm not," Holden admitted. "As my mom says, things just have a way of working out."

He squeezed his hand around Rachel's and she gripped back. Her eyes lifted, something he couldn't quite pinpoint in her forget-me-not blues.

"As many of you know," the Mayor started in again. "Every year, we select a tree from the yard of one of our community members to serve as our official town square Christmas tree. It takes years—decades, even—for these trees to reach their full height. And each holiday, it's a competition to see whose will be chosen. But every year, we have had fewer and fewer trees entered. This year in particular, unfortunate circumstances led to a last-minute scramble to secure a tree for the lighting. For a moment, we feared there would be no tree at all."

Holden felt Rachel's fingers tighten around his. Her body leaned into his side and he swore she bounced a little, like a child with a secret they couldn't keep contained.

"But in the eleventh hour, Rachel Joy came through with this glorious, thirty foot, artificial noble fir, and we could not be more thankful for her generous donation," Mayor Thornton bellowed over the cheers his announcement elicited. "This tree will allow us to continue our holiday tradition without altering the very landscape that makes our beautiful town what it is. So, without further ado, let the countdown to the lighting begin." The Mayor led the crowd. "Ten…nine…eight…"

Holden's gaze dropped to Rachel. "You arranged this?"

"I asked if I could adjust my holiday bonus a little," she said with a humble shrug. "Apparently, I'm the first to request a Christmas tree instead of a check. Go figure."

"You are amazing."

The chanting around them rose in volume until everyone shouted excitedly as one. "Three…two…*one!*"

Flashing on in brilliant unison, the strands on the tree and a kilowatt of power lit up the entire square. Possibly even the mountainside. Holden had never seen a lovelier sight, but some of that had to do with the person by his side who lit up his spirit, his life, his whole world. His heart felt like it could burst. And when the ladder on the fire truck parked off to the side began to lift, followed by his father cautiously climbing the rungs with a glittering star in his grip, Holden knew that everything—each moment leading up to this very one and all the ones to come—worked together for good.

And in the end, that made them all winners.

EPILOGUE

One Year Later

Rachel clasped her hands around Holden's waist and held on for dear life. She couldn't believe Scout could keep their pace as the snowmobile zoomed down the hill. The dog loped happily along, snow spraying from her paws meeting the powder.

She was such a great pup. In the year since her validation as an Avalanche Rescue Dog, she'd already put her skills to use in two lifesaving efforts. And all she'd asked for in return was a game of tug-of-war.

Rachel couldn't possibly be more proud. That pride transferred to Scout's handler too. Holden often shied away from being called a hero, but that wasn't a label he could dodge anymore. She always knew he was one, but those rescues just made it official.

But today, they were out on the slopes purely for play, not work. Rachel had taken the day off from the floral shop. In recent months, she'd picked up a few shifts here and there until Trinity eventually extended the invitation to partner with her in the flower shop endeavor. The metal sign above the door with their new name, Joyful Blooms, still made her heart skip each time she walked beneath it.

It was close to the same exhilarating rush she felt as they careened down the mountain.

"You want to take a break for a bit?" Holden angled his head back and shouted over the hum of the snowmobile.

Rachel nodded her reply.

He slowed near one of her favorite lookouts and clicked off the engine. She loved this view. From here, they could see all of Snowdrift, their sweet mountain town with its snow-tipped trees and cozy cabins, along with a quaint downtown at the heart of it all.

Scout plopped onto the snow, then rolled on her back, swishing side to side. She looked like the golden retriever version of a snow angel.

"You hungry?" Holden asked. He removed the backpack from Rachel's shoulders. With Rachel at his back for the ride, it only made sense that she wore it instead. She hadn't asked what was inside, and her growling stomach was relieved at the thought that it might be food.

"I am," she said. "Always prepared, huh?"

He smiled. "Most of the time."

They found a seat on a fallen log, and Holden unzipped the pack. He pulled out a plastic bag of cookies, all frosted with holiday reds and greens. Scout perked up and trotted over, and Holden ruffled up her ears and said something Rachel couldn't quite decipher.

The dog scampered away.

"When did you have time to bake?" Rachel took a bite out of the sugar cookie on top of the stack.

"You know me. I'm a baking machine." There was an odd quality to his tone that Rachel didn't recognize.

She went in for another nibble when a shower of snow flicked across her face. Scout dug furiously, kicking up layers of powder as her front paws burrowed into the soft ground just a few feet away.

"What have you got there, girl?" Holden stood and came to her side.

Rachel crammed the half-eaten cookie into the bag and raced over too.

As if locating something beneath the surface, the dog continued to dig frantically until she finally came upon the object that had her so riled up. Rachel couldn't quite make it out, but Scout passed it off to Holden as she dropped it from her mouth and into his hands.

And then Holden dropped to one knee.

Rachel gasped. In his palm was a small, green velvet box, and in his eyes were tears that mirrored her own.

She shoved her hand to her cheek and sniffed.

"Rachel Joy?" He looked up at her, his gaze a tender

question. "Will you marry me?"

There wasn't a long speech to accompany it, but they didn't need one. The shared years between them said it all, and her heart could read his like it was her own.

"Yes!" she shouted, certain all the town below could hear her elation echoed throughout the summit. "Yes, I will marry you, Holden Hart!"

He lifted to his feet and pulled the glittering solitaire diamond from the small box. Then he reached down for her left hand, gloved in the very mittens she'd been wearing the first day they reconnected.

He slid the ring onto her bare finger.

"See? These gloves do come in handy!" She wiggled her fingers and beamed so broadly her wind-chapped cheeks hurt.

Chuckling, Holden drew her into his arms and kissed her with all he had. When he pulled back, he said, "So, I'm not sure if you noticed, but those cookies were cut out in the shapes of letters. I was going to have you arrange them. They spelled out *Marry Me*."

Rachel sputtered a laugh. "I think it's good you cut to the chase. History shows I'm not that great at unscrambling things."

"Oh, I don't know. We managed to unscramble all the tension between us and create something beautiful in its place," he said. He laughed a little to himself before asking, "Did you ever think you'd share my last name? I mean, for a while there, you couldn't even stand the sound of it."

"I'll admit, there was a time when the thought of sharing anything with you made me cringe," she said, her eyes still affixed on the shimmering jewel adorning her finger. "But now, the thought of *not* sharing my entire life with you is one I can't even comprehend." She pulled in a breath. "My grandma always said the sky was the limit for my dreams, but I have to disagree. I think the summit was. And here I am, at the top of it with you…my dream come true."

He rubbed his finger over the stone and met her gaze, the depths of his moss green eyes tugging at her soul.

When it came down to it, it wasn't the height of a tree or a score in a contest that mattered, but the enduring love they shared, which was something beyond measure.

In the end, love conquered all. And that was, and always would be, the sweetest victory.

* * *

Thank you so much for reading **Homegrown Holiday**. *If you're like me and can't get enough of Snowdrift Summit and its lovable cast of characters, I've got great news!*

Lance and Sarah's story continues in **Snowdrift Sunrise**. *Here's a sneak peek:*

Snowdrift Sunrise:
A Snowdrift Summit Romance

Lance Major thrives in the great outdoors, always chasing that next exhilarating rush. The thought of settling down is as distant as the snow-covered peaks of Snowdrift Summit until Sarah Hart, his best friend's sister, returns to town after a recent divorce.

Suddenly, he finds himself in the hushed aisles of the library where she works, spending more time between the pages of a book than carving up the snowy slopes. Sarah has taken notice of Lance, too. In truth, she's always been inexplicably drawn to Lance's carefree spirit. Stolen moments between the stacks quickly evolve into hot chocolate sunrises and late-night book clubs.

When the opportunity to organize a reading retreat at the local Snowdrift Inn arises, Sarah seizes it with the same spontaneity she's learned from Lance. Gathering fellow literature enthusiasts becomes her passion project, but Lance's winter sports business feels the repercussions. The Inn's rooms, traditionally reserved for his adventurous clients, are now occupied by authors seeking peace and quiet.

And when a renowned travel writer attends the retreat and offers Lance a chance to embark on a globe-trotting expedition that would take him far from Snowdrift, he must choose between following his heart or pursuing the thrill of the unknown.

Can Sarah and Lance strike a balance that allows their passions to coexist, or will the clash between the love of literature and the allure of adventure ultimately drive them apart?

ALSO BY MEGAN SQUIRES

Snowdrift Summit Series
Homegrown Holiday
Snowdrift Sunrise
Sweetheart Season (Coming Soon)

Holiday Reads
Christmas at Reindeer Ranch
A Winter Cabin Christmas
Christmas at Yuletide Farm
An Heirloom Christmas
A Lake House Holiday

The Harmony Ridge Series
Detour to Harmony (Book One)
In Sweet Harmony (Book Two)
Match Made in Harmony (Book Three)

The Seascape Shores Series
The Seascape Retreat
The Getaway House
The View by the Shore

Stand-alone Sweet Romance

In the Market for Love

* * *

Join Megan Squires' Reader Group!

Join my corner of Facebook where I share sneak peeks, host giveaways, and get to know my readers even better! I'd love to have you there.

* * *

ABOUT THE AUTHOR

When Megan Squires isn't writing, thinking, or dreaming all things sweet romance, she's caring for the nearly sixty animals on her twelve-acre flower farm in Northern California. A UC Davis graduate, Megan worked in the political non-profit realm prior to becoming a stay-at-home mom. She then spent nearly ten years as an award winning photographer, with her work published in magazines such as Professional Photographer and Click.

In 2012, her creativity took a turn when she wrote and published her first young adult novel. Megan is both traditionally and self-published. She can't go a day without her family and farm animals, and a large McDonald's Diet Coke.

To keep up with Megan online, please visit:

- facebook.com/MeganSquiresAuthor
- x.com/MeganSquires
- instagram.com/megansquiresauthor
- bookbub.com/authors/megan-squires

Made in the USA
Las Vegas, NV
04 March 2025